A DESIRE
FOR DEATH

A DESIRE FOR DEATH

SALEEM

PARTRIDGE
A Penguin Random House Company

To order additional copies of this book, contact
Partridge India
000 800 10062 62
www.partridgepublishing.com/india
orders.india@partridgepublishing.com

My sincere thanks to Dr. jayalakshmi and Mrs Sujatha Gopal for editing the novel.
—saleem

'Thoorpu Palem' in Ongole district of Andhra Pradesh . . . the time was five in the evening. The school had closed for the day just then. Children were rushing out in a cry of pleasure, outshouting each other. Siddhartha, with a schoolbag hung over his shoulder walking at a slow pace toward the school gate, looked at the students nudging and pushing each other impatiently. It was the same every day. They would be running in ecstatic joy once it was time to go home, like prisoners released from a jail. Even the school principal's reprimands to maintain discipline would be of no avail. They would form a queue only up to the school gate. Once out of the gate, they became like birds just freed from the captive cages.

Siddhartha had shared his feelings with his grandmother. 'Children behave like that for different reasons. Those who have little interest in studies or dislike going to school may leap in joy at the end of the day. They perhaps think of it as a good riddance to be let off,' she had explained.

'Then why don't I feel the same way?' Siddhartha had asked. She had pinched the boy's cheeks affectionately and said, 'There you are. You are worth a mountain of gold. You are an endearing child of learning!'

There was a temple dedicated to Lord Rama on the way to home. A flight of pigeons . . . came flocking . . .

devotees visiting the temple threw millets at them. The birds fed on the grain, cooing in delight. The sight of the birds charmed Siddhartha so much so that, he wanted to see more of them every day.

Siddhartha stood at the spot transfixed, staring at the pigeons pecking at the grain. The graceful movement of their necks fascinated him. Perhaps some children had disturbed the birds with a hush and they took wings into the sky, making the sky appear ashen in a jiffy. They sat on the ramparts of the temple for a while staring eagerly at the grains scattered on the ground below. Slowly, one after another, they scooped down and began pecking at the grain once again.

Having watched the birds peck at the grain a little longer, Siddhartha headed towards home. Clusters of babul trees lined up wildly on either side of the path. Children feared to take this road in the dark. Siddhartha saw something moving under a tree, so he peered closer. It was a black cat. He bent forward to inspect the scene. Lo, there was a pigeon's wing in its mouth. Later he noticed another cat loitering nearby. The black cat that held in its mouth the wing of the pigeon let go of it and chased the other cat. . . . The latter held the pigeon's neck between its jaws. A fierce battle ensued between the two cats for the prize catch.

The commotion had already attracted the attention of the rest of the children. Picking up stones, the boys began pelting at the cats. Soon, the cats fled the scene, leaving the wounded pigeon behind. The children flocked around the wounded pigeon. The poor pigeon was bleeding all over. One of its legs was broken too, and appeared to be half dead with its neck bitten in a deep gash. Its heart was still palpitating.

'Hey, take a look . . . how badly it's bleeding . . . it's unlikely to survive. It is bound to die in half an hour's time or at best in an hour,' said one of the children.

Siddhartha took the bird in his hands. It appeared to have looked at him pityingly through its half-closed eyes . . . in endless pain. Siddhartha ran his fingers along its body lovingly. It seemed to be in misery and Siddhartha again felt the bird to have looked at him appealingly . . . he felt as though he understood the mute language of the bird . . . asking him to liberate it from its mortal suffering, as it were.

It was then that Siddhartha remembered his grandmother's words. Every morning and evening, twice a day, as a ritual she prayed before their family deity with great devotion.

Once he had asked her, '*Nanamma*, what do you ask God for, when you worship Him with such devotion?'

She smiled at his words. Her toothy smile appeared beautiful ever since her dentures were fitted.

Smiling softly, she had answered Siddhartha's question. 'I ask God to bless my grandson to become a great doctor and treat the kind of diseases elders like me get afflicted with, and earn a good name.'

'Now tell me *Nanamma*, for yourself what do you ask!'

'What would I need from God for myself? I ask Him to bless my son and daughter-in-law.'

'Not that . . . what about you . . . won't you ask anything for yourself?'

'I ask Him to grant me a painless death,' she replied after a pregnant pause.

'What does that mean?'

'It means death bereft of pain. It's like painlessly reaching the lap of death while still in sleep . . . do

3

you know, such fortune is ordained to favor only the virtuous . . . to die quietly and peacefully without being afflicted with any kind of disease, while being physically still active.'

For thirteen-year old Siddhartha, his grandmother's words made little sense. Isn't everyone afraid of death? Doesn't everyone weep over someone's death? That means no one likes to die. Then why does grandma wish for death to come to her? Why does she talk about dying peacefully?

'You should never die *Nanamma*! Don't ever say those words. I can't bear to hear those words. I feel like crying.'

Grandmother drew her agitated teary-eyed grandson close to her warm hug. For him, she was the dearest of all. She always came to his defense whenever his mother scolded him or father tried to punish. Whenever she came to his rescue, even father couldn't say anything. Only grandmother fought on his behalf to get what he wanted from his father.

'My dear Siddhartha, no one can escape death. I have spent my life in happiness. Now I have grown old. One day or the other, I'll have to go to God's abode. It's better to die before my near and dear wished I were dead, or I'm laid up in bed with sickness and my people are unable to tender care. The reason why I pray to God everyday is that he should take my life without subjecting me to miseries that lead to a painful death.'

Breaking away from his thoughts, Siddhartha took another look of the pigeon that seem to be appealing to him to deliver it an easy and speedy death. From its half-opened eyes, it seemed to be praying, '*won't you release me from my suffering and this physical pain?*'

The children who gathered around Siddhartha waited eagerly to see what he intended to do with the pigeon. Like the Siddhartha of earlier times who saved a swan's life plucking out an arrow from its body, will he save the life of the wounded pigeon . . . will he take it to a Vet . . . else, will he take it home to give care . . . or abandon it to its fate uncaring?

Siddhartha lifted the pigeon by its legs with his right hand. As one of the bird's legs was broken, he could not get a firm hold of it. Moving towards a nearby boulder, he dashed its head against the stone. The bird died that very instant.

Those around him let out a shocked cry 'ah!' . . . some looked at Siddhartha in awe . . . some in sorrow . . . some others in disbelief. The girls among them could not bear the sight of that ghastly action. They fled.

As for Siddhartha, he jerked up his head proudly as though he performed a great deed and threw a casual glance at others before heading for home.

He wished to share that incident with his mother; however, he feared that she would scold him. After dinner, he snuggled up to his grandmother and settled by her side.

'*Nanamma* . . . do you know what happened today while I was returning from school?'

'How do I know unless you tell me? Do I have any divine vision?' she smiled as she asked the question.

She was all ears through his narration of the incident.

'*Nanamma* . . . did I commit any mistake in killing the pigeon . . . have I committed any sin . . . will God punish me?' Siddhartha asked towards the end with a pale expression.

No answer came from grandmother immediately. She pondered over the matter awhile to know if there was anything unnatural about her grandson's action.

'Why did you get the idea that you should kill the bird dashing its head against the rock?' she queried.

'It was heartbreaking to see the bird wriggle in pain, *Nanamma*. I was moved to tears, moreover, the bird was about to die. Did it have to go through that terrible pain until then? Did you not say that it would be better for one to have an instant easy death, instead of a painful and miserable one? I felt immense pity for the poor bird. I put down the poor bird to help ease its pain.'

'Okay! You wanted to kill the bird. You thought you should liberate it from its mortal pain. Then your action of dashing the pigeon against the boulder could have appeared cruel to those around.'

'No, *Nanamma*! Initially, I wanted to strangle the bird . . . well, the cat had already bitten into its neck, and what if it had to throb on with pain? I found that to be the best possible way to kill without causing much struggle and pain. Tell me, have I done anything wrong?'

After a long pause, grandmother affectionately touched Siddhartha's cheeks. 'No. You did the right thing. You possess a heart filled with ardour and kindness, but people may not look at the situation the way you have. I know you very well . . . my grandson has a very sensitive heart.'

That night Siddhartha slept well. He even dreamt of the dead pigeon thanking him.

Next day on reaching the school, the principal sent for Siddhartha. A ninth standard student by then had promptly taken the matter to his notice.

'Is it true you did a mighty good thing, on your way home last evening?' Siddhartha observed the principal's eyes turn red with anger.

He could not get the expression 'mighty good', so asked, 'what have I done, sir?'

'Rascal, are you asking me what you did? Do you think I will let you off if you act innocent? Haven't I heard of how you had killed a pigeon dashing its head against a boulder?'

'Sir, its neck was bitten into by a cat. It had also lost a wing. One of its legs was broken. I could not bear to see its pain hence I killed it,' Siddhartha confessed.

'Scoundrel, did the bird tell you of its pain? If you can display such monstrous and violent nature at this tender age, you may even grow up to commit murders as an adult. You will become a ruffian or a rowdy. Well, tomorrow bring your father along! I will have to talk to him!'

'Sir . . . I was moved by the pitiable state the pigeon was in. It was bleeding all over. With a broken neck, it was suffering immensely. I could not see it suffer in pain. I eased its pain so that it may die in peace. It had to die a painful death a little later anyway. The bird too must have desired a speedy death. I only helped it fulfill its last wish.'

'Shut up, you idiot! You are trying merely to justify your actions. It is as though the bird had a mind of its own, and you executed its wish . . . do you take yourself to be next to God or what!'

Siddhartha said in defense, 'the bird cannot voice its desire, sir!'

'You can speak since you have a voice, so you are now trying to justify your savage act. Over that, you are trying to convince me it was not a mistake at all on your part . . . that itself is a bigger mistake . . . . I wouldn't be going through this trauma had you confessed to your mistake saying, 'what I did was a mistake and I'll not do it again!'

Siddhartha had not even finished his sentence, 'sir, I did nothing wrong,' he was struck hard on the cheek. The principal was further infuriated, 'I've to suggest your father to have you examined by a doctor to see if are sick in mind. It's going to be dangerous if it gets worse.'

Tears turned in Siddhartha's eyes, besides he was angry with the principal . . . 'why should he face punishment without having committed anything wrong . . . who is the principal to punish him . . . what authority did he have to punish him?'

When Siddhartha's father came to know of the issue the next day, he caned him severely to punish him. He did not even pay any heed to the pleas of the grandmother.

Siddhartha's father worried no end about his son's future as he shared with his wife his worst fears, 'what would become of this fellow when he gets older and knifes somebody for the stated reason that he killed only to free that someone from physical pain?'

*   *   *

Prasad was wearing his school uniform. 'Come on my son, make it fast . . . your school bus will be here any time!' His mother prodded him waiting with his tie ready in hand.

'It's over, Mummy. Now hand me my tie. Where are my shoes? Have you polished them? They have to shine, or else I'll be made to stand in a corner during the school assembly, and over that made to pay a fine,' saying so, he wore his tie and put on his socks. Finding his shoes already done, he nodded his head in approval even as he was putting them on and slung his schoolbag over his shoulder. 'Bye Mummy!' He took one long step and was out soon running towards the spot where the school bus picked him up daily.

'If you run like that, the *dal* in your lunch box would spill! Wasting time and waiting until the last minute . . . and thereafter running at such great speed! Oh, what a boy . . . failing to explain to him really kills me!' He could hardly wait to hear his mother out to the end.

Five to six children of Harvard School were already at the bus stop, waiting for the bus. Prasad's spirits brightened as soon as he saw Ramya, his classmate, who was among them. After greeting her 'Hi!' he quipped, 'Are you done with your homework? As it is, our Mathematics teacher is quick-tempered. He beats black and blue until the cane in hand breaks.'

'Oh, Yes! I am done with homework yesterday itself. Besides the teachers don't beat girls,' she said batting her eyelids at him.

He had heard his mother mention many a time to his father, 'That girl's eyes . . . have you observed, how beautiful they are . . . eyelids like bee wings . . . don't they remind you of Savitri, the yesteryear actress?'

Ramya and Prasad studying in eighth standard were immediate neighbours. Ramya's father worked as a lecturer at Nizam College. Prasad's father was an officer with Canara Bank while his mother worked as a clerk in the same bank.

'Your father helps you with all subjects. He should be helping you with your homework too. No wonder you stand first in the class. My father is not so good at Mathematics. He only did his B.Com.'

'No. You are all assuming that my dad teaches everything. I'd rather study all subjects by myself. See, I did the homework too by myself. My dad didn't help with it . . . true!' she replied rolling her eyes.

Finally, the bus showed up . . . the children formed a queue to board the bus as per their Principal's instruction. Ramya stood behind Prasad . . . two other boys were behind her.

Those in front of Prasad boarded the bus first. When Prasad's turn came, he was about to place his right foot on the footboard when he found he could not move his leg. For a moment, he could not understand what was happening to him. He gathered all his strength and tried to move it again. *'No use. What is this? Why is my leg not in my control? It is as though it were dead . . . fell to ruin . . . . Are my legs like those of the cursed hero in that folklore movie on TV turning to stone?'*

'Move fast!' Ramya's impatient voice came from behind.

Now Prasad lifted his left leg. To his great relief he could. He thought to himself . . . *'Oh, boy . . . how afraid I was a moment ago!'* He put his left leg on the footboard and lifted his right leg after that. Once inside, he could run as fast as Ravi who was rushing towards the first available seat. About to grab the seat in just another leap, Prasad fell down with a thud. Every student in the bus fell silent, but soon they all burst out laughing.

Shame, anger, pride and sorrow . . . a myriad of emotions overtook Prasad at once. He grabbed Ravi's shirt collar who took his seat by then. 'Why did you thrust your leg forward as to trip me up? I'll report this matter to our Principal,' he quipped in anger.

Ravi looked at him surprised. 'How could I knock you over, when you were way ahead of me? You ran and I after you. That was all. I had no idea how you fell down,' Ravi replied who was in the tenth standard.

Ravi did not get angry with Prasad despite the latter grabbing his shirt collar. He bore only sympathy for him for getting hurt in the melee.

'No. You must have tripped me up on purpose. Mind you, in the past did I ever fall when we scrambled for seats?' Prasad asked with pride mixed in anger.

'I swear on my mother. I was not the cause for your fall. You fell all by yourself,' Ravi tried to pacify him.

'Why should I fall? Am I crazy to fall for no reason?'

'Perhaps.'

At that, everyone fell to laughing yet again.

'Wait! I'll settle a score with you later, but not now."

Prasad forgot all of it the moment their bus entered the school campus.

The next day was Sunday.

Prasad in fact loved riding bikes. His passion for bicycle-ride deepened when his neighbor, Ramya, bought one for herself.

Prasad had approached his father who was reading a newspaper.

'Won't you buy me a bicycle, Daddy?' Prasad pleaded.

'Bicycle? Why do you need one?' Prasad's father frowned.

'You know Daddy, most of my friends come to school on bicycles . . . I too will go to school on a bicycle . . . that way I will be sparing some expense for you on transport.'

'Son, don't try to outwit me! Never mind about that expenditure! You'll go to the school by bus itself.'

'What do you lose if you buy me a bicycle?' Prasad's voice turned teary already.

'Yes, a lot. Firstly, you will hurt yourself falling from the bicycle, and every day, we have to wait eagerly for your safe return. For us, the bus is more convenient. It arrives at our doorstep, and brings you back safe and secure."

'Even girls come to school on bicycles, Daddy! Ramya's father too bought her one. Haven't you seen her practicing every evening?'

'Why should I concern myself with others' matters . . . I'll not buy you a bicycle. I cannot bear to see you hurt yourself!'

'Daddy, it's common to get hurt while learning to cycle. You had told me that you fell off the bicycle three or four times when you were young, didn't you? *Tatagaru* bought you a bicycle all the same.'

'Hey . . . don't you try your crooked logic on me! My father had six children. I was the fourth one. But you are my only child,' Prasad's father protested.

His mother too joined her husband, 'besides you're our long awaited offspring. You were born after eight years of our marriage. No temple or shrine went unvisited and no god spared without saying a prayer, all for the sake of having a son. If anything untoward happens to you, neither your father nor I can endure.'

Prasad knew that it was easier to convince his mother than his father. That day he took care not to press further.

Next day he returned from school as usual at four-thirty in the evening. Two hours later, his mother returned from the bank. Father was to return home anyhow after eight.

Mother got down to her work in the kitchen.

'Mummy! Shall I help you in cutting the vegetables?' saying, he entered the kitchen.

'No, my son! The cut vegetables are ready in the fridge,' his mother said fondly looking at her son.

'Any other help, Mummy?' Prasad asked, his eyes expectantly shining.

'Yes . . . studying well secure good marks and become a District Collector . . . I can't ask for more.'

'Mummy . . . for your sake I shall become a Collector. Sure, Mummy! With my salary I will buy you a car . . . a Scorpio . . . in that you can commute to your bank in style.'

'Hey, wouldn't I be retiring by then!' Saroja said looking at her son proudly.

'So what? Then you can as well take a ride to Necklace Road in the evenings for an outing,' he added.

After a brief while, he ventured, 'Mummy . . . I have a small request. Will you please grant it?'

'Oh, didn't I know it coming! My darling son is about to make a wish. Well, tell me what your request is.'

'Please recommend to Daddy to buy me a bicycle.'

'Didn't we tell yesterday that there was no question of buying you a bicycle? You can't balance while riding.'

'I'll balance it well, Mummy. I rode Ravi's bike two or three times . . . Ravi, who lives down the lane a couple of houses away.'

Prasad's mother looked at her son in wonder. 'You rascal . . . didn't you fall from that bicycle? How could you learn cycling without falling off? Did you hide your bruises after a fall?'

'No, Mummy . . . Ravi held the bicycle for me while riding. Besides, I pedaled it slowly. My legs could easily reach the ground.'

'Even so, there's no bike for you. You've to go to school only by bus.'

Prasad lowered his head and remained silent. He expected his mother would think he was sulking when he sat that way.

As hoped, his mother came to him and stroked his head. 'Will you please listen to me as a darling son? When you grow up, Daddy will straight away buy you a car . . . is it okay!'

'Mummy, please. Even if Daddy buys me a car then, he'll still have the regrets, that he couldn't buy me a bicycle now.'

At his words, she burst into a loud peal of laughter.

'Oh, how brainy is my boy . . . . Well, on one condition, I'll convince your Daddy, you have to go to school by bus.'

Prasad thought over the proposal for a few minutes. He came to a compromise. Anyway, he could ask for permission later, to ride to school after he gained enough practice.

'Okay, Mummy! As you wish' he finally agreed.

'See my son's over smartness! You're seeing your wish fulfilled now. Yet you make it appear as though we have a vested interest in your wish,' she said rejoicing over her son, inwardly.

*   *   *

Ten days later . . .

The time was around six in the evening.

Prasad was waiting for his mother in all eagerness. By then he could have stepped in and out of the house at least ten times impatiently. 'Mummy is always like this . . . she's never prompt in doing things she promises,' he said to himself. Resignedly he squatted at their doorstep looking out into the street. His mind was set on the bicycle his mother would be bringing . . . 'how will the bicycle look . . . which color will she select . . . oh, didn't he ask for black colour?' He also told her that it should be more magnificent than Ramya's.

The moment an auto stopped in front of the house, Prasad jumped up. The auto driver offloaded the bicycle from the vehicle. His mother, Saroja, paid him the fare.

Prasad rushed forward and grabbed the new bicycle from the driver's hands. He did not even heed to his mother's caution, 'Relax . . . why that tearing hurry?' His eyes glimmered as he admired the bike . . . *Yes, it's the same black one but not the same . . . still fine with me. It's glittering new.*

'Mummy, I will be back in a moment,' Prasad set off pushing the bicycle along.

'Where to, son . . . won't you wait until Daddy returns?'

'Just a minute, Mummy! I want to show it to Ravi. I'll be right back,' Prasad told his mother.

Instead of going to Ravi, he headed straight to Ramya's house. 'Ramya, see my Daddy bought me this bicycle.' He was all smiles with his face flushed with happiness.

'Wow . . . it's so good . . . do you know how to ride . . . or do you have to practice?'

'Oh, I know it . . . will you also come . . . let us take two rounds.' He was enthusiastic to show off his expertise to Ramya.

'Okay. Let us go. I will fetch my bike,' Ramya reciprocated.

While Ramya was on the bike, Prasad tried to keep pace with her, riding alongside her. He felt his heart afloat on the clouds. They finished making a circle round the colony. During the second lap, Ramya raised the speed of her bicycle. Prasad tried pedaling harder. He felt his right leg go stiff. Then he tried with his left leg but of no avail. Soon fear gripped him and he started to sweat.

'Why are you that slow? You're lagging behind!' Ramya said without turning her head.

Prasad's bike slowed down. He pedaled hard. It slowed down further and he fell off the bicycle.

Ramya stopped. 'What happened, you fell off the bicycle . . . have you lost the balance or what?' She helped him to his feet.

His face reddened with shame and insult. He picked up his bicycle and walked back home without answering Ramya's call from behind.

'Where did you get this dust all over your person from . . . did you fall off your bicycle or what . . . Oh! Look at your arm . . . you got a bruise there!' Saroja cleaned the injury with an antiseptic lotion and later applied some ointment.

Prasad looked baffled. How was it he could not pedal the bicycle? He wanted to tell his mother. He took bath and had his dinner. Then as he sat down to study, he forgot all about it.

*   *   *

Saroja was back from work early.

Prasad who was riding his bicycle in the front yard, rushed forward to greet his mother. 'What a pleasant surprise, Mummy! You're home an hour before your usual time.'

'Another surprise awaits you! I've taken off from work tomorrow. Ask me why!'

Prasad beamed with happiness, his face blooming as a melon flower.

'Yes, Mummy I know! Tomorrow is my birthday.'

'Don't I have to celebrate my prince's birthday in style? I plan to cook for you some yummy dishes tomorrow so I am home early. You like *garelu* and chicken curry, don't you? Besides, I will also make *pulihora* and *payasasm* too. Now, tell me what will you have for breakfast?'

'Will you prepare whatever I ask?'

'Yes, you only have to order,' Saroja said smiling.

'How about having *dosalu*?'

'You are asking for *dosalu* since your dad likes to have them with chicken curry. I knew it . . . don't I know you always take your Daddy's side?' she said, seemingly annoyed.

'No, Mummy. I like you very much . . . I like Daddy too but only a centimeter less.' He put his hands round his mother's neck, 'You're my life Mummy!'

'Enough of your filmy dialogues! Words won't suffice . . . you'll have to show in action.'

'Tell me, Mummy . . . what I should do for that. I'm ready to do anything for you. Do you want me to give up my life for you? I'd do that with a smile.'

'Shut up, you rascal! How many times did I tell you not to speak such ominous words? Now–a-days you have become a chatterbox. Blame it on your grandmother who overdosed you as an infant with that sap of *vasa* that you are now over-talkative and annoying me to no end.' Saroja walked towards the kitchen.

Prasad followed her, 'Mummy, let us go to a movie tomorrow. It's been quite some time since we went for a movie together.'

'Okay! You suggest which one, but don't suggest one of those newly released movies. It's hard to secure tickets for them. The crowds suffocate me. More, I've to ask your father to be back early at least tomorrow.'

Prasad felt as if he were on cloud nine. For some time he looked fondly at the new clothes mother bought for his birthday. Later he fetched from the nearby store, Cadbury's chocolates to be distributed in the class. His father bought a birthday cake on his way back from work.

Prasad's father made his mind clear at the very outset. 'Listen Prasad, I'm telling you this beforehand. You know I dislike the practice of getting up at midnight hour only to cut the cake and wish 'Happy birthday!' It makes no sense to stay awake until midnight when you have to wake up early the next morning. Of course, it is all right on New Year eve. Personally, I don't like cutting the cakes on birthdays either. I bought this only to please you. You'll therefore cut the cake only before going to school. Keep some pieces to treat your close friends. Is that okay?'

Prasad nodded his head obediently and added, 'but Daddy, you have to be home early tomorrow. Otherwise we won't get tickets for the movie.'

'That's okay . . . you told this a dozen times already.'

'You tend to forget Daddy once you are immersed in work! How many times has that not happened . . . at the time of my admission, when I had to pay my school fees, and at the parents' meets . . . only Mummy had to take care of all these.'

'Oh, I left you in her hands knowing her capability of managing matters,' Prasad's father winked at his wife.

'Daddy, don't think you can escape with those excuses tomorrow.'

'Okay . . . okay! I'll not take long. I will be home by five in the evening, then accompany you people to that stupid movie. I got one more thing to clarify. What kind of movie have you selected? Instead of a Viswanath or Balchander movie, did you select one of those violent movies where they axe and stab one another?'

'No, Daddy! I heard it is a good movie. Most of my friends have already seen it.'

'So be it. I am letting you have your way. After all it's your birthday.'

Next day, Saroja gave him a special bath applying oil to his head. Prasad wore his new set of clothes for the special day, instead of the regular uniform. He said his prayers to the family deities at the altar in the house. When his mother tried giving him some *payasam,* he asked her to wait a moment and touched the feet of his parents seeking their blessings.

Pleased, Saroja commented, 'Look at my son. How devoted he is!'Siddhartha's father too felt happy but interrupted, 'Well, an expert at the art of pleasing others!'

Prasad packed some cake in his lunch box while placing the packet of chocolates in his school bag. At the bus stop, his eyes looked for Ramya. He wondered why she was late. Usually she reached early. Will she come at all? Is she unwell? He turned anxious seeing their school bus approaching. He looked to check if she was coming. He saw her at a distance running toward the bus. Instinctively he beckoned to her,'Why this delay? Here comes our bus.'

Ramya placed a packet in his hand. 'Happy birthday, Prasad!'

'How did you know it's my birthday?' he said with happiness overwhelming him.

'Last year you brought a piece of cake for me. I remember it very well. I will never forget my friends' birthdays.'

'Okay, thanks. I brought you some cake this time too.' He was about to take out a piece, Ramya told 'Prasad, you better get into the bus. We can look into it later.' Both boarded the bus. Once in the bus, he offered the cake to Ramya once again, but she made a gesture to say it was not time yet.

No sooner had they crossed the school gate than Prasad gave Ramya piece of the cake. 'Now, it's your turn. Won't you open the packet I gave you?' Ramya asked him. He opened the gift wrapper to find a coffee-coloured 'Hero' pen . . . with a gold cap. How beautiful it was! He exclaimed enthusiastically, 'I love it!'

'You know, Prasad, fountain pens were in vogue before ball pens came into existence. Formerly, 'Hero' pen was a status symbol I heard my father say and that people loved this colour. I bought it for you as a special gift. I went to the nearby store to get it gift-wrapped. That was the reason for my delay.'

Prasad promised that he would keep the pen for its rarity. Ramya laughed as a shoe-flower in full bloom.

That day Prasad saw his entire time in school pass by happily, chitchatting with friends and teachers joining in to wish him a happy birthday. At four, the school closed for the day. He was home by four-thirty.

He alerted his mother that she should call his father. 'Have you called Daddy . . . unless he starts now he won't be here by five!'

'Son, I called him twice already, but there's no response. Perhaps he is in a meeting. He must have kept his cell in the silent mode.'

'He is forever the same, Mummy!'

'It is pressure of work, is it not? After all, one has to listen to the boss when at workplace.'

'Mummy, work is routine. My birthday comes only once a year!' Prasad said, controlling his tears.

'Son, don't worry over a petty matter such as this . . . where will the movie go? If not today, you can watch it tomorrow. There is still time left anyway. Don't be tense.'

Saroja rang her husband again. Still there was no response.

With a long face, Prasad sank into the sofa.

It was five in the evening. Saroja too began feeling impatient. . . . When it was quarter past five, she called off for that day the plan of going for the movie. At five-twenty, a call came from her husband.

'The meeting is just over. I could not skip the meeting since it was a very important one. Now, are you ready? Do one thing. Immediately, start for the theatre. Isn't the movie running in Shanti theatre? Take the tickets; I will join you right away.'

Saroja reassured her husband. 'Never mind. Should we have to watch the movie in great hurry? It takes at least half an hour to reach the theatre. In the meantime, the show would have begun. Better still, we watch the movie tomorrow. I prefer you rather return home.'

'No Mummy, not tomorrow. We'll go only today,' Prasad screamed standing close.

Prasad heard his father's loud guffaw coming over from the other end. 'Did you hear what our gem of a son is saying? Why should we disappoint him on his birthday? You both start now. He'll feel bad if you fail to get tickets.'

By the time they locked the house and engaged an auto, and reached the theatre, it was five-forty. Going to the ticket counter, Saroja bought three upper-class tickets.

'You're lucky, in spite of our being late the tickets are not sold out yet,' Saroja said to cheer Prasad.

Prasad felt very happy since his will prevailed. The only bother was they had to wait for his father. He kept squinting and peering at every scooter that entered the theatre compound anticipating his father's arrival.

It was six. The show had begun. 'Mummy . . . I am told there's a great fighting scene at the start of the movie. We may miss it,' Prasad rued.

Saroja was at a loss. In normal course, her husband should have reached the theatre by then . . . was he stuck in a traffic jam? In that case, he would have called her.

It was soon quarter past six. Saroja called his number yet again but there was no answer from the other end.

It was half past six. 'Mummy . . . half the movie would have been over by now. Dad is always like this.' Prasad was getting agitated. Fear began to grip Saroja. Did anything happen to him on the way to the theatre . . . did his scooter break down?

She dialed his number again. There was no response.

'Let's go inside, Mummy. Dad will anyway call us once he arrives. Then I will go out to hand over his ticket and bring him in,' Prasad urged his mother.

Saroja did not know what to do. Unable to stand Prasad's pestering she started to climb the stairs and move toward the entrance. Through the doors kept ajar, the sound of the film's dialogues fell on their ears.

'Move on, Mummy. Let's get inside!' Prasad said.

She let out a long sigh staring at the silent instrument in hand. She moved towards the door saying, 'okay, let's go in.'A call came the moment they entered the theatre. Yes, no doubt it was he.

With anxiety-ridden voice she asked, 'where are you? What caused you so much delay?'

There was no prompt reply from the other side. 'Why aren't you speaking?' she said raising her voice.

'Madam, my name is Sudhakar. I am Sub-Inspector of Police. How are you related to this person?' Saroja heard a stranger's voice coming over the cell.

Saroja felt her legs stiffen. *How is it someone from the police is speaking on my husband's cell? Did my husband by any chance lose his cell? Did the finder hand it over at the police station? Is he in the police station too?* Several questions rose in her mind all at once.

'I'm his wife, sir. What is he doing now? How did his cell come to your hand? Can I speak to him?'

'I am sorry, madam. Your husband met with an accident near the Old MLA Quarters. A *Qualis* collided with your husband's scooter.'

'My god . . . how is he now? Is he injured? Where are you calling from?'

'Madam, he suffered some minor injuries. We admitted him in the Apollo hospital at Hyderguda. I'm calling you from the hospital.'

'I'm rushing there right away. How is he doing now, is he alright?'her voice trembled.

'Not bad. Please reach the hospital as soon as possible.'

Prasad noticed his mother's face turn anxious and he sensed the fear and sorrow in her voice. 'Mummy, what happened to Daddy?'

'I hear your father met with an accident and is admitted in the hospital.' Her son tagging along, Saroja quickly exited the theatre and engaged an auto to reach the hospital. She cursed the driver for not driving faster. Strange fear took hold of her. *Are they minor injuries as stated by the police . . . why did he not use his cell . . . is he unable to talk . . . does it mean, he suffered injuries badly?* 'Oh, God! Don't be unjust to me!' she prayed to each of the gods in the pantheon.

On reaching the hospital, she ran towards the Sub-Inspector who was waiting in the lounge. 'What happened to my husband? Where is he right now? I intend seeing him immediately,' she asked in an anxious tone filled with tears.

'Are you the same person who spoke over the phone?'

'Yes. My name is Saroja. He is my husband. Show me where he is now. Please take me to him,'Saroja said agitatedly holding his hands.

'Madam, sit here for a while. Please relax.' He showed her a chair next to him.

'I will sit down, but not now. First allow me to see him, talk to him for a minute at least.'

'Right now your husband is in the ICU. It is not possible for us to go there. Please be patient. Everything will be alright.'

'Have they taken him to the ICU? Is he so badly wounded . . . you had said he only suffered minor injuries. Then why is he in the ICU?'

'Madam, you sit down for some time. Doctors will take good care of him. Good, the hospital was close by.We admitted him soon after the accident without losing time. I again beg of you, better sit down. Once the doctors come out we'll ask their permission to visit him,'the police officer tried to assure her.

Saroja slumped into a chair and made Prasad sit next to her. She held his hand hard in her hands. She was not quite conscious of what had happened or what was going to happen. To her everything appeared a vacant existence as though darkness was engulfing her life like a tidal wave with despair staring at her face like an open-mouthed python.

Hearing the news of the accident, some of Saroja's colleagues from the bank rushed to be by her side and stayed back to extend her their moral support. Later the doctors took Saroja's consent on some papers for conducting an operation.

At eleven-thirty that night, the doctors finally declared, 'despite our best efforts we failed to save his life.' That very instant, Saroja fell unconscious.

* * *

The sprawling campus of the Law College . . .

A few final year law students are engaged in casual talk gathered under a tree.

Another twenty minutes left for the next session to begin.

'I think, Kiran, it is justified to book under Section 306 those who instigate and abet suicides. It is not so with regard to those unfortunate ones booked for attempt of suicide under Section 309. It is cruel. I feel Section 309 took effect without much thought given to it. There is every need to repeal it from Indian Jurisprudence. What do you say?' Ramana quizzed.

'Isn't that the topic of the debate scheduled at three this afternoon? Are you participating in the debate?'

'Yes, that's the reason I raised this topic with you for discussion. I beseech you to throw some light on the topic. As my best friend, won't you be happy to see me win a prize in the competition?'

'Ramana, how selfish you are . . . what if I too participate?'

'You'll not participate . . . I know.'

'How can you be so sure?'

'Because Akshara too is participating'

Kiran's face reddened hearing that name. Nevertheless, checking himself, Kiran added, 'so what if Akshara participates? After all, anyone can participate in the competition. Akshara cannot thwart my right to compete.'

'Keep bragging Kiran! I am your best friend . . . don't I know you . . . your capability and your spirit of sacrifice.'

'What capability and what sacrifice? Don't run on in Greek and Latin. If you go on like this in the debate the judges will be at their wit's end to get the hang of your arguments.'

'No Kiran, you have eloquence. You can debate well and convince skillfully, swerve audience to your side. You are capable of analyzing any given issue from different perspectives, that beside, you have good grasp of the subject. Everyone in the college knows how many times you won first prize in our college debates.'

'But you are forgetting Akshara too won many times,' Kiran quipped.

'I know that is the reason you are giving a skip to the contest this year, isn't it?'

'True . . . I don't like to taste defeat at her hands.'

'No. That is not true. You only want to see her win. You always wish her to stand first in every competition. It is all your love for her my friend and sacrifice that is in love. Do you think I am not aware of it? If Akshara wins, you feel happy as though you won it. Tell me the truth. Isn't that the reason?'

For a few seconds, Kiran remained silent and replied softly gathering words. 'I've seen pain in her eyes rather than satisfaction whenever I stood first and she second. I like her determination and desire to win. She is a great woman.'

'I don't agree with you. You are great . . . to love a girl like her. At a time when films based on love cause disgust of the very word love, the thought of your love for Akshara is noble. . . . I applaud you raising my hands! How honourable is your ideal!'

'Hold, what ideal? It is a meaningless word. By calling me great, are you not belittling Akshara? Never again, talk of someone in a demeaning manner and call it love. In love, there is nothing high or low. If I love Akshara it's not for any ideal, but for her and my heart yearns for her only.'

'Then . . . tell me one thing. What have you seen in Akshara to love her so much?'

'I love her cheerful attitude toward life . . . her passion to win against all odds . . . her spirited nature of enjoying each day as a God-given gift . . . and her celebration of each day as if savoring a favorite fruit, in short, her zest for life . . . her intelligence and her beauty. . . ."

Kiran stopped mid sentence as something caught his attention just at that moment. Ramana too turned his glance in that direction.

Akshara was entering the campus just then. . . .

Kiran watched keenly the softness in her face. Her small mouth . . . beautiful chin . . . that tiny mole as a beauty spot to the left of her lower lip adding charm to her . . . above everything, the radiance on her face . . . a brightness seen only in people who live life relishing it . . . that self-confidence adorning certain faces as an attractive jewel . . .

Seeing Kiran, she greeted him with a 'hi' and waving her hand in the direction of Ramana, she moved on to enter the classroom . . . rolling her wheelchair.

Ramana looked at his watch. 'Oh my . . . I've just six minutes left! We are yet to discuss the topic of the debate. We digressed from the topic.'

'No deviation . . . it's the direction I've to follow.'

'Oh you magnanimous! Now answer my question on Section 309.'

'You know I dropped out of the competition to allow Akshara to win. Then why should I help you with tips on the subject?' Kiran asked with a smile on his face.

'Now, don't betray your friend! Rest assured first prize is going to be Akshara's. Second and third prizes will suffice the rest. Coming to the topic, tell me how a suicide or its attempt be considered a crime?' Ramana persisted.

'Certainly it's a crime. A man has only a right to live, but there's no such right to take one's own life.'

'My life is my concern. How can a government stop me from taking my life? What big crime have I committed to deserve punishment?'

Kiran explained, 'The government takes responsibility of its people just as a father does of his family. Take the example of the police. The police fines motorcyclists for not wearing helmets, since failing to wear one is an offence. If one foolishly questions the police, 'what do you lose if I do not wear a helmet . . . if I hurt myself, I am the one who will suffer and I am ready to face the consequences, now, who are you to question?' Then the motor cyclist's argument is termed perverse. It is the responsibility of the government to see that accidents do not take place on the roads. In the same coin, it is the responsibility of the government also to prevent suicides. That's the reason there is Section 309.'

Ramana countered, 'for a moment think of the man who decided to end his own life. Left with no choice, with defeat staring at the face or vexed with life, he wants to end his life or say, he is tired of the devious and envy-ridden world. Then how justified is the government in booking him and imposing punishment on him? It amounts to adding insult to injury. When the government itself is not capable of offering any solution, it has no right to stop one from choosing death as a way out.'

'When incidents of suicide are analyzed, it is proved that not more than ten per cent of those dead had sufficiently strong grounds for suicide. In the majority of cases, only the weak-minded were driven to suicide on frivolous grounds, such as getting reprimanded by one's mother, for scoring low marks or failing in examinations, a wife failing to return from her parents' home, or not allowed to watch TV. If the government does not consider these as crimes, there are chances of one committing suicide for no apparent reason. Just as a smile is infectious, suicidal tendencies can also be contagious. One suicide inspires another to commit the same . . . like sheep that jump into a well following the leader blindly. The increase in suicides reflects the failure of the government. There arises, hence, a need for the government to effectively check suicides and enact necessary laws in this regard,' Kiran said.

Continuing his argument he said, 'in addition to this, you have touched upon another important argument on whether the government has the rightful authority to intervene when it is not capable of providing a solution to the hardships and problems that troubling mankind. What can the government do when people are distressed or are weak in mind, unable to repay debts incurred beyond their means and as a result commit suicides? Any government will only provide facilities to its people to lead a decent life and expects them to avail themselves of government help. The government also introduces many welfare programs such as free healthcare, loans at concessional interest rates, loan waivers, supply of essential commodities at subsidized rates etc. In spite of that, if people say they want to die, is it not a crime?'

Seeing their lecturer arrive, Kiran and Ramana put an end to their conversation for the time being, and entered the classroom and took their seats. Kiran sat right behind Akshara. He listened to the lecture, while admiring, off and on, the charm of Akshara's lustrous hair flowing down to her waist.

In the afternoon, the debating competition commenced.

Ramana's turn came after four candidates had finished theirs.

Ramana began to speak.

'How can suicide be a crime? It is not proper to treat it as a crime without going into the root of the problem as to know why a person decides to commit suicide. Moreover, who faces punishment in the end . . . the victim who attempts suicide! No body wants to know about the suffering that drove him take such a decision. However, as per our legal texts, isn't the punishment to be given to one who inflicts such suffering on them?

'In the case of the weak-minded who could not face misery and tackle life's problems and commit suicides, do you know who has to be punished . . . the parents of the children who raised them as such . . . the education system that does not train them to deal with the problems of life. Besides, the teachers have to be punished for not training the students to face the bitter facts of life. Lastly, the society has to face punishment for pushing its members to a situation where left with no choice they attempt suicide.

'Laws have to be in place only to punish cruel people, but the law should not be cruel. Formulate laws that have a humane touch so they may last long. In conclusion, I am of the opinion that there is every need to repeal Section 309 from the Indian Penal Code since it is inhuman and heartless.'

The next name called was Akshara.

The lecture hall fell silent as Akshara wheeled her chair to the podium and geared herself up to speak.

'I don't say suicide is a sin because I don't believe in the assessment of good deeds versus bad deeds or that one's deeds on earth determine one's place in heaven or hell.

'Life is for living. Life is a struggle. The cowards escape life, attempt suicide. Whatever be the problems in life, one has to overcome the same with courage. In fact, life is a game. It is our duty to keep playing that game without giving a thought to winning or losing. At the same time, we have to play the game with determination that we will win. We should not lose faith in ourselves. Even when we face defeat, we should be prepared to play the game all over again. We should keep playing till we win. Quitting the game midway is inexcusable.

'Some of the speakers before me contended that it was unjust to commit suicide on petty grounds. Does that imply suicide is not wrong when one has a strong reason? Whatever be the reason, big or small, it is a crime to commit suicide.

'In my opinion, there's no problem without a solution. Why sit in darkness and complain there is darkness all around? Dispel that darkness by lighting a candle. If no candle too is at hand . . . get on to your feet, look around, you will discover light somewhere!

'According to the Article 14 of our Constitution, all people have equal rights. Through Article 21, our Constitution has guaranteed the right to life of dignity to everyone. . . . In the case of Gian Kaur on the right to life of dignity, it was held by the Five-Judge Bench of Supreme Court, that 'the right to life' guaranteed by Article 21 of the constitution does not include the 'right to die'. The Bench clarified that 'the right to life' meant living until the arrival of moment of natural death. It overruled the judgment of the lower court in the case of P. Rathinam and held that Section 309 is constitutionally valid. So I strongly advocate the need for Section 309 of IPC to stay,' Akshara concluded her speech.

Everyone was spellbound by Akshara's eloquence . . . her voice cutting through hardened silence like a sharp knife . . . diction that was impressive . . . lines that had a poetic flow . . . articulation in English like gushing waters of a stream . . . she knew where to heighten or tone down casting a spell on the audience like a magician.

The lecture hall reverberated with a loud applause.

The results were announced at four in the evening. As everyone expected, Akshara won the first prize.

Once everyone finished congratulating Akshara, Kiran approached her last and said, 'I won't congratulate you.'

Akshara smiled. 'Didn't you like what I said?'

'No, not for that, one should be surprised if you don't win, what is so odd about your winning the first prize? Be it studies, debate or essay writing competitions, the first prize has always been yours, isn't it?'

'Why aren't you participating these days? You used to give me a tough fight. Had you participated, I may not have won the prize. Besides, there is no satisfaction in winning unless it is against a competent opponent,' she said pushing her wheelchair towards the room's exit.

'Even if I had participated, only you would have won the prize.'

'Then I would have felt happier than now.'

'Oh . . . so you say happiness lies only in defeating me?'

'No, it is in winning against you. Well . . . you have not answered my question. Why aren't you these days participating in the competitions?'

'I felt it is better to listen to others instead of speaking.'

Akshara turned her head and looked at him quizzically as though to say, 'say that again!'

'I mean . . . in my view . . . that means . . . okay . . . why beat around the bush . . . I love to hear you speak. Your voice sounds sweet as the strumming of a string instrument . . . it is soothing to listen to you, do you know?'

Akshara laughed out loudly. 'Lies too should be relevant . . . I wonder how you will fare in your profession in future! Even if you participate, could you not have listened to me still? Reason does not lie in that.'

Kiran did not reply. They had already reached the main road.

Akshara asked Kiran who was walking beside her, 'Where is your bike?'

'I didn't bring it today. I gave it to the mechanic,' he lied.

'Is that so? Nevertheless, you have to go on that route . . . why are you coming this way?'

'I have got some work on this route. If you don't mind . . . can I walk along with you?'

'Okay . . . no big deal.' Akshara adjusted the motor attached to the chair to suit the walking speed.

'I didn't get an answer for what I had asked,' Kiran asked walking by her side.

Akshara knew what he had asked, but feigning ignorance, she queried, 'What did you ask?'

'I beg for your love.'

'Do you watch Telugu films often? The phrase sounds good.'

'It's no laughing matter. I am telling you the truth. I like you. Don't refuse my love.'

'I'm afraid you seem to lack clarity in this regard.I told you that day itself . . . not to bring up the matter again.'

'I will bring it up a hundred times, till you accept . . . I'll keep bringing it up till I get you to accept my proposal.'

She looked at him, at first, with some irritation. Soon, comforting herself, she looked at him as one would reprimand an infant threatening to go near the fire. She turned her glance to the road. 'Yours is not love, Kiran . . . but pity. I loathe those who shower pity on me. I don't think I am in so pathetic a condition for others to show pity. I am living happily within my bounds.'

'It isn't pity Akshara . . . it is adoration. Your mental strength and your attitude impress me immensely. My love for you is true . . . a love that loves you as you are.'

'It is natural, Kiran, to feel that way at your age. Your mind misses the mistruths of your thoughts. Your eyes refuse to notice the truth before you. Love is a trick of your mind deluding you into thinking what you imagine as real. As days pass by, each of those delusions will get cleared and as each misgiving reveals itself, those layers covering your eyes will peel off, and the bitter truth will stare at you and you will realize that you were deceiving yourself through out.'

'What's that bitter truth?'

'The truth of what you consider as love wasn't love at all!'

'You're mistaken. My love will remain as fresh as now for eons. You'll come to know the sweet truth after a while.'

'What's that, Kiran?'

'That my love is true . . . pure . . . unique . . . and eternal.'

'Do you know poetry too?'

'No poetry . . . it's a truth surging from my heart.'

'Kiran . . . in another year's time we're going to be lawyers. It isn't proper to prattle like children anymore. You don't quite know about me. If you knew, you wouldn't be talking like this.'

'Akshara, whatever I may hear of you, however dreadful it might be, it will not alter my love for you. I love not your beauty or your body. I love your mind, hard and firm as steel . . . your heart whiter than snow . . . your personality, which is like a treasure house of boundless sweetness.'

'You forgot another thing, Kiran.'

He continued, interrupting her. 'I haven't forgotten anything . . . I remember everything. I have enormous trust in my memory.'

Akshara could not help laughing despite the seriousness of the subject.

'Kiran, won't you allow me to finish? Memory is something I too possess. Isn't it for that reason, everyone is expecting one of us to top in the college? I'm not referring to that. What's the end result of love?'

'Marriage'

'A heart is enough for love, but for marriage both body and heart are important. Do you agree?'

'You aren't any disembodied spirit, are you? Doesn't that mean you have both a mind as well as body?'

'You aren't getting what I am trying to say Kiran. Some day, I will share with you all the details about me. I don't think you'll get me right till then.'

'Why postpone to another day? Tell me now . . . I am here to listen.'

'Not now and even if I start now, I may forget some details, or I may not put them in proper perspective. . . . I need to put everything down on paper. We'll discuss once you finish going through it.'

'Okay. Then when do you plan to put the whole thing down on paper?'

'Can't say, but I will soon as my mood directs. I will hand it over to you when I finish. Is that okay?'

'Can I dare to disagree . . . I have already committed the sin of loving you, haven't I'

'Look . . . already there is a change in your tone. You've come to accept it was a sin to have loved me.'

'Hey, it was just a casual remark. . . . Okay, I correct myself. Can I dare to disagree for having gained the merit of being in love with you?'

Akshara burst into laughter hearing him. The stars from above seemed to have dropped down on the earth in her peal of laughter. Her laughter seemed like moonshine scattering its warmth all over. 'All in all, you proved yourself to be a lawyer. See how you changed your words in a second.'

Kiran too laughed hearing her words.

*   *   *

Prasad, tying his shoelaces called out to his mother who was in the kitchen, 'what is there for today's breakfast?'

'*Upma*,' she replied from inside.

'Oh, Mummy! How many times do I have to tell you that I don't care much for *upma*? You can as well make *dosas* or chapattis.'

'There isn't enough flour in the house. I will buy some today on my way back from office. Tomorrow I will prepare whatever you suggest. Is it alright?' she said while carrying a plateful of *Upma* and tomato chutney to go with it.

'I don't want it. I can't have it,' Prasad protested.

'My son, make do with this for today.'

'No Mummy. . . . Please!'

'I can say 'please' as well . . . don't you know that if you do not eat, I feel bad and I can't have my lunch too?'

'Oh, Mummy! How you bring me round with your sentiment!'

'This is what you taught me,' she retorted adding a smile.

'Then we shall arrive at a compromise. I will eat bread and jam, instead. Is it okay?'

Saroja looked at her son affectionately and said, 'obstinate fellow . . . look how he sees to it that his word prevails.' She placed the packet of bread and the bottle of jam on the dining table. Pulling his chair closer to the table, Prasad started applying jam to the bread slice.

'Mummy . . . you promised to buy me a cell phone . . . when will you buy it?' he asked applying jam slowly to the bread slice.

Saroja sat in the chair next to Prasad's and pulled the plate of *upma,* she had earlier brought for her son.

'Why do you need a cell phone so soon? Didn't I say I would buy you one once you secure above five hundred in the examination and before you move to the Junior college?'

'Everyone in my class has a cell phone, Mummy. Do you know how ashamed I feel at not having one?'

'You need not be ashamed for not having a cell phone or a motorcycle. Only children who don't do well in studies or conduct themselves well need to be ashamed. You study well. You do not indulge in any mischief. Hasn't your principal recently given you a certificate of good conduct?'

'Mummy! Please, don't change the topic. We are discussing here about buying a cell phone, not about my conduct.'

'You're now in your tenth standard . . . don't forget that. Tell me what use are cell phones, but for wasting time and indulging in useless chatting? So, listen to me . . . I will buy you one when you come to Intermediate.'

'Look, Mummy. I will study well irrespective of whether you buy me a cell phone or not. I will also secure above five hundred marks Mummy, if you buy me a small cell phone in advance.'

'Don't play smart with me. Even a small cell phone is cell phone all the same . . . there is hardly any difference in the damage it can cause.'

'Please Mummy! Cell phone has advantages too. You are very dear to me, aren't you? I can talk to you anytime I wish to. I can even know when you plan to get back home from your bank. If I take ill, I can inform you over the phone.'

On hearing the word 'illness', Saroja writhed in agony. 'No, my son, don't talk that way. I can't bear to hear it. I pray God everyday that you should remain for ever healthy and happy. Who is there for me beside you? I am struggling to stay afloat only for you.' Tears welled up in her eyes as she said those words.

'Please Mummy, don't weep. I can't bear to see you in tears. Sorry, I hurt you. Please forgive me. I don't wish to have a cell phone.' Prasad began to weep wiping his mother's tears rolling down her cheeks.

Saroja's heart melted like butter hearing his words. 'Okay I will buy you one. Anyway, your birthday is round the corner. You can have it then.' Having said those words, the next moment she realized the mistake she had committed. She unwittingly raked the wound the boy had just been forgetting. *Will the wound ever heal at all in his life? Certain wounds remain raw forever.*

Staying silent for a while, Prasad gathered his words. 'Don't ever remind me of my birthday, Mummy. The guilt haunts me to no end that I was the cause of my father's death. Didn't I tell you before, that I cannot celebrate my birthday as long as I remember it is also my father's death anniversary?'

Before Saroja could say something, the doorbell rang.

As Saroja was about to rise to answer the door, Prasad offered, 'I will open the door, Mummy.' He tried to rise from the chair. Some invisible glue seemed to have fastened him to the chair . . . he tried to rise again. He felt his legs go limp. A vague fear lurked in his mind. Placing both his hands on the table, he tried again with all his strength to get up. He could not.

The doorbell rang again. Saroja was having her breakfast and was expecting Prasad to open the door. Exasperated, she looked at him as if to say, 'how long . . . open the door quick!' Looking at his paled face, she knew at once that something untoward had happened to her son. She saw in his eyes sorrow she never saw until then . . . despair . . . helplessness of being defeated . . . an element of disbelief . . . a fear that it could be true. . . .

In a quick movement, Saroja rose to her feet and opened the door. Ramya entered greeting her, 'Hi, Aunty!'

'Hi Prasad . . . I came to remind you of my Math notebook lest you forget to get it. Can you give it now, so that I can keep it in my schoolbag?'

Prasad looked at her giving a blank stare as if he were a wooden doll, but did not reply.

Saroja intervened. 'I saw him putting it safely in his school bag. He will give it to you on reaching the school.'

'Ok, Aunty,' Ramya then turned to Prasad. 'Come quick. It is time for our school bus.'

'He will follow you in a minute Ramya. You go first,' Saroja replied.

'Bye, Aunty!' Ramya left. Closing the door after her, Saroja sat beside her son. 'What happened . . . what are those beads of sweat gathered all over your face?' She touched his cheek and stroked his head lovingly.

Recovering a little, Prasad tried rising on his feet pressing his palms against the table. He managed to stand on his legs, but then why couldn't he do so earlier, as though someone cast a spell on him . . . checked if there was any gum stuck to the chair. There was none. All the same, felt nothing as he ran his hand along the chair's surface. Saroja looked at her son confused. 'What happened, my son . . . what are you looking for . . . what happened to you in the first place?'

Prasad looked at his mother once and then looked at the chair with some disquiet. He sat down and stood up again.

Saroja cried out impatiently, 'Tell me, what happened . . . why do you behave as though crazed?'

'Mummy, when Ramya came here a few moments ago, I tried getting up from my chair but I couldn't.'

'What?'

'True, Mummy. I felt as though I was stuck to this chair.'

Saroja laughed out aloud. 'Did you heed to my words when I asked you not to watch that horror movie last night . . . didn't I tell you that there is nothing occult or magical . . . you must have merely imagined things.'

'Is it so, Mummy?' Prasad asked in a weak tone.

'Definitely . . . you scared the daylights out of me for no reason. Get moving fast. Ramya must be getting worried,' Saroja hurried her son.

As Prasad remembered that Ramya's notebook was with him, he slung the school bag across his shoulders and walked briskly towards the bus stop. By then the bus had arrived. Ramya seated in the bus called out to Prasad to run. Once he boarded the bus, Prasad forgot all about how a few moments ago he was unable to stand on his feet.

*　　*　　*

Akshara was up before sunrise. She did not sleep well the previous night . . . she spent the whole night eagerly looking forward to the daybreak. Her cherished dreams were about to fructify, it was a long awaited day to repay the debt to her parents. The result of her final year law course would be out that very same day.

Akshara tied her disheveled hair with an elastic band. Gently brought together both her legs and let them hang down the side of her cot. Then managing to pull the wheelchair lying behind the cot's headboard, she shifted her body into it. She succeeded in meeting that task after about fifteen minutes of effort. Though it had been a daily routine, she always heaved a sigh of relief at the end of it and mumbled to herself, '*at last!*' Because of its wheels, the chair never stayed in place. It was no less than a feat, a circus feat at that—to hold fast the chair with both her hands and use the very same hands to shift her inert body into it. Formerly, her mother or father lifted her and seated her in the chair. Having decided not to trouble them unless and until required, as she grew older, with unsparing resolve and continuing practice, she succeeded in doing certain tasks herself, that seemed impossible initially.

Even such small victories had been cause for immense satisfaction and happiness, and made Akshara say each time, '*I am the winner!*'

As Akshara thought of the results that were to be out that day, she mumbled to herself, '*so far, I never knew what defeat is. I am always a winner. Success should be mine this examination too.*' At that thought, a smile flashed on her lips.

Akshara maneuvered her wheelchair slowly and entered the bathroom. It was a bathroom re-designed keeping in mind her physical disability. Due to the efforts of her father who got some minor changes done as per her needs, she congratulated herself everyday for being in a position to perform certain tasks all on her own. That gave her infinite strength and worked like a tonic. It was her father who suggested that positive thinking would give her necessary mental strength to surmount any obstacles that she might face in her life.

Squeezing the toothpaste on her brush and brushing her teeth slowly she thanked her father. The toothbrush fell on the floor due to the slackness of her fingers. With great effort, she retrieved the brush and finished her chore. In the past, whenever the toothbrush slipped from between her fingers, her mother gave her a success lesson picking it up for her. '*The question ought not to be how many times the toothbrush fell to the ground, but how many times you tried to pick it up.*' Except two or three times, the toothbrush was no longer slipping to the ground as before. Akshara vowed softly, '*another few days, I will brush my teeth without dropping the brush to the floor even once. Definitely!*'

To bathe, Akshara has always depended on her mother's help. Her bedroom door was always open. To call her mother, she only had to press the button on the wheelchair for the buzzer to go off. What could be the time . . . did her mother wake up by now . . . she herself might have woken up early unable to control her enthusiasm or her anxiety, but her poor mother worked till late in the night! She might have retired for the day round midnight. She might not have woken up yet. Akshara felt for the talking clock fixed on one side of the chair with her right hand. She heard it say, 'five forty two a.m.' Akshara's mother normally was up by six. Even so, to check, Akshara pressed the buzzer, but no answer came in reply. When she pressed a second time, she could hear her mother's voice, 'coming!'

'*Amma*, are you up already . . . It isn't even six yet,' Akshara greeted her mother who entered the bathroom.

'Today I woke up at four-thirty,' Akshara's mother looked at her daughter fondly.

'So you were up long before me. What's up?'

'Yes, it is a special day. Today our daughter, Akshara, will become a full-fledged lawyer. The results of her final year examinations will be out today. You do not know about my Akshara, do you? She may not have even slept a wink last night. She might have woken up as early as five in the morning. Moreover, she will set me on a spin till she is readied. Today I had to be up early for that.'

'*Amma*, I did really wake up at five. How do you come to know of these beforehand?'

'Well! Who else will know better than I about my daughter who I bore for nine months and raised with love?' Akshara's mother said switching on the geyser.

'*Amma*, I might have earned some merit in some previous birth that I should be born to you and *Nanna*. . . . I am so lucky,' Akshara said, with a thin tear film covering her eyes.

'How many times will you repeat those words in a day?' moving close, she adjusted Akshara's hair affectionately.

'I will not be satisfied even if I say it a hundred times . . . seeing all the effort and sacrifice you people make for my sake.'

'What sacrifice? What we do for our daughter can not be called 'a sacrifice' . . . it is rather 'a responsibility.' You are our life. We will face any problem of any nature to see you happy.'

Akshara put her head in her mother's lap and burst into tears. '*Amma*, I shudder to think what hell I would have had to go through with my physical disabilities, had I been born to someone else.'

'Our only concern is you should never grieve over your disability, Akshara. If you do, we will have to take it that we failed in our efforts.'

'No *Amma* . . . it is years since I stopped grieving over my disability. I never rue over my incapability, instead I am blissfully happy every moment that I am born to parents like you. The tears are nothing, but water lilies gratefully placed at your feet.'

'Wow . . . my Akshara is getting into poetry too! Perhaps, she will become a great poet following her father's footsteps!'

Akshara laughed merrily at her words. 'Whether or not I write poetry like my father, surely I will become a lawyer. One day I should give a historic judgment as a Supreme Court judge. That is my life's ambition!'

'Okay . . . to see you realize your ambition, your father and I will transform ourselves into a ladder . . . you only need to climb the ladder and reach your destination. Okay! Now the water is warm enough. Come, I will bathe you.'

'But I cannot climb the ladder, can I?'

'We will carry you up then.'

'It is exactly the reason why I said I am fortunate, *Amma*.'

'Come, enough of all this praise!' Akshara's mother said pushing the wheelchair forward.

'It is not praise *Amma*. Thinking of it over and over, I am overwhelmed with happiness.'

Akshara's mother bathed her, as if she were an infant. She had bathed her, placing the infant Akshara on her outstretched legs. As Akshara grew, she made her stand to bathe her. When Akshara grew up to be five, she would demand in an insistent tone, 'I'll bathe on my own, *Amma*. Please don't enter the bathroom!' and spill all the water down. Pity! The weird disease afflicted her in her seventh year. Since then, it had become a practice for her mother to bathe her once again.

Akshara's mother wheeled her back into the bedroom after toweling her dry.

'What will you wear, *Churidar*? Better, choose the dress yourself. Anyway you will not like what I select for you.'

'I will wear jeans and a T-shirt today, Amma. Give me that dark blue jeans and black t-shirt, I feel comfortable in them.'

Akshara's mother helped her wear the inner wear and the dress. She combed her hair and braided the hair in a loose plait. When she was about to apply talcum powder to her face Akshara forbade her. 'What you did till now is enough, *Amma*. At least now allow me to do these small chores myself.' Akshara applied some cream over her face along with a dash of talcum powder. Then she put a crimson dot on her forehead and looked into the mirror for a final touch up.

A round face . . . wheatish brown complexion . . . wide eyes, well-arched eyebrows, little mouth . . . a v-shaped chin . . . Akshara admired her beauty reflected in the mirror. As a child, her mother cuddling her would ask her husband, 'have you seen my daughter good as gold . . . isn't she moon-faced . . . a moon without a blemish?' '*True . . . I am spotless but for one major blemish in my body . . . a scary blemish . . . a terrible one at that.*'

Akshara shut out in an instant the dark thoughts about to overtake her. She remembered the inspiring words instilled into her by her parents since the time her lower body was parlayzed. *There are strengths and weaknesses in every person. The one who constantly dwells on his weaknesses achieves nothing. He who moves on with a positive attitude consolidating his strengths and overcoming his weaknesses, he alone meets with stupendous success.*

It was not Akshara's wish to face defeat in life. She needed to win.

Often Akshara recalled her mother's encouraging words! *'You triumphed over death itself . . . rather you defied death. Do all other issues matter?'* Every recall of those words breathed into her a renewed confidence.

'See you, *Amma.*'

Waving her hand out, Akshara was about to leave for the college.

'Take care, darling. Watch out for the vehicles and keep to the side always. Go slow. Don't raise the speed of your wheelchair. Heavens won't fall if you are late.'

'Please, *Amma*! This you tell everyday . . . I remember every word you say. Repeating those words may not tire you, but I feel bored hearing them.'

'Like it or not but I won't tire out telling you this . . . I can't help it. After all, it is a mother's concern . . . I have my own fears. I fail to understand why you should go to the college to know the results. You will come to know about it even if you stay back at home. Why are you so anxious? You secured distinction in the first two years. I am sure, you will pass the final year too in flying colors. If you show anxiety, there is every danger for others to think you lack confidence.'

'*Amma*, the reason for my anxiety is not whether I will get distinction. I know I will get it. I told you about a boy who competes with me, haven't I? I am eager to know if I have beaten him. Another reason is my professor has offered to guide me regarding admission into postgraduate studies.'

'Who else can stand first in the college other than you?'

'Come on, *Amma*. You don't need to be so confident of your daughter. That boy is giving me a tough fight. I fear with one or two marks he will upset the cart.'

'No, it can't be. Success will always be yours. I wish you all the best.'

As Akshara reached the college, she found quite a number had already gathered there. They mobbed her with their greetings. 'Congrats, Akshara . . . true to your name, rightly chosen by your parents, you are indeed 'the invincible one'. You stood first in the college. Do you know, they say, the marks you scored created a record in the history of our college? The Principal had sent word that you should meet him in his office as soon as you arrive.'

As Akshara received their greetings with thanks, she mumbled thanks silently to her mother, *'Amma . . . I have achieved it . . . thanks to you and Nanna!'*

As Akshara wheeled toward the principal's room, she saw Kiran waiting for her with a bunch of two roses . . . one yellow and the other white.

Kiran moved forward and presented her the roses. 'Hearty congratulations for standing first in the college.'

'Thanks . . . the roses are beautiful . . . .'

'You told me you like yellow roses, didn't you? That's why I got a yellow rose for you.'

'Why this white one then?'

'It is the colour I like.'

She smiled softly. 'Nice . . . so one rose represents me and the other you, don't they? You tied them together with cellophane tape . . . does it also have any symbolic expression?'

'You guessed it right, Akshara . . . it is an attempt at expressing what is on my mind.'

'Stop there. Anyone hearing it would laugh.'

'Why should they?'

'That your madness has reached heights. Forget it! Who stood second? It has to be you . . .'

'Will I allow anyone else . . . I may have given up on the first rank for my Akshara.'

'What do you mean? Did I stand first because you gave up your right over it? Do you take yourself to be an epitome of sacrifice?' Akshara retorted with a wee bit of anger showing in her eyes.

'Oh . . . I was only joking. Who else can get the first rank other than you?'

'Good. I agree with what you say. Now let me congratulate you for coming second,' she said extending her hand for a handshake. Kiran took her hand in his and held on to it.

'Hey . . . let go of my hand . . . what will anyone think seeing us?' she pulled back her hand.

'They will think we are in love.'

'No, they will take us to have gone mad. You do not understand how foolish it is to love me. You will not pine for my love as you proclaim to now, if you knew the whole truth about me.'

'Well, you promised to put everything down on paper, didn't you? I am looking forward to that auspicious moment.'

'Today that moment has arrived. I have put down everything about myself in this letter. Can you wait for some time? Our principal has sent for me. I will not be gone for long'

'Why only for some time . . . if you wish, you may find me waiting here for a lifetime.'

'As a modern day Casablanca?' Akshara smiled heartily. She added, 'don't have to do all that, just half an hour's wait.' She wheeled towards the Principal's room carefully placing the roses in her handbag.

Seeing Akshara, the Principal rose from his seat and shook her hand. 'Hearty congratulations, Ms. Akshara . . . we are all proud of you. Our college is fortunate to have a brilliant student like you,' he greeted her with a bouquet of flowers. Overwhelmed, Akshara mumbled, 'thank you sir!'

The other lecturers and professors present there in the room joined in congratulating her.

'All the credit goes to our college, sir. I owe it to the committed lecturers who taught us . . . it is my good fortune to have studied under the tutelage of such competent staff. I owe special thanks to you for having permitted to shift the classes from the first floor to the ground floor all these years. I am grateful to you for that.'

Taking his seat, the Principal asked, 'what do you plan to do next?'

'Sir, first I will enroll myself in the Bar Council, but I won't take up practice yet. I wish to do my post graduation. I will think of the practice only after finishing my LLM course.'

'Good idea. In fact, I thought of suggesting you the same. Students such as you need to pursue postgraduate studies.'

Professor Kishan Rao, who was present there, intervened. 'Sir, As promised earlier to Ms Akshara, I will offer appropriate guidance to her in this matter.'

'Good, Ms. Akshara . . . coffee or tea which would you prefer?'

'Thank you. I want neither, sir.' She felt embarrassed.

'No choice. You choose one. You have created a record for our college . . . the percentage you scored is a record in our college. You not only stood first in the college, you also topped the university. I called you to treat you to a cup of tea.'

'I don't take either tea or coffee, sir.'

'In that case, I will send for some fruit juice. The rest of us can have coffee.' He called for an attender and asked him to get pineapple juice.

Having had the juice, Akshara, thanked the Principal, she turned her attention to Prof. Kishan Rao. 'Sir . . . I will wait for you in your chamber.'

'Okay. I will be there in ten minutes.'

Akshara came out and saw some students in small groups standing under the trees discussing something seriously.

Kiran was standing at the same spot where she had left him. Ramana was by his side. They were discussing about something. Smiling, Akshara turned her wheelchair toward Prof Kishan Rao's chamber. The corridor appeared deserted. Moving to the end of it, she pulled her wheelchair to a side and removed her cell phone from a leather pouch, and called home.

Akshara's mother picked the phone at the first ring and said at once, 'Akshara . . . aren't you the one who stood first in the college . . . you are calling to convey that piece of good news, aren't you?'

Tears welled in Akshara's eyes. 'What confidence *Amma* . . . I will never fail you in your trust . . . besides standing first in the college, do you know, the first rank in the university is also mine.'

'Wow . . . Great! I feel proud . . . get back home fast . . . we will have to celebrate. You know the news calls for a grand celebration?'

'Don't break this news to *Nanna* yet . . . I will call him myself.'

'Okay. Convey this good news fast. He will feel elated.'

'When my life seemed waste to friends and relatives, who always looked down upon me, as my parents you shaped my life in a wonderful fashion, *Amma*. You helped me prove to the world that even my life has some meaning and fulfillment. I don't know how I can repay the debt I owe you!' Akshara could not contain her feelings any longer. Copious tears rolled down from her eyes as from a breached dam.

'Akshara, what we did is very less . . . As your mother I bear testimony to how much you suffered to prove yourself worthy against all odds. Your efforts have borne fruits due to God's grace.'

'*Amma*, how many times I told you not to raise the subject of God in my presence? There is no God . . . if He were there, why did He have to create persons like me to suffer from disability? What sin have I committed that instead of walking normally, He confined me to this wheelchair? If there is really a God, He is a cruel

God. He must be a sadist to have created people like me only to take pleasure at our misery.'

'Akshara, it is wrong . . . don't say such words.'

'Please, *Amma*. Please don't say it is God's grace . . . rather say He is an unkind God. The Gods that I know are only two in this world . . . you and *Nanna*. I recall how *Nanna* carried me to the classroom. I also remember how you, giving up your job for my sake, even now bathe me and clothe me as a child.'

'Why do you recall such things this happy hour, Akshara? Don't you know how disturbed I would be to see you sob so helplessly?'

'I know it, *Amma*. It is at this moment of joy that all those things are coming to my mind. This happy occasion when I turned a law graduate all those incidents are moving before my eyes as on celluloid. It's inhuman not to remember the two important persons in my life who have helped me hold my head high with pride. I don't know if there would be another birth, *Amma*, if I have a chance to be reborn again, I wish to be born only as your daughter.'

'Akshara, my child! Why do you turn so emotional? Come home quickly . . . or shall I come there . . . we can get back together.'

'No *Amma* . . . I am all right . . . . I will come home on my own. Here comes my professor! I will call you back. Bye.'

After having met the professor, Akshara came out. Swirling thoughts swarmed her mind once again. What a long journey leading to this success . . . what relentless struggle . . . how many sacrifices lie hidden behind this success of hers . . . .

Memories, one following the other . . . so many of them . . . how many bitter memories . . . standing alongside with those are sweet memories standing testimony to the sacrificing love of her parents.

Ramana seemed to have left. Kiran was waiting at the spot alone.

On seeing Akshara, he moved forward and began walking at a slow pace by her side. 'Where is your letter? Come on, give it to me now!'

'You mean right here? You're always in a hurry,' she said discomfited.

'Hurry? Do you know how long I have been waiting for this letter? Accept, you have delayed it inordinately.'

Past the college compound, they reached the main road.

'There is no one in sight from our college around here. Will you give it to me now or will you make me walk till your house?'

Akshara pulled her wheelchair to the side of the road. She took out from her handbag a long envelope. Handing it to Kiran she said, 'read the contents of the letter seriously . . . this is no fictional story . . . this is the story of my life . . . read it in all seriousness. Give your opinion only after giving it a careful thought.'

*　　*　　*

Kiran opened the envelope. It contained quite a few written sheets. Putting them back into the envelope, he shoved the envelope into his pocket.

Setting aside all other engagements, Kiran returned home straight and settled down to read the letter.

'Kiran . . . I don't know where to start when it comes to telling you the story of my life.

I can't tell how wonderful my early childhood was . . . I remember my parents showering on me their overwhelming love. In fact, Nanna loves Amma very much . . . theirs was a consanguineous marriage, meaning she married her maternal uncle. When Amma was born, the families on both sides decided that she was going to be Nanna's wife. Amma loved to study. As a child, she longed for higher education and take up job, for which reason she refused to marry early. Fighting against the will of the elders in the family, who wished to get her married soon after her tenth standard, she followed her ambition successfully.

If anyone tried teasing Amma, 'what does he care, he is a man. How long do you think he will wait for marriage? You don't want to get married till you finish your graduation and if he decides to marry someone else, your future will be doomed. What will you do then?' Amma reacted sharply, 'why should my future be bleak? If he dares do that, his own future will be in a soup. Can he get another girl like me . . . do you think I will be done with this graduate degree? I wish to do my post graduation too . . . marriage will take place only after that!'

'Oh . . . no . . . poor man! You have punished him enough until now. He's even taken up a job as a lecturer. Who will look into his daily needs? He's eager for marriage!' they lamented.

Amma gave them a fitting reply, 'that doesn't bother me. He has already confessed his love for me. If it is true, he will have to wait for me. If he can't wait it means he is not fair in his love. Then there is no reason for me to regret. I might as well marry another man and live happily ever after.'

Amma did her postgraduate studies in Psychology and joined in job at the Secretariat. Four months later, she got married.

When Amma conceived two years into her marriage, my grandmother had a huge celebration. When I was born, they believed Goddess Lakshmi herself had set foot in the family and celebrated my coming into this world grandly. Until I turned seven, they allowed me to make merry in a carefree manner.

I fell sick one day while I was in school. Amma came immediately taking leave of absence from work to take me home. When the fever did not subside even after four days, they got me admitted into a hospital. After various tests, the doctors diagnosed that I suffered from a genetic disorder. They said it would increase in severity and as days passed by, that my legs and hands will become paralyzed and ultimately I will lose control over my bladder and bowel movements. Another thing the doctors had informed worried my parents, that I would survive only till my fifteenth year, and that there were no instances of patients with this kind of disease living beyond that age. Though my parents took care to hide this from me, I came to know of it as I grew older.

From then on, there was quite a change in our family atmosphere at home. Suddenly a pall of gloom descended on the house where once fun and frolic reigned everywhere. An icy silence of a tomb reigned in the house. I experienced a change overtaking me. I felt myself suddenly growing older . . . as if I had lost my childhood somewhere. Though my parents did not tell me a thing, still I could guess something abnormal was about to happen. Normally elders assume that the children know nothing about the challenges life poses, but children always study every nuance of life around them as well as people's behavior which creates everlasting impressions in the minds permanently.

When I was in my third class, my legs went limp. I used to crawl dragging my feet behind me. Nanna used to carry me every day to the school. He brought me home carrying me on his shoulders. I used to burn with envy seeing my friends rush out for lunch during the recess. I would wait for Amma to feed me my lunch in the classroom. Then she would carry me to the washroom.

Meantime, I took all precautions not to feel the need to go to the washroom. I drank minimal quantities of water. It took me about six months to train my body not to use the washroom except during the lunch hour. I used to shed tears looking at the children playing merrily in the evenings. The words of Amma came good at such times and made me take certain resolutions in life. She taught me how to see life through different, yet practical perspectives.

Once Amma explained, 'do you know this, Akshara? Earlier, the physically handicapped like you were termed as 'physically disabled'. Now it is wrong to call them as such.'

'Then what do they call us now, Amma?'

'Now they are called 'physically challenged' or 'differently abled'. Tell me Akshara, how life would be, if there are no challenges? It would indeed be a dull life, you see. Will it be great if someone achieves something when everything is all right? If they achieve, there is nothing great. Now take your case. Whatever small thing you do is a great thing. Hence, now on you focus your mind on things you have to achieve. When others are playing, you study hard. Then, you alone will stand first in your class. Also, keep thinking how to overcome whatever obstacles come in your way. For that, you will have to keep trying

always, but you have to compromise over things that are beyond your capabilities. Take them to be part of the game of life. For that, you have to accept your condition completely. It is tough not to be cross with someone, but if you learn to be tough, it will cease to bother you.'

I began to accept my physical drawback from that moment. Surprisingly, it ceased to bother me after that.

Now pressure mounted at Amma's workplace. She was getting late for work since she could reach the place only after feeding me my lunch in the school. Twice or thrice the section officer fumed at her for being late for work. One day, she got back home in a fit of anger.

Amma narrated how her boss reprimanded her, 'madam, you have to decide for yourself what is important . . . work or your daughter. We are not going to allow you claim the pay without work. We can understand if it happens every once in a while. If you are late to the office every now and again, we just cannot tolerate.'

'Sir, my daughter is important to me, neither the damned job nor the pay I draw,' was her reply. That day, when Nanna returned from work, they discussed if she needed to continue in her job, and more importantly whether they could manage with the financial burden.

Amma told Nanna, 'after all, we have only one child to feed. If we are frugal in our lifestyle, what you earn should suffice. I don't want to continue in that job. I feel the pressure is getting to be too much. While I am at work, I keep worrying about my child, if she is facing any problems in the school. When I am with her in the school, I keep worrying about my office. I am vexed with this predicament. I feel my daughter's welfare is of paramount importance. I shall henceforth devote my total time and attention only to her.'

Nanna was in total agreement with her. Next day my mother went to her office and put in her resignation letter.

Not even a month, Amma came up with a new idea . . . if only she could work in the school where I studied she could still earn some money and be with her child as well.

Nanna agreed to the idea. 'Well, it's a good idea . . . you are an MA in Psychology . . . over that a gold medalist. If there is a job opening in the school, you can perhaps apply for that. Tomorrow I shall meet the principal and discuss the matter with him. Besides, I am also worried about leaving our child at the school all by herself. If you join the school I can peacefully attend to my work.'

I was elated the day Amma joined my school as a teacher . . . I felt as if someone lifted a mountainous burden off my chest. It gave me infinite joy since no less than my mother herself came to teach my class. She also visited me after finishing her classes, only to greet me. She would then inquire, 'how are you my child . . . do you need anything?' Though I did not need anything in particular, still I looked forward often to those inquiries. My mind would relax in peace whenever she greeted me that way.

When the other kids played games, Amma would engage me in some indoor activities, like chess, caroms, word games, and dumb charade. That way, my mother became my best friend. When Nanna got back home from work we played cards together. With the help of Amma, I could overcome feeling of inferiority for not being able to play like the other kids.

I was happy that at least my hands were of use, forgetting for a while about my legs. Even that happiness did not last long. When I was in my sixth standard, the disease started affecting my hands. To begin with, I found it difficult to hold anything firmly. In due course, I totally lost grip in my hands. I could not move my hands at all.

Amma attended to my homework, but I was worried where my handicap would affect my studies. My concern was how I should take my exams. Even at that time, Amma stood by me giving me courage. She told me that there was a facility of engaging scribes to write the exams for the handicapped.

Amma chided me, 'Akshara, you are still in your sixth standard now. There are still four more years to go before you take your tenth standard exams. Moreover, doctor said the problem of your hands is not as severe as that of your legs. He said physiotherapy would considerably improve your condition. I am sure you will be in a position to give your tenth standard examinations.'

'Amma, what am I going to do, if there is no change in my condition?' I asked.

'You know, I always think positively. If you think positively about the things that are due to happen, at least you will have some peace of mind until something actually happens. Now, I will take on that responsibility and see that you appear for your tenth standard examinations successfully. Leave such worries to your parents and proceed with your studies.'

Just as Amma hoped, with the help of therapy, I could move a few fingers. When I got promoted to the tenth standard, my confidence boosted and believed truly that I could take my examinations. Amma made me practice writing for hours on end, only to make sure I write with a good speed. Nanna used to take me out in the evenings for my therapy exercises. Even at home, he supervised if I was following the exercises correctly.

I used to break down looking at the burden my parents shouldered. They had stopped living for themselves . . . it was as though they were living only for my sake, my well being alone mattered. I was in their thoughts all the time.

Kiran, don't you see my fate . . . once I got used to the existing problems, some other problem used to crop up close on the heels of the earlier ones. This was after I had learnt to live with them with a certain level of dignity and quality.

I was studying at home soon after my tenth standard quarterly exams. Amma was preparing dinner in the kitchen and father was watching the news on TV. I felt something wet under my chair. Then I felt my pajamas were wet. I was shocked that I had wet myself.

I was ashamed to disclose this to Nanna who was sitting nearby. I called out for Amma and whispered into her ears. Tears welled in my eyes, but Amma did not panic. She went about as if she anticipated this phase of me. My parents discussed at great length about it.

Amma bathed me and changed my dress. She cleaned the place with a disinfectant.

'I feel embarrassed looking at you cleaning the mess, Amma. I am ashamed of myself. I feel like putting an end to my life.'

'Why my love . . . did I not indulge in this activity when you were an infant? I can still do it. Don't feel sorry and hurt yourself.'

'Amma, but I was not aware of it then . . . now I have turned sixteen!'

'My dear, children are always children to parents.'

Next day my parents took me to the hospital to consult the doctor.

The doctor informed that I had started losing sensation from below the waist. Further, he said that I would henceforth be having no control over my bladder and bowel movements. He guided my parents with precautions they needed to take while caring for me.

I had my own fears and confided them in my mother, 'when this happened at home I didn't feel so much embarrassed since you were around. Being my mother, you cleaned up the place, but, Amma . . . whatever am I to do, if I face the same situation while I am in school? In that case, how can I suffer the humiliation? Amma . . . I might want to die at that very instant.'

'Akshara, you should not say such things. Life is something that God has blessed us with.'

'No, Amma. In my case . . . it is a curse.'

'Child, it is all in your hands, whether to take life as a curse or a blessing. I will train you to see that you do not have to face such a situation in future. Our body is like a clock too. They call it a biological clock. It can be set to tick away, the way we desire. Each day you have to schedule your visits to the washroom. For that we need the resolve . . . the will . . . and the self-belief to succeed.'

As promised, Amma took a lot of care in my case. She saw to it that I developed the habit of visiting the washroom only at certain predetermined timings. I felt elated for having won over the problem that embarrassed me so much.

Next fear of my death took root in my parents' mind deeply. The facts of my disease had begun to gain clarity that hitherto was unknown when I was a child. I also came to know about the prognosis the doctors came up with, that I would die before I turned fifteen or sixteen. My parents did not know I was aware of that terrible truth. Taking me to be asleep around midnight, they would talk to each other. I frequently heard Amma sob uncontrollably.

I often thought at length. What is death? What is there after death? I never believed in theories of heaven and hell nor reincarnation, because I believed there was no god. I believed that there was merely nothingness in the beyond or total darkness that thought cannot pierce through . . . or some deadly silence reigning after death. I was frightened to dwell on such matters.

Am I going to really die . . . but what about the things I wanted to achieve . . . am I to die without achieving anything . . . then why did I, in the first place, take birth at all . . . is it only to trouble my parents? How unfortunate it is to die a premature death without having added meaning to my life!

My interest in studies receded. I wondered why I should work hard when I had to die soon anyway. What would I achieve in my educational career? Will it matter if I secured five hundred fifty or more marks? I cannot do my Intermediate course anyway. Even if I joined the Intermediate course, will I live to take the examinations? Why face this anxiety? What use would I gain other than giving avoidable trouble to my parents? Should I not give them a bit of rest and peace as long as I lived?

Owing to such brooding and unable to concentrate for any length of time on studies my scores began to go down. Whatever Amma had coached, it was of no use in the face of my fear of impending death.

An incident took place ten days before my pre-final examinations. I was in my Physics class. Students were all listening keenly to the teacher's lecture, but engrossed in my thoughts, I was not paying much attention.

I heard one of the girls sitting behind me exclaim 'Ah.' One of them scratched my back. 'Check the floor below!' she seemed to say. I thought I dropped my pen or pencil and looked under the desk. There was water all over . . . . I failed to understand from where the water appeared on the floor. Did water spill from my water bottle . . . or someone else spill *water there . . . a sudden fear seized me . . . did it happen to me . . . no, there was no chance . . . to clear my doubt I checked my dress . . . it was wet all over . . . . The entire classroom came to know of my condition. The teacher stepped down from the dais. 'What's the matter?' he shouted. Coming to know what had happened he threw a sympathetic glance at me and left the classroom. Soon, the teacher returned accompanied by a sweeper with instructions to clean the place.*

The word reached Amma. She was engaging another class. She came running to me where I sat frozen in my seat in the classroom alone.

First time ever it occurred to me . . . I wished I dropped dead. Strangely, my fear of approaching death disappeared. Why doesn't speedy death swallow me up now . . . why does it take so long?

I cried out when Amma lifted me up from my seat. As we reached home, I did not speak a word despite Amma trying her best to draw me out. A single thought, kept returning to my mind that I have to die . . . but how? Whether I should hang myself . . . swallow sleeping pills . . . or drown myself.

Amma seemed to gauge the storm raging in my head. She kept convincing me that I was not at fault for what happened. 'Such things happen even to healthy people. What happened to you is not a matter of shame at all.'

I reacted sharply. 'Amma, do you still insist it is a matter deserving sympathy? For that matter, I hate to live a life of pity.'

'Pity apart, Akshara, it is a matter of understanding. Those who are civilized will understand. Those who are not . . . well, we have nothing to do with them.'

I thought of it at length: I have to do something about it, Mom. I do not want this life of contempt. I do not want to be at the receiving end of people's ridicule. Any way the doctors declared I will die this year . . . but I want to die sooner. I will rush towards death invitingly.

That night I decided to commit suicide.

After supper, Amma made me wear my nightdress. Later she tucked me into the bed. To my surprise, she lay beside me. She turned towards me and placed her warm hand on me.

'What, Amma . . . are you still worried . . . I am not feeling that depressed . . . please leave me alone.'

'Akshara, I want to tell you a thing. Life is very precious. There is no single life that is not worthy in this world. Those who cannot accept even a slight failure alone want to escape from life. I don't say that suicide is a grave sin. I would instead say that it is a cowardly act, escapism, amounting to running away from problems, lacking courage.

'Do you know what most people think? They believe that it requires courage to die. Absolutely wrong. Death comes easily, if one closes one's eyes for a moment. It is as easy as that, whereas it calls for tremendous amount of courage to want to live. Life punishes humans in all possible ways! Inscrutable are the ways of life. We never know what happens the next moment. That which we expect to happen with certainty may not happen at all, and that which we expect never to take place might really happen. Those who face the predictable as well as the unpredictable in life they alone are the courageous. Life is a relentless struggle . . . they alone live who can fight till the last breath. Success belongs to only the brave. Cowards achieve nothing.

'Akshara, now I want to tell you yet another thing. It is not a right attitude to worry about what others think. After all, we are not sure if others are also thinking on those lines. It is all in our imagination, a feeling born of insecurity and inferiority complex. The so-called others don't have much time to spare for others or they have least interest to care. Most of us miss out this aspect, yet simple logic. We think about ourselves all the time, so do others.

'Akshara, four months ago one of your teachers fell down having sat on a broken chair. That day you told me that the incident evoked laughter from some students and sympathy from some others. Did you ever recollect the incident since it had happened? No. You may not have. I say there can be no worse fool if your teacher were to think that everyday his students would be recalling, time after time, that incident of his falling down and are still laughing. Life has a very large canvas, my child. No single incident . . . not even a slight insult . . . or a minor humiliation should receive importance more than what is due . . . it is foolish to let it to rule our life. Treat everything by its worth . . . not an iota more than that. I am telling you this, because winners need to imbibe this quality. I want you to become one such winner.'

'Amma, don't think I am not aware of it. You say I need to win for your sake. Why should I? Why should I bother, when I am not living beyond my sixteenth year? When I am destined to die before my time, is it worthwhile I exerted myself to study well?'

Amma looked at me for a long time before resuming her talk. 'I knew you would come to know of this fact of your life one day or the other. I have been waiting for you to come out with this question. After all doctors are not gods. They too are human. There are instances of patients who died when doctors said they were on the path to recovery. Conversely, there are patients who recovered in a few hours as by a miracle in spite of being ticked off.'

I countered, 'Amma, don't try to trick me into believing your words. I know pretty well about my disease. It has no cure. It is fatal, and the severity is bound to increase as days pass by. I have gathered enough information from the internet. There are no known cases of patients living beyond their teens. I am certain to die in two or three years, if not this year.'

I embraced Amma and wept.

Amma did not try to console me. She kept staring at the ceiling until I stopped crying. After I calmed down, she continued. 'Shall I tell you a story, Akshara . . . the one I heard in my childhood? I heard it from your grandmother. The story continues to inspire me to this day.'

I did not understand why Amma wanted me to listen to a story, when we were discussing a serious topic concerning my life.

Without waiting for my assent, Amma started narrating the story.

'Once upon a time a king wished to own a flying horse. He called all the carpenters and artisans in his kingdom to his court. He offered one hundred thousand gold coins to whosoever came up with a flying horse. None was brave enough to say it was impossible to make one, but for a carpenter named Jayanth who stepped forward to say: my Lord . . . it is impossible to make a flying horse. The king was furious: Jayanth, you being the best carpenter we have in our kingdom you shouldn't be saying that. You have to make a flying horse in six months, or you will face the sentence of death.

'Jayanth gave a quick thought to it. There was no use arguing with the king. Jayanth merely needed to buy time. So he said: yes, it is my duty to obey you, Your Highness. I shall certainly make the flying horse as ordered, but the time you granted is too short. I need at least two years to make it. That aside, my Lord, kindly arrange to pay me *half the amount to start the work right away. The king ordered his treasurer to pay Jayanth fifty thousand gold coins that very instant.*

'*Everyone pitied Jayanth for inviting death but took his decision as grown out of stupidity.*

Jayanth however was elated and busied himself making investments in property for the future of his children. Jayanth told his wife: anything may go wrong before the deadline, my dear wife. The king may die due to some illness or I might die a natural death.

'*A year passed. Jayanth showed the king a wooden horse in the making and took the balance amount. His wife got alarmed. He told her: don't you worry. I have one more year to go. I think the horse will fly.*

'*After six months, the king summoned Jayanth to the court. Jayanth informed he was still in the process of preparing the special wings for the wooden horse. Coming home, he told his worried wife: I still have six months on hand. With the wealth in hand, we know no worry now. Once I attach the wings to the wooden horse, it may even fly.*

'*Soon only a month was left to meet the deadline. Jayanth did not hurry with his work. He remained his usual cool self. His friends thought he was condemned for hanging. His wife alerted him: oh dear, only a month is all you got before the deadline. He pacified her: I know, darling. A moment's time is all that is required for anything to happen.*

'*The king called Jayanth to remind him of the deadline for one last time. He told the king that the wings were now ready, but he was only waiting for the machine that would make the wooden horse fly. Time ran out fast. There were mere two days left to complete the job. His wife and children began to weep thinking of his approaching end. Next, it was only one day before the deadline. Without* losing his cool, Jayanth told his wife: well, I still have twenty-four hours on hand. He ate his meal and slept soundly. The same night the neighboring king invaded their kingdom. The king lost his life in that invasion and the kingdom annexed. In the end Jayanth gifted away the wooden horse to his grandchildren.'

After a brief pause, Amma continued. 'Akshara, do you know why I narrated this story to you? I have to tell you one more thing. Whatever you do, I leave it to your discretion, but keep this in your mind. What others think should not concern you. You have to think only about your parents who consider you as their entire world. Think whether your actions will cause happiness to them or sorrow, but as parents we like to see you happy as always. We are ready to do anything for that. We care least for what others think. To us our daughter is our whole world. Good night darling.'

Amma rested her hand on my forehead and pushed back the strands of hair lovingly.

I was puzzled how Amma knew I was thinking of suicide. Now that she plainly explained, it made me believe how true she was. Why should I die for the sake of others and bring suffering to my dear parents? Though I was unable to give them happiness, I should not be the cause for their sorrow. I decided not to commit suicide.

How wonderful was the story Amma had narrated! Yes. Hope should never die. Why should one invite death before its time? Let it come whenever it has to. Why invite death prematurely? After all, who knows someone may invent a medicine in the meantime as a cure, someone else may come out with an alternative medicine that may work wonders in the days to come. Besides, they say our genes mutate, so my defective gene may mutate and I may really recover. True . . . the wooden horse may even fly.

That night I had sound sleep. In my dream, I rode a flying horse. I goaded asking the horse: 'Fly . . . fly on!' The students in my class surrounded me and heckled me in my attempts to make the wooden horse fly. Unmindful, I kept goading the horse to fly. The horse started to take wing. I clung to its mane and the horse took off into the sky. Everyone, who till then took it to be a flight of fancy, was astonished. It circled four times in the sky. The students down below clapped gleefully. My joy knew no bounds at the experience of riding a flying horse in my dream.

That day I refused to go to the school. I told Amma, 'I will go to school only after four days. By that time my classmates would have forgotten the incident.'

'Akshara, did you forget what I told you yesterday? Go to the class and see what happens. You will be surprised,' Amma encouraged me.

Unable to say 'no' to Amma, I went to the school and sat in utter trepidation. Everyone seemed to be preoccupied with one's own activities. No one bothered about what happened the previous day. Yes, what Amma told was very true. I was petrified unnecessarily imagining things.

Setting aside everything, I started preparing afresh for final year examinations. Amma sat by my side helping me with my studies in every possible way. The exams had commenced. I had taken two of them. On the night before my third examination, I studied until midnight. When my parents took me to the examination hall I felt giddy and lost my consciousness on my way to the hospital. Once in the hospital, the doctors said my days were numbered and cautioned that I would survive at best for four days.

My parents gave up on me. Mentally they were prepared to face my end, but I proved the doctors wrong and survived through a miracle, as it were. The doctors told my parents that they were lucky since their daughter was out of danger for the time being.

Nanna asked them what they meant by saying 'time being'. He was told, 'Haven't we told you, sir . . . there is a chance to extend her life but it isn't in our hands to pull her back from impending death.'

Since I missed my exams, it took me another year to clear them and get through my tenth standard. I took ill once again during my Intermediate Course. I had to stay away from college for three months at a stretch. However, all said and done, I could successfully take the examinations.

Now I am twenty-four years old. Twice I had a close brush with death Yet, I am aware of it hounding me all the time. Kiran, it is your foolishness or say, naivety, that you are unable to understand me. You are a gentle soul with a kind heart. You have a bright future too. I don't wish to spoil your life for my sake. I don't know when my life would end.

Think well. Life is very precious. Desist from inviting misery into your life by mistaking your emotions as your ideals. Let us part as friends. Trust me next to my parents you are the one to whom I will turn for help in time of crisis.

Your well-wisher

Akshara

The letter moved Kiran and his eyes filled with tears.

* * *

They were the preparatory holidays for Intermediate examinations to commence. Prasad was preparing for his final year examinations that were away by another fortnight.

Though Prasad was trying hard to concentrate, he could not. Whenever he opened his book, all that he could see was Ramya's smiling face. The mere mention of Ramya's name tickled him pink. Their friendship was not a recent phenomenon, many years old going back to preschool days. They played together and indulged in mock fights, challenged each other and ended up in sulks, yet they patched up sooner as frequently. What sweet memories!

It was high time Prasad said to her, 'I love you'. Already it was late. He ought to tell her his mind before she joined Engineering course. Until now, they studied together in the same class, but now she may go to another college to study Engineering and opt for a different stream. Once before, she had made a mention casually that she wanted to pursue engineering in the Electronics and Communications branch.

'Why don't you take up Computer Science? I think of applying for the same myself. After we do our Engineering course together here, we can do our MS in the United States. There we can take up a comfortable job and happily settle down,' Prasad had made his mind known.

'Isn't ECE the first choice of all top rankers? Job opportunities are aplenty in that discipline. I will surely get good rank in the Entrance Test that will assure me a free seat in any of the prestigious engineering colleges,' Ramya had replied.

Prasad had been thinking about this for the past few days, if he too should choose Electronics and Communication stream like Ramya. He was in dilemma as to what to do, a veritable dilemma indeed. Should he sacrifice his own choice for Ramya's sake? He resisted the temptation since becoming a software engineer had been his dream. His other dream was to marry her.

Prasad remembered what his mother used to say about Ramya. 'Which ever home she steps into as a bride, that house would be blessed to have her. She is as good as gold . . . those eyes . . . large as almonds . . . like the white roses grown in our flowerpots . . . . She is well educated and more beautiful . . . so goes her goodness . . . whoever will marry her, might have worshipped god with golden flowers in his previous life anticipating such a virtuous girl for a wife in this birth.'

Prasad thought within: *Mummy, I am that man who prayed to God that way!All her beauty, brains and good behavior all have to be mine own. In fact, she is born for my sake, I am that lucky man!*

Can he change his stream for Ramya's sake then? In that case, he can be always with her in the same college. They can do their college assignments together. The thought sounded wonderfully romantic.

In the end, Prasad arrived at a conclusion. Both his dreams were intense, viz. becoming a software engineer as well as marrying Ramya. They were like his two eyes having equal importance. Hence, he decided to pursue computer science stream. Come what may, he strongly wished to join the same college where Ramya joined so may the two go to the college together. His mother had promised to buy him a motorbike when he joined the engineering course. He would go for some *vroom-vroom* joy rides on the bike. Didn't he see that happening in the movies? Engineering college students gave priority to love than anything else . . . his love that lay dormant hitherto would now bloom on his entry into a college campus just as shown in films.

Prasad was waiting for Ramya's visit to his house that evening. She would visit him twice or thrice a week and chat with him. If he had any difficulty at studies, she would explain and leave.

Now Prasad looked at his watch . . . 7.15 p.m.

Prasad could hardly wait. He closed the book he was reading and pranced around the house impatiently. He watched TV for a while. An anchor from a Reality Show was asking a college student, 'hey, you guys out there! Aren't you from the first year? How many girls are you chasing these days?' Prasad thought to himself that he did not chase girls.He was only in love with one girl. Then he peered into his watch again. It was 7.30 p.m.

Normally, Ramya came on a visit to their house between six and six-thirty. They arrived at this schedule on his suggestion. In the past, Prasad made his mother ask Ramya, 'Ramya, I understand you stand first in the class . . . why don't you come in the evenings and solve the doubts my son may have . . . especially in Mathematics. If you find it difficult coming to our house I will send my boy over to your house.'

'No aunty . . . I will come to your house myself. That way, I can take a break from my own studies. It offers me some relief too, but I can't come every day . . . I will come as and when it suits me or my mood."

Mother goaded Ramya, 'don't say mood and all . . . after all you are teenagers. Your moods will not be in your hands. Don't you think my boy too deserves to pass in first class? Any way, he is your best friend. Do as it suits you.'

'Sorry Aunty. That was not what I meant. I will come to your house in the evenings thrice in a week without fail. I think you underestimate your son. He is very intelligent and is sure to score distinction without my help.' While saying this to his mother, Ramya threw a kind glance in his direction. *Was it kindness or love?*

'In that case your help would add a ten percent to his aggregate score,' Saroja said beaming.

'Sure, aunty!'

Despite that arrangement, Ramya did not come that day . . . she didn't visit them for two days. Prasad checked the time again. It was 7.45 p.m.

What if Ramya does not visit him? Prasad was eager to see her. He restrained himself for two days already. He could not contain any longer his anxiety. He had to see Ramya.

'Shall I serve you dinner?' Saroja asked.

'I am not hungry, Mummy.'

TV bored him. He switched it off.

'Your food is getting cold, son. Why don't you eat and begin your studies?'

'Mummy, I am unable to understand this Quantum Theory in physics. I thought Ramya would come and explain. Without understanding that topic I cannot proceed further.'

'Why do you say that, my boy? You have scored well in your tenth standard. Deliberately you are glorifying Ramya's help. Read it once again, you will understand it better.'

'No, Mummy. I did not attend college the day my teacher taught it in the class. I will go now to Ramya's house and ask her to explain.'

'Okay, come back soon. Don't be late for dinner.'

Prasad picked up the book and left for Ramya's house.

Ramya's mother greeted Prasad. 'How are you, child?'

'Fine, aunty,' Prasad said while looking for Ramya.

'Did you have your dinner?'

'No, Aunty. I did not understand a particular lesson in physics. I need Ramya's help.'

'Ramya is studying in her room. You can go in, my child.' It seemed they had their food. Ramya's mother cleared the table and proceeded with the rest of her work.

Prasad knocked on Ramya's door and entered.

'Hi Prasad' Ramya looked up from the book she was studying.

Prasad sat beside Ramya. 'Will you please explain some problems in quantum physics? I am unable to solve them by myself.'

Ramya put aside the book she had in hand and picked up Prasad's physics book. He was not listening to her. He was just watching her rosy lips move. He was looking at her big round eyes and her beautifully curved chin.

The more Prasad looked at Ramya, the more restless he became to tell her his mind without any further delay.

Prasad asked, 'the day after tomorrow is your birthday, is it not?'

Stopping her lesson midway, Ramya looked at him in surprise.

'Prasad, you came to me to have the lesson explained. Instead of listening to me why do you raise the topic of my birthday?' Clearly, Ramya was annoyed with him.

'What are your birthday plans? Are you going to any movie?' Prasad persisted.

'No chance. Do you think I can go to movies when I have exams in another ten days? Are you crazy?'

'Then how will you celebrate your birthday?'

'I will have my special bath and have *payasam* my mother prepares. Then I will settle down to study. It's as simple as that.'

'Is that all? I wanted to give you a special gift.'

'Give . . . I will accept it with pleasure. What is the big deal?'

'Not in your house. Do you know how long I have been waiting for your birthday? I wanted to give it to you in the most picturesque and pleasant surroundings.'

'Oh, is it going to be so special?'

'Find it out for yourself how special it is. Shall we go to some park and sit there for an hour and come back?' Prasad said pleading with folded hands.

'Do you have to beg me for such a simple thing?' Ramya laughed. 'Is it only to a park? We will go, but not for an hour, a half hour will do. It takes fifiteen minutes to reach there anyway. We will go there at five-thirty in the evening, return by six thirty. Okay?'

'Thank you . . . Thank you very much,' Prasad grabbed his book from Ramya's hands.

'Will you not allow me to finish the lesson? I am halfway through it,' Ramya tried to snatch the book back.

'I didn't understand the lesson only to the extent you explained. Thanks once again!' Prasad jumped with joy and reached home excitedly.

That night Prasad could not sleep well. He wondered what gift he should buy. In the same breath, he also rehearsed endlessly how he should convey his love to Ramya.

Next day, Prasad scouted around for hours on end to buy the gift: what should he gift her? Should it be heart-shaped? It is outdated in its symbolism! How about Taj Mahal . . . a symbol of love . . . still an outdated idea . . . his love has to be expressed in a brand new way . . . it should be different . . . it should make a poetic statement of his love . . . and thought-provoking too, a mesmerizing thing . . . and mystical too.

A message written on a plaque interested him. On a black-coloured surface, the words were itched in golden letters: 'My love is as true as you are. My love is of the blooming smile of a white rose. My love is of your stately gait as of a swan. The glow of thousand suns shining in your eyes . . . the waves of perfumes rising with your breath . . . the zillion sweet nothings engraved in your bosom . . . all these are witnesses of my eternal, pristine and exotic love . . .'

The writing reflected exactly the feelings Prasad held in mind . . . as though they found right expression . . . as if the feelings were engraved into the letters opening his heart . . . there can be no other meaningful gift than that.

Prasad got the article gift-wrapped.

*   *   *

It was Ramya's birthday.

Prasad felt he was contained inside a steel jacket right from the morning.

Prasad texted a message to Ramya . . . 'Many Happy Returns of the Day!' He received a reply that said, 'thanks'. He feared it might be a day without an evening in his life. He was angry at the time that ran slow.

Prasad tucked a pink color shirt into his dark trousers. He polished his shoes hard to the extent of wearing them out. He was ready by four in the evening and his eyes were following the movement of the minute hand of the wall clock.

From five onwards Prasad pricked his ears to hear the ring tone from the mobile for a message and alternately fixed his eye to the clock checking time.

No sooner than the message from Ramya flashed on his cell phone, than Prasad left home like a bullet released from a gun.

By the time Prasad reached, Ramya was already standing at the street corner looking out for him.

With all the running he did, Prasad managed to say 'hi' even as he was gasping for breath.

Ramya checked the time on her cell phone. 'You are late by four minutes . . . haven't we agreed to meet at five-thirty?'

'You delayed in sending me the message. I am here as I saw the message,' Prasad said laughing.

'You seem to have forgotten to wish me on my birthday,' Ramya said as she moved forward.

'No, not here. I will wish you on reaching Indira Park in the midst of the greenery and blooming flowers.'

They engaged an auto and were in the park in no time.

Young couples occupied the benches round the lake twittering away as birds in love.

A couple settled on a bench seemed oblivious of the surroundings. Crossing the limits of decency the boy began to kiss the girl.

Prasad warmed up to the sight and thought about his own prospects of doing that to Ramya at least in the near future when they got closer.

Ramya whimpered, 'Hmm . . . what a shameful thing to do in a public park. Why don't the public condemn such behavior? Had I known I would have to see these riveting scenes, I would not have come in the first place. What uncivilized people are they! This couple has neither shame nor discretion in a public place.'

Prasad thought, 'my god . . . Ramya doesn't seem to like such sights. Good, I did not make any advance. She would have expressed her displeasure right on my face. I will go out with her next when we join the engineering college. I should be careful then to sit a distance away from her. Never should I commit the mistake of embracing her.'

Soon Prasad and Ramya walked further inside the park.

'Now, tell me. How many subjects you have studied and how many you have revised,' Ramya asked.

'Why talk of studies now Ramya? Don't you have any other interesting topic?' Prasad said impatiently.

'Do we have to talk differently since we have come to a park? You remain Prasad and I Ramya. We are after all students of Intermediate who are about to take our final year examinations commencing next week. What other important things do we have other than exams?'

'Agreed. By the way what is your birthday resolution?'

'I have to study hard and get a good rank, then become an engineer of repute and do my bit for my country. Now, come on, where is your birthday gift you promised? You promised to give me something special.'

'Ramya, wait a minute, I will give it to you. Won't it be nice if we moved to that bench on the lakeside?' Prasad said smiling. In fact, his idea was she should sit on the bench and he knelt down before her and said, 'I love you' . . . just like in movies.

'But there are no vacant benches, are they?'

'Don't worry. There should be a vacant bench somewhere. Let's go and see!'

'Okay, as you please,' Ramya rose.

Prasad was walking alongside Ramya. He wanted to hold her hand. No, not now . . . later, it will be in the near future, he hoped.

The couple who hugged each other sometime ago rose and started to leave.

'Ramya . . . look . . . the bench there is vacant now. Let us take it before others occupy. Let's run.'

Without waiting for Ramya he lunged forward and started to run.

'Hey! Prasad! Easy,' Ramya shouted after him from behind.

Another ten steps, Prasad would have reached the bench. He turned to check if Ramya was following. She was indeed following him, walking with a smile on her face.

Prasad looked on all sides. No one was looking for the bench. He stopped running and walked slowly.

After three steps, Prasad fell to the ground.

'Prasad!' Ramya shouted.

Prasad tried to get on to his feet, but in vain. His legs refused to co-operate. He found his back go weak.

Ramya came running to him and lent her hand for help.

Prasad took her hand but slumped to the ground again.

'Did you hurt yourself, Prasad? Did you sprain your leg? Could it be for that you are unable to rise?' Ramya inquired.

Ramya's words were clearly audible to Prasad. Her image was also clear. He also noticed the faces of those who laughed watching him. His mind was working fine. That was not the reason why he fell, nor did he trip up on anything on the ground. Yes, he was walking slowly before he fell down. He wondered what made him fall down. He examined the place where he was squatting on the ground. The ground too was even. There were no stones or weeds to impede his way. Then why did he fall down? Why was he not able to get on to his feet . . . as if he lost sensation from below his waist . . . as if his body from below the waist paralyzed. . . .

Ramya used all her strength to pull Prasad on to his feet gently. He turned around in circles but could not rise.

Ramya got worried.

By that time, a few people gathered around.

Prasad felt greatly embarrassed. He felt ashamed too. Tears came to his eyes.

'Could you please help him to get on to his feet?' Ramya pleaded with men around.

Together, they all lifted him and made him sit on the bench.

Ramya thanked the men for their help.

After they left Ramya asked Prasad, 'what happened to you? Did you twist your ankle or what? Do you have pain?'

With tears in his eyes Prasad said, 'I don't know . . . I don't understand.'

Prasad moved his legs . . . they were working fine. He stood up. Yes, his back too was working fine now.

Prasad remembered a similar incident that had happened in the past. For the first time in his life, he was concerned and troubled about his health. Unknown something terrible seemed to be happening in his body. The body for that reason was giving out specific signals.

Prasad lowered his head. 'I am sorry, Ramya. I am angry with myself. I am ashamed of myself.'

'It is okay, forget. I feel sad it had to happen on my birthday. After all, it is not a shameful thing to fall. It's common . . . so take it easy.'

'Let's go home, Ramya,' Prasad said.

Ramya looked at her watch. It was ten minutes to six.

'We still have some time left. Now, let's sit for a few minutes until you relax.'

'No, Ramya . . . let us go.' Ramya looked into Prasad's face. He looked pale . . . due to fear or anguish . . . as if someone caused injury. All his vitality drained out.

'Okay Prasad. Can you walk? Let's move.'

Prasad held Ramya's hand and stood up.

Prasad walked slowly at first. Looking at Ramya, he said, 'It is okay . . . I think I can walk straight now.' He walked out of the park with the support of Ramya.

*　*　*

Initially, Prasad's mother did not take the incident seriously when Ramya told her about it. Saroja took it that her son might have tripped on something and that had embarrassed him since it happened in Ramya's presence.

Saroja chided her depressed son, 'Didn't you know you had better watch your step, son?'

'But I walked carefully, Mummy. There was nothing to knock me down. The ground was not uneven either.'

'Prasad, forget about it . . . it is a small thing.'

'No, Mummy . . . something is going wrong with my body.'

'Nothing is happening to your body. Didn't you see me slipping many times in our house?'

'Mummy! In fact, I am not worried about my falling . . . it is about my inability to rise despite my efforts . . . I am afraid of that. I felt nothing worked from below my waist . . . my legs went out of my control. Mummy, do you remember about the time Ramya came to our house one morning? Then I told you how I was unable to stand up on my legs and you laughed it off. Even now it is the same . . . something is happening to me, Mummy.'

Hearing of it, a vague fear began to take hold of Saroja.

'Mummy, nowadays I am tripping many times simply for nothing. It is as if I am knocking over something?'

Immediately Saroja remembered her colleague, Krishnaveni, whose husband was a doctor. He practiced from home. They lived on the first floor and he ran his clinic on the ground floor below. She checked the time. It was not even six-thirty. The doctor would not have gone to the clinic. He must be still at home, so she thought and rang up her friend.

'Hello, Krishnaveni! This is Saroja. I have to talk to your husband regarding my son's health. Will you please connect me to him?'

Saroja, while telling the doctor about her son's complaint, added, 'I called you to seek your advice, doctor . . . why is this thing happening to him? Do I have to take his problem seriously or is it due to any general weakness?'

'To me it looks like a neurological problem. It is not good to have such symptoms at his age. You better consult a neurologist without further delay.'

Next day Saroja took a day off from her work.

By nine-thirty, Saroja reached the Apollo Hospital along with Prasad.

People gathered as at a fair in the waiting rooms . . . after two hours of waiting, a call came from the doctor.

Dr. Satish Rao . . . reading the name outside the consultation room, Saroja mistook him to be a young doctor. He appeared as approaching sixty. His hair grayed, had fair complexion and wore an affectionate smile.

'Yes, tell me, what is your complaint? Incidentally, who is the patient . . . you or your son?' Initially, to the doctor's question, tears came to Saroja's eyes.

Saroja controlling her emotion, explained to the doctor of Prasad's complaint. She added, 'doctor . . . he is our only child, born after many years. I can't take anything happening to him,' Saroja broke down.

'Why do you trouble yourself imagining things even before he is examined? There may be many causes for illness to attack the body. It could be merely due to general weakness too. You are educated and working. How can you give in to despair so easily?'

The doctor asked Prasad to take a walk. He noticed some shift in his gait . . . he observed him from close another time. He noticed Prasad walked on his toes with his heel hardly touching the ground.

The doctor examined Prasad's legs. His calves looked swollen than normal.

'Can you recall when exactly you began to feel weak in your legs?'

'I suddenly fell over once when I was in eighth standard while running to occupy my seat in the bus. I thought I fell down due to someone tripping me up. Although I fell down a few times later, I never paid much attention to it. Once I could not pedal my bicycle. I forgot to tell you yet another incident, doctor. Two months ago, there was a function in our school. During the arrangement for the function, we had to shift a few tables. That day, I could hardly move the table despite exerting myself. My friends even laughed at me.' An unmistakable sorrow showed in Prasad's face as he remembered the incident.

The doctor asked Saroja, 'Did anyone in your family from your husband's side or from yours have this problem?'

'What kind of problem, doctor?'

'Like the limbs going limp . . . or unable to hold things?'

'No one had such problem to the best of my knowledge, but my mother-in-law had arthritis.'

'Is your marriage consanguineous?'

'No. Why do you ask, doctor?'

'Take it easy. It was one of those routine questions to clear a few doubts. For now, I will prescribe a tonic to boost his strength in addition to a few multivitamin capsules. I recommend certain tests. Get me the reports at the earliest. After seeing the findings I will prescribe the necessary medicines.'

Collecting the fee that Saroja gave him, the doctor asked Prasad, 'What would you like to be Prasad, an engineer or a doctor like me?' The doctor's question visibly brightened up the otherwise gloomy face of Prasad.

'No doctor. I want to become neither. I will become an IAS officer and work as a collector.'

'Best of luck, my boy.' The doctor stood up and shook Prasad's hand.

Saroja, with Prasad in tow, moved to another room where a technician took the necessary blood sample of Prasad and gave a date for collecting the reports.

Two days later, Saroja went to the Apollo Hospital with Prasad. As usual, the hospital lounge was teeming with patients. She collected the reports at the counter and while waiting for doctor's call, she glanced through the reports, but could not make out anything of them. One report related to serum Creatine Kinase levels. Another related to Dystrophin levels.

When Saroja's turn came to see the doctor, she entered the consultation room and presented the reports to the doctor with her heart in her mouth. Scrutiny done, the doctor asked, 'could you ask the boy to wait outside for a while?' In the same breath, he turned to Prasad. 'I will call you in again, young man. Wait for a while outside.'

It broke Saroja's heart, *did that mean Prasad's condition is serious . . . is it something that Prasad cannot hear? Oh, God, how many upheavals should I face in life? I have not recovered from the loss of my husband as yet . . . which tempest is waiting to engulf me now?* Wondering what news the doctor was coming out with, Saroja looked into his face in dread.

'Madam, my suspicion proved true. Pull yourself together to listen to what I say.'

'Don't say that, doctor. I am scared. I cannot take anything terrible befalling my son.'

'It can't be helped, now. So listen to me carefully. The condition of your son is called, Muscular Dystrophy.'

Saroja who never heard about it earlier, asked, 'what does that mean, doctor?'

'Genetic disorder is the cause for the condition Prasad is in. There are no suitable medicines available for the disease. Due to this, the muscles in the body gradually weaken, and a situation may arise when the patient finds it difficult even to move his limbs and his back will lose its function. Eventually he will find it difficult to even breathe.'

Saroja's heart plunged into a shock; genetic disorder to my son . . . he who looks handsome and healthy as a prince, how could he get such a disease? Something somewhere has gone terribly wrong. The reports may have come out wrong. Did she not see that lab technician collecting the blood sample disinterestedly while carrying on conversation over his cell? He may have swapped the sample with someone else's. None from either side of my family suffered from such a disease. Then how can my son . . . never.

'Isn't it better he undergoes the tests all over again? A mistake may have occurred somewhere. How can my son carry a genetic disorder? Both my husband and I are healthy. He merely died in an accident otherwise he could have lived a full life since having a body strong as steel. Even I am hale and healthy like my husband, doctor. I do not know of any ill health. Neither my parents nor my husband's parents had any genetically acquired diseases,' Saroja said to the doctor.

The doctor looked at her for long thoughtfully. 'There is no mistake in the tests. I can understand your anguish. We do not know why these kind of genetic disorders afflict people. There is no rule to say that a man has to inherit them. They may also occur when genes mutate. For muscles to remain healthy and function normally, a certain protein called Dystrophin is required. Either due to genetic disorder or due to error in genetic information, or when the signals required for producing this protein are absent, then, there is a chance of a disease such as Muscular Dystrophy to occur. Even under this, there are many types. I have to decide through some more tests which type of muscular disease has affected your son. I will recommend those tests. Get them done soon.'

'Doctor . . . I am prepared to face any ordeal for the sake of my son. I will bear any expense. If no suitable medical treatment is available here, tell me if I can take him to America. Will there be better treatment available there?'

'No, not necessary . . . you may take him anywhere, but there is no cure for this. You have to take good care of your son, as if he were an infant. We will treat him the best way possible, keeping in mind the complications that may arise in future. Even if it is painful to hear, I have to tell you this. The life span of such patients is very short.'

'Is it very short, doctor? Then how short is it? Am I going to lose my son just as I lost my husband? Why is God punishing me this way?' Saroja sobbed.

'I cannot tell you that unless I conduct some more tests to determine the type of Muscular Dystrophy your son is suffering. Whatever, he may live for another ten to fifteen years. That is all. You have to keep courage only at such times. As a doctor, I will extend all support necessary to you. Is that okay?'

Saroja did not know what to say. She walked out of the room as a statue that gained movement.

Seeing her come out, Prasad rushed forward showering questions on her. 'Mummy . . . what did the doctor say? What is the problem? Did he prescribe any medicines?'

'Nothing, my son . . . it is only a minor problem. The doctor feels your problem is you are not eating right. He recommended some more tests. That is all,' Saroja said, taking proper care to hide the depression that started to swell within her all at once.

'More tests? Do I have to give more blood sample then? Didn't you say it is a small problem? Then, where is the need for so many tests? As it is, I am scared of those needles. Enough of these tests Mummy. Let us go. I am fine. I will eat well as you say from now on.'

'Don't say that, son! If you don't follow as the doctor suggested, he will be angry. He won't allow us to see him again.'

'If he does not, the loss will be his, Mummy . . . he will not get his fee. What do we lose? We will find another doctor. Is there shortage of doctors in Hyderabad? There are four such doctors practicing in our own street.'

'You are right, but he is a very good doctor . . . and very reputed. Do I take you to any ordinary doctor? He must be the best in town.

Prasad smiled happily. 'Is that so . . . am I also not the best one?'

On reaching home, Saroja went into her room complaining of headache, and sobbed her heart out. One factor stood out clear to her. It was no time to shed tears, but time to muster all strength to stave off the challenge. When her husband was alive, she wondered if she could ever live without him, but she managed to withstand the pain of his loss. This problem too was no different . . . an unavoidable problem, a crisis she had to fight off fiercely.

That evening she sat up wiping her tears, and got down to cooking the dinner. She was determined to face her son's ill-fated disease with courage and determination.

* * *

It was the first day for LLM classes.

The class strength was less than twenty. Vibrancy and a characteristic buzz hung in the air typical of any university. Akshara looked closely at the faces of the other students. Most appeared unfamiliar to her. Some came to introduce themselves to her.

Akshara's eyes looked around for Kiran. How many days it had been since she met Kiran . . . didn't he apply for postgraduate study? Did he by any chance go to a different college or give up further studies and begin practice as a lawyer? Did he realize how unfair it was for a bright student like him to give up higher studies? Didn't anyone tell him so? Rather, he did not give her the opportunity to advise him . . . he did nothing wrong. She forgave him long ago.

Seeing Ramana enter the class, her face brightened. What a relief, she thought . . . there was at least one familiar face from her previous batch to give her the needed company.

'Hi! Ramana!' Akshara greeted him.

Ramana occupied the seat next to her.

The professor had not shown up yet.

'Are you the only one to join this course from our batch?' she inquired.

Ramana smiled to say that he understood what she was driving at. 'Why, Akshara . . . will you feel better if someone else had joined the class in my place?'

Akshara was baffled. 'No, no . . . it isn't that. I just inquired. I merely wanted to know if there was anyone else familiar to me.'

'Why can't you be more open? I know . . . you are anxious to know about Kiran.'

Akshara gave it a deep thought, 'What you said is true. I thought of getting the first rank just as I did in my graduate exams. Kiran is an intelligent man. If he were to join I would have to double my efforts,' she smiled uneasily.

Ramana reflected, 'what a beautiful smile she sports . . . perhaps the same smile floored Kiran too. How well she is justifying her statement!' Still, Ramana felt it to be a one-sided love from Kiran's side. It seemed her feelings for Kiran lay dormant in her mind's deeper recesses. A little nudge is all that is required to bring those feelings out.

The class commenced.

Since it was the first day, there were formal introductions . . . a brief preliminary about the faculty . . . the details of syllabus in LLM . . . advice as to how best to cope to score well . . . and finally a roundup on library facilities available in the college.

Akshara listened absentmindedly. She remembered the unusually long letter she wrote to Kiran and how she handed it over to him on the day their results were out and what followed later. She got a reply from him in the form of a SMS, 'I understood what you wrote. Knowing you now fully, my love for you has doubled. Can we go out next Sunday . . . I have to discuss with you many things. I will message you the venue.'

Akshara felt vexed reading the message: *how crazy and stubborn he is! He is the type to invite trouble foolishly.*

But the next moment she realized that: *he is not a fool . . . maybe he likes me. Even if his love for me is true, I should not give in. He is just a good friend. I cannot be cruel to spoil his life.*

The next Saturday Akshara expected the promised message to arrive and wondered how she could avoid meeting him, but she did not get any message. Even at ten in the night, she checked her cell phone for the message. There was none. She expected the message to come on Sunday morning. There was no message by afternoon either.

Eyes fixed to the message screen of the cell phone, Akshara had waited until night. Still there was no message that she had so much expected.

Akshara was anyway determined not to go to meet Kiran even if he were to ask her. Nevertheless, now that there was no message itself, she felt some hopelessness shrouding her. She felt humiliated at his rejection . . . rejected as an unwanted thing . . . discarded as if she were ruining his life.

Kiran's initial response in reply to her letter could have come in a fit of emotion, which he might have later revised on a leisurely re-think. He might have thought it to be foolish to share life with a person who could neither walk nor move since paralyzed from below the waist and whose life was fated to be short-lived.

On thinking along those lines, Akshara's mind had agitated under unbearable sorrow, *it was true she was not worthy of his love. It was also true that she could not have given him any pleasure even if he was ready to marry her, but the idea that she too had a lover in her life, the thought that there was a person in her life to give her sweet taste of love . . . that though raised her desire to live multifold. What sweet joy that feeling gave her . . . what comfort that thought gave her!*

Nonetheless, Akshara's life was not lovelorn after all. Her mother showered upon her all the love that was sweeter than honey. She received the same pure love from her father. There was, however, something unique about Kiran's love. The experience was novel, a wonderful sweetness that she had never known until then.

Kiran appeared very handsome to Akshara's eyes. He was five feet six inches tall . . . had large eyes . . . since being slim he looked taller. How much she loved those eyes! There was adoration for her in those eyes. His love, soaking wet, shone forth through those eyes. Those eyes showered moonlight as twin moons . . . as a wood nymph granting benign wishes . . . perhaps eyes that exude love always appeared so.

How many times did Akshara not suppress her desire that surged as a wave to look into those eyes for hours on end! After Kiran declared his love for her, she learnt how much joy there was in love . . . and how much satisfaction in that desire . . . .

The despair of not receiving any message from Kiran that day and later pushed Akshara into darker and deeper despondency.

When Akshara was doing her Intermediate course, she came to hear about love blossoming between youngsters. She heard much gossip: who was after whom . . . which girl was moving with which boy . . . who sat on whose pillion . . . who were together in picture halls . . . how they were seen . . .

Realizing how Akshara missed playing with others of her age, her mother used to play various indoor games with her. Nevertheless, what could her mother do in this regard? She alone knew into what depression she plunged into watching her classmates having love affairs. It was something she could not share even with her mother.

Despairing over her life, Akshara wished she were dead. There was no place for such love in her life nor could she ever dream of marriage. She was destined to lead a lonely life. At such times, when she felt increasingly depressed unable to put up with that despair . . . did not know how her mother came to know of it . . . she would cajole Akshara and calm her mind that was on a boil.

'Child, at your age it is but natural to have such thoughts. Blame it on your hormones that make your blood seethe like lava. All that girlish talk among your friends . . . their curiosity to know about sexual experience, and the desire to own that experience soon . . . I agree, has certainly a strong impact on you.

'Listen to me. The attraction between a boy and a girl at your age is nothing but infatuation which is born out of desire for sex. Sex is a basic instinct in all living creatures. Sex is not anything unreachable or unrealizable. In my opinion, sex is the only cheapest and most easily available commodity in this world. From a District Collector down to a labourer, everyone has access to it as per one's level. Even lepers seek sex from another beggar or a leper.

'Sex is not as wonderful as shown in movies or as written in books. In the beginning, one knows not due to its freshness and novelty . . . and as time passes by, it becomes bland and routine . . . that is all.

'What is so great about gaining sexual experience? It is the most mundane thing available to all creatures including riffraff. What is truly great is to acquire certain things in life that are unique and precious. Imagine how great you would feel when you deliver landmark judgments as Supreme Court Judge. Your father and I will then feel proud to have given birth to you. As your parents, we would think our lives indeed are blessed. If you have to achieve such things, you have to forgo certain other pleasures,' Akshara's mother explained.

'*Amma*! What about love between a boy and girl?'

'All love is the same. Those who could not receive love from their parents will seek it out elsewhere. Don't you know how much we love you? If you seek love other than ours, it means our love is deficient.'

'Oh, don't say that, *Amma*!' hugging her mother, Akshara wept.

From then on, Akshara never allowed her mind to dwell on thoughts of physical love or love of boys.

However, the moment Kiran began to express his love for her, Akshara saw through her mother's ill-founded reasoning on love. Certainly, she saw difference between Kiran's love and her parents' love.

A parent's love was cool and quaint whereas Kiran's love felt as warm as staying close to a winter hearth. While her mother's love was sweet, Kiran's appeared intoxicatingly sweet.

Akshara was not in sulks because Kiran did not send her a message, or that he distanced her. At the same time, she would not charge him with selfishness. She understood Kiran well. Anyone in his place would have done the same. After all, Kiran was not an extraordinary man.

Whatever Kiran was, he was most dear to her. He was the one who for two years gave her taste of sweetness of love. He also gave her an experience hitherto unknown to her. She would remain grateful to him till the end of her life for that one reason alone.

It mattered little if Kiran did not love her. It sufficed if he only joined the course . . . if only she could see him every day! Akshara did not desire anything further, except to see him at least once in a day.

'You don't seem to be in this world . . . where is your mind wandering . . . miss, where have you gone amiss?' the professor turning to her asked.

At first Akshara did not get it.

'Hello, miss . . . my question is directed to you,' the professor rapped at her.

Akshara pushing aside her thoughts, turned round. The rest of the class was staring at her in wonder. Ramana, who sat next to her, tapping her shoulder with his pen tried drawing her attention, 'Akshara, the question is to you.'

By then tears had already welled up in Akshara's eyes thinking of Kiran. Noticing tears in her eyes, the professor was embarrassed. 'Why are you crying . . . any problem?'

'None sir! Something fell in my eyes. My eyes are watering since I rubbed them.'

'Okay . . . okay. Aren't you the same who stood first in the university? What's your name?'

'Akshara'

'Keep it up. You should get a first in postgraduation too. All the best to you!' he said.

After two sessions, an announcement was made that there would be no further classes for the day.

Akshara stopped Ramana as he was about to leave. 'Why didn't Kiran come? He promised me many times that he would join the postgraduate studies . . . did he join another university?'

'No. Kiran is apprenticing with a lawyer having decided to stop pursuing higher studies.'

'Was it so . . . why did he do that?'

'Akshara, don't you know . . . he lost his father!'

'Did he lose his father . . . I didnot know . . . when did this happen . . . how did he die?'

'Do you remember the day our results were out? You came to the college too. That same week on Saturday evening . . . he hanged himself from a ceiling fan.'

'Oh . . . why did no one tell me of such a terrible thing? What problems drove him to commit suicide?'

'He was in share business, wasn't he? He incurred heavy losses.Unable to clear the debts or show his face to the debtors, he committed suicide. The burden of the family has now fallen on Kiran's shoulders.'

'Kiran must have been in a great shock at the time. At least you should have called to inform me of this, or messaged me Ramana.'

'On hearing from Kiran, I rushed to be by his side. We both were extremely busy until Tuesday afternoon attending to one thing or the other. Police arrived on the scene, since it was a case of suicide. They refused to hand over the body to the family until after the postmortem was over. Kiran did not want that. He told them that it would be unbearable for him to see the already emotionally shattered person go under the knife. Meantime, the debtors too descended. They were adamant on first clearing their dues before taking the body for the funeral. It was Tuesday before they could arrive at a peaceful solution to the impasse. After that, do you know how many times Kiran tried calling you . . . there was no response from your end. He even sent a number of messages to your cell phone. Yet, there was no response. Even I tried calling you from my cell phone . . . I too drew a blank. A recorded message said the call was not reachable.'

'Oh . . . is that so? What a mistake! Kiran must have got me wrong.' Akshara started to weep quietly.

'Kiran likes you very much. He will never talk ill about you. He told me of the letter you wrote to him. Even so, I heard he sent you a message of love to you. He thought you were angry with him for going after you against your wishes, for which reason perhaps you stopped answering his calls.'

'How odd . . . I forgot to tell you, Ramana. That Tuesday morning I had lost my cell phone. I was a little depressed that morning and to divert my mind, I wanted to go along with my mother to the market to buy vegetables. On my insistence, she too agreed to take me with her. On our return, I found my cell phone missing. I did not know where and when I lost it. I got myself a new cell phone and a new number altogether. What a mistake . . . it has led to a slight misunderstanding.'

'Akshara, you could have called him.'

'Haven't I told you . . . that was all due to a misunderstanding? After he read my letter, Kiran

100

sent me a message promising to meet me on Sunday. He even told me he would inform me of the place and time. I had waited eagerly and no message came. I looked forward to it even on Monday. There was neither a call nor a message. I thought he changed his mind upon learning about me and decided to distance himself from me. I deliberately avoided calling him in order not to embarrass him,' Akshara sobbed.

'How you two manage affairs between you! He took it that you were angry with him and you thought he had changed his mind. . . . This shows how deeply you love each other. If you keep your love to yourselves, this is how you will suffer. So what are you planning to do now?'

'I have to meet Kiran at once. First, I have to pay him my condolence on his father's death. Besides, I have to tell him of my lost phone.'

'Akshara, you also say one word about accepting his love! He went into severe depression. Only you can help him to get over it.'

'Ramana, why do you also talk of absurd things like Kiran? There is no room in my life for love or marriage.'

'Why do you deceive yourself, suppress your love for him Akshara? Your anxiety shows plainly how much you love Kiran.'

'When did I say I don't like Kiran? I like him very much but it is not love. He is a good friend of mine. That is all. I told you I cannot think of love and marriage in my life, haven't I?'

'Akshara, for how long do you wish to remain in self-denial? Love is very much there in your life. That Kiran has been in love with you since the last two years is something that we both are aware of . . . how can there not be place for marriage when your love is sincere?'

'Please Ramana . . . let us end this here. Now tell me, is it possible to meet Kiran now? Can you take me to him, please?'

'Kiran will be in the court now. Please come to Minerva Hotel at six in the evening. Together we shall go to his house. I will message him of our coming.'

Akshara agreed thinking she could meet Kiran's mother too. By six-thirty, both of them reached Kiran's house. Kiran by then was waiting at the door. He came forward to greet her, 'Hi, Akshara . . . how are you?'

Akshara took his hands in hers and said, 'Sorry, Kiran . . . I didn't know of your father's demise. I am very sorry really. I lost my cell phone. Maybe, there wouldn't have been this misunderstanding had I not lost the phone.'

'Ramana called me and conveyed everything. Come to think of it, why will there be misunderstanding between close friends?'

Kiran led her inside.

In the hall, Kiran and Ramana settled on the sofa. Across the sofa, Akshara was in her wheelchair.

Kiran's mother came out of her bedroom. Introducing his mother to Akshara, Kiran told her, '*Amma* . . . this is Akshara. Remember I told you that she always stood first in the class.'

'Not just first in the class, she topped the university,' Ramana corrected Kiran.

Akshara folded her hands and greeted, '*Namaste*!'

'My son never misses a mention about you. Wishing to see you, many times I asked him to invite you over to our house. He never obliged . . . it doesn't matter. You've come at least this way,' Kiran's mother responded.

Akshara felt very uneasy. She felt guilty to have had to come on such an occasion, a time when one knew not what to say. 'Kiran is a very intelligent man. To tell the truth, he should have got the university rank. He having missed it narrowly by a few marks, it came to me.'

'Fate is taking it on us. How much my son desired to study further! Now he had to give up abruptly to feed our family. To see him take on the burden at a time when he wished to continue his education joyfully, I suffer the pangs of it.' Kiran's mother wiped her tears with her sari end.

Akshara realized the mistake she committed however careful she tried to be. Kiran interrupted, '*Amma*, why talk of all that when Akshara is visiting us for the first time?'

'Don't think otherwise, Akshara . . . I was beside myself unable to control my heart-breaking sorrow,' saying Kiran's mother brought coffee for all.

Taking his cup in hand, Kiran said, '*Amma*, I forgot to tell you. Akshara does not take coffee or tea.'

Kiran's mother went in and brought for Akshara a glassful of thick buttermilk.

Kiran's mother fondly looked at Akshara. 'Just as my son said, you look very beautiful. You are as a lamp that brings light to any family.'

Akshara knew very well what would follow those words generally: *the girl's face is beautiful . . . it is a pity only her legs . . . how sad, what happened? Can't you walk at all, since when?* Those words of sympathy and of concern hurt her. . . .

Akshara loathed people who pitied her condition.

Kiran's mother did not bring up the mention of it at all. Ramana rose to say that it was time to leave.

'If not my son, at least you study well . . . I will not then regret that my son missed his postgraduate study.'

Akshara could not help but appreciate her culture.

'*Amma*, I will see her off,' Kiran said leaving the house with his friends.

Akshara gestured to Kiran not to bother.

'I mean to go with you a little distance . . . that is, if you don't mind.'

Akshara smiled.

Kiran's mother said from behind, 'Please keep visiting us once in a while . . . that will make me happy.'

Once they were out, Ramana left saying, 'Kiran, I will take leave now, you are here anyway to take care of Akshara.'

Kiran was walking slowly alongside Akshara's wheelchair. Both of them remained silent, but the silence between them was turning insufferable. Each one wanted the other to break the silence. Akshara thought it proper that she speak first as Kiran was just coming to terms with the grief of his father's loss. 'Kiran, I feel sad that you cannot do your postgraduation.'

'Aren't you doing it instead? Not just my mother, I too feel happy for you.'

'How can both be the same? Your education is yours. It's unfortunate for a bright student like you to stop with graduation.'

'Why do you think I am going to give it up that easily, Akshara? No chance. I am joining the evening college. Don't ever think I will not stand in competition with you.'

'That's the spirit!' Akshara gave him a thumbs-up sign.

'Whatever I desire, I desire in all sincerity Akshara! I will give my all to realize what I desire.'

104

'You seem to be alluding to something Kiran.'

'Alluding to something? What is that? I am not well versed in language as you are. Come out clear.'

'Meaning, you are beating round the bush without coming to the point!'

'There is nothing in this to beat round the bush. I want you. Think seriously, Akshara. Truly, I like you . . . sincerely, it is love.'

Akshara did not respond.

'Why aren't you speaking Akshara? Do you want me to wait until you finish your post graduation? I will wait . . . if you want me to wait for some more time even after your postgraduation . . . even so, I will wait . . . if you so desire, even until the end of my life!'

'Did you say, till the end of life Kiran! For that matter, I don't know when my life would end. You know my life is destined to be very short. Why do you want to stake your entire life for my sake?'

'You are boring me telling the same thing over again, Akshara . . . don't I know all these? It is all right then. Listen to my side of the story too. Are you going to live another five years . . . three years . . . a year? If I can win your love, it will do even if it is for a few months. The rest of my life I will live out with memories of the glorious moments I spent with you. I will live with memory of your love.'

'Your lines are superb! Do you take life to be a movie?'

'Movies too are made based on real life. Think coolly, Akshara. Tell me the truth. Don't you like me?'

'Yes I like you a lot. That is why I say this. What pleasure do you get in marrying an invalid like me who can't even walk, Kiran?'

'The reason why I asked for your hand is not for any physical pleasure. Your presence in my life will give me endless joy.'

'Kiran, do you remember to have come across anyone in this world who asked for a wish such as this? If you take me as your wife, the world may take you to be crazy.'

'It is wrong to say we are venturing into something that none till now has. If you turn the pages of history . . . how many great persons . . . all illustrious men deserving reverential worship . . . haven't you heard of Stephen Hawking, the world-renowned physicist? He is living since many years confined to a wheelchair. He cannot speak, communicates through a keyboard on the computer. His own student married him having fallen in love with him. They have children too.'

'Please, Kiran . . . why do you force me to do a thing against my will?'

'Sorry, Akshara! I don't compel you. At the same time, I cannot help but love you. It doesn't matter even if you don't, I will continue to love you. I shall wait until you come up with a positive response.'

'Okay . . . we'll think of it if I survive till then,' Akshara said with a vague smile. There was no sadness in that smile, only a determination to face reality fearlessly.

'Didn't you in your many debates argue fervently that one should think positively?' Kiran reminded Akshara.

'Thinking positively is different from thinking practically. I am now thinking practically.'

'Whichever way you think, Akshara, don't forget that I love you.'

Akshara mumbled to herself: '*I too*' and *appended a silent thank you too to it.*

*   *   *

That night, Doctor Siddhartha was on night duty. He had joined the Lifeline Hospital the previous month. During this one month, he noticed new patients moving in and those cured leaving the hospital happily. The surgeries took place in a routine manner. Where they failed, the patients left the hospital in sorrow, and where successful, the patients left cheerfully looking on the doctors as veritable gods. An atmosphere, Siddhartha was well acquainted with, prevailed there. However, there was one patient whose condition remained the same since the time he came to this hospital.

When Siddhartha heard of the patient, he initially pitied her. Discussing the patient's history Dr. Wali told him, 'It's two years since I came to this hospital. I have been observing her since then. There is absolutely no change in her condition. Do you know another thing . . . it is said she had been admitted on the day this hospital was inaugurated. She has been here since then, meaning, it is over ten years since she came here.'

Siddhartha exclaimed in an open agape. 'Ten years?'

'Yes, ten years it is . . . haven't you noticed the patient's condition? She is on a liquid diet. The hospital kept her alive feeding her food ground into a paste, through a pipe into her stomach.'

'Is there no improvement in the patient's condition? Aren't the medicines helping her?'

'She is not afflicted with a disease that can be cured with medication; She came to this vegetative state with oxygen denied to the brain. It is better we say she is kept alive per force instead of saying she is a living corpse.'

'What happened to her in the first place? Please give me all details, Wali bhai.'

'Her name is Kiranmayi. While she was doing her Engineering Course, a youth from her neighborhood by name Naresh used to stalk her claiming to be in love with her. He was a vagabond who made a small living by running an auto. Kiranmayi's father was a head master in a government school. Unable to put up with his harassment they lodged a complaint with the police. The police gave him a good thrashing and sent him on remand. With that, he turned vengeful. He decided that what could not be his could not belong to anyone else, so once he was out of police custody he began to threaten her that he intended to disfigure her beautiful face by throwing acid at her.

'Fearing the worst, Kiranmayi's parents admitted her into a hostel. Even so, he did not give up on her. One day, he barged into her hostel room and threatened her saying, 'I went once to the jail because of you. I am ready to go to the jail for you any number of times. Call anyone you want . . . If I can get you I am prepared to even dare a noose round my neck with a smile. It does not matter if I cannot marry you, at least spend a night with me. I have to be the first person to deflower you. After that, I promise to stay away from you. At least agree to this or else I shall do you and your parents in.'

'That is the result of the evil impact of present day movies, Dr. Wali. The film directors and writers who make heroes of anti-social elements deserve to be stoned to death in the street. The society will not correct itself until that day. Tell me what happened next,' Siddhartha asked.

'When the girl was in her final year, this fellow entered her hostel room one night between one thirty and two by clambering up the pipeline behind the hostel building. He raped her dragging her to the bathroom. He tied a rope round her neck, lest she cry out for help. The blood supply to her brain stopped for a few minutes and she went into coma. She came to this hospital fighting desperately for life. The doctors here could save her life, but what we see before us is only a corpse with a heart beating within.'

'Dr. Wali, what have they done to that man?'

'He was arrested and sent to jail. I saw him on TV. Do you know what he said without any remorse as though he did a great deed: I wanted her first before anyone. I am satisfied and very happy. Now you do what you want. Do you wish to mincemeat me? Please go ahead.'

'What a horrific incident . . . and how monstrous . . . eliminating him in one go or death at the gallows is not enough for such people. They have to pay for their crime through taste of hellish torture, every moment of their life craving for death. Why has this society turned so ugly and violent Wali bhai? Just because some lecher demanded to be loved should a girl oblige him . . . or else would he kill her . . . rape her . . . throw acid on her . . . what authority does he have on that girl's body or on her mind?'

'What is the use of our worrying about it? Where are moral values today in the society? Girls too are not lagging behind here. Haven't you seen this morning's newspaper? A girl had been in love with a man for the past five years. She was also in love with another for the past two years and she claims to like both of them.

To the query from them, as to whom she would now marry, she asked the suitors to settle between them . . . she would marry whoever won, so both men attacked each other with daggers. One died and the other went to the jail. That is what happened.'

'They think life takes after films. The girl may have thought she would choose her future husband by garlanding the survivor of the fight for her hand as a princess of lore. Finally hasn't her life too ended in misery?'

'At one time, parents were scared of having daughters for fear that they would have to shell down heavily toward dowry. Situation has changed these days. It's become a challenge to protect and shelter the girls till the time of marriage,' Dr. Wali averred.

From that day, it became a habit for Dr. Siddhartha to observe Kiranmayi from close quarters standing by her bed for a few minutes. She must be close to thirty years of age, but to look at she appeared over fifty. She lost her hearing and her vision too was affected, the blood vessels damaged, she lost her speech. She was not in a position to recognize anyone since her brain too lost its functioning. She cannot however be called brain dead. The brain is partially functioning.

Every time Siddhartha stood by Kiranmayi's bed and looked at her, he remembered that incident in his childhood when the white pigeon was mauled by the cats. He thought Kiranmayi mutely prayed to him, *'won't you give me release from this mortal pain?'*

Finishing his round of visits, Siddhartha came to rest in the room allocated for the resident doctor. . . . Soon he slipped into deep sleep. In the dream . . . was a white pigeon badly mauled . . . he took it into his hand . . . . Blood covered his hand . . . a red bleeding pigeon . . . its eyes pleading pitiably to grant it a speedy death. . . . The eyes were not those of the pigeon . . . those eyes were of Kiranmayi's . . . lifeless glass beads . . . lacking in vision . . . misery-reflecting eyes . . . pleading eyes . . . the entire body of Kiranmayi reduced to a pair of folded hands . . . turning into a pool of tears swirling round his feat.

Siddhartha woke up all of a sudden. He felt thirsty. Taking a bottle out from the fridge, he gulped a few sips of water . . . his grandmother's words flashed across his mind. *'You've a heart full of ardour and kindness; a very sensitive heart . . . not every one understands you.'* Yes, his mind was very sensitive. It was unbearable for him to see others suffer. The responsibility of saving Kiranmayi from her pain and misery was now on him.

Siddhartha checked the time. It was one-thirty. Coming out of the room, he looked around the ward. The patients were all in varying states of sleep. He approached Kiranmayi's bed. Her eyes were half-open. As a sign of putting up with endless intense pain, her skin wrinkled intricately and there were signs of beastly old age that pounced on her and left behind a half consumed body. A tube passed through her nose to support her life artificially. The only evidence to say that she was still breathing was the intermittent expansion of her chest.

Siddhartha moved further a little, and rested his hand on the tube supplying oxygen. He just had to pull it out. Kiranmayi would die in a few moments struggling for breath. He surveyed the surroundings another time. Making sure no one was watching him he bent down to pull out the tube, when he suddenly drew back as though someone held him by his hand. A feeling of committing a wrong, somewhere in his mind: *is that his conscience . . . what he is doing is right, is it not? It is not wrong to take someone's life, is it? He might be wrong . . . .*

Siddhartha's hands that could at one time easily dash the pigeon against a rock, were now trembling. Was killing a human being not as easy as killing a pigeon? The patient was a fellow human being . . . now in a vegetative state. She was absolutely of no use to the society. Had not the entire world condemned the Nazis in unison for planning to exterminate the old and infirm just because they were of no use to the society? What he was about to do, was it a gruesome act . . . how many were not in the society who were worthless . . . . Was it possible to do away with all of them? Their lives were of no consequence to the society. Were there not many others too who were harmful to the society? Was it better for the world perhaps to eliminate all of them?

No. Killing Kiranmayi would be in her own interest. It would be a release from a life that is bereft of any happiness and meaning. True! It was one thing not to be useful to the society, but another not to be of use even to oneself. It was a worthless life, as good as dead. For how many long years should she bear this punishment? Sentenced to live out her life as a punishment, she endured her torture enough this far. The hell she went through until now was enough. He only had to pull out the oxygen tube that stood between her life and death.

Siddhartha stepped back having tried placing his hand on the tube once again. He felt as if Dr Wali stood before him, rebuking him, '*what you are doing is wrong doctor . . . God will punish you!*' He rubbed his eyes to check if Dr. Wali was around. He was not there, only a delusion.

Siddhartha got back to his room and reclined on the cot. He could not catch a wink and needle—like thoughts pricked him. He felt as if crowbars blasted his heart. . . .

Siddhartha recalled the conversation he had with Dr. Wali two weeks earlier. Siddhartha commented, 'how many more years? What is the point in keeping her alive artificially? There is every need to amend laws to legalize mercy killing in our country like in Holland.'

'It is barbaric to kill. What is this merciful killing? As man's birth, his death too should be in the hands of Allah. God is the owner and giver of life. Man has no right to condemn another man to death,' Dr. Wali replied in answer.

'Where is justice, then, in allowing patients to suffer from incurable diseases, to endure the dreaded pain living for months on end for death to embrace? We are not to concern ourselves here with what religion says on this point but with what humanity says on this . . . what our conscience holds forth on this.'

'How can you seperat life from religion? After all, religion is an important and integral part of our lives. According to our Quran, suicide is a great sin. I quote '*Do not kill or destroy yourself, for verily Allah has been to you most merciful*'. Likewise, there is no worse a sin in other religions also than to take life of another man. Allah rules our life. I quote Quran '*Take not life which Allah made sacred, otherwise than in the course of justice*,' Dr. Wali shot back.

'Dr. Wali! It is no sin to take worthless and meaningless lives. In fact, it is the greatest good we can do to that life, a permanent release from pain.'

'According to Islam, there is not a single life that is worthless and has no right to life. It is against Islam to desire death as an escape from physical pain.'

'Then what is the way out? Should one be condemned to live a life ridden with pain and suffering? Don't you feel anything when you see cancer patients during their terminal moments of pain? Left to me I feel like presenting a peaceful end by giving them a lethal shot that will free them from physical pain in an instant.'

'Doctor, your thinking is on a wrong path. We can control pain largely through palliative care and therapy. Our duty is to save lives, not to take them. If there is no cure today for a certain disease, there are chances of discovering a drug some day. Since there is no medicine and death is certain, who are we to invite death prematurely? What authority do we have? Don't forget Allah is watching every one of our actions.'

'My brother, I don't believe in God.'

'That is your personal affair. I am not here to debate with you that there is a God. Don't you recognize godliness that is in fairness and humanity? Is it fair to kill men quoting some bizarre reason? It is monstrous . . . barbaric . . . inhuman . . . and criminal,' saying thus, Dr Wali stormed out of the room.

Thoughts swarmed Siddhartha, 'Like Dr. Wali stated, is Allah or some God keeping watch over us all . . . is there a god at all . . . are there heaven and hell . . . is there a life after death that assesses one's merits and sins, metes out rewards and punishments to men? Trash . . . it is only a figment of man's imagination . . . if there is really a God, then why are innocent children too dying of dreaded diseases like cancer or AIDS? How is the wicked continuing to live? Why is not god sending down thunderbolts to destroy them all? Even they who are stealing God's jewelry and his income, how are they living in happiness? Everything is an illusion . . . even life after death is an illusion!

As a doctor, Siddhartha saved the life of many a patient from pain and disease . . . so the responsibility of saving Kiranmayi was also on him. If only she could talk, she would be begging him in thousand different ways to grant her death . . . if she had vision, glancing him variously, would be begging to put her out of misery. She would be wishing fervently to put an end to her wretched life.

Siddhartha rose and stood again by Kiranmayi's bed. He felt as if she was pleading with her hands raised: *won't you please grant me a speedy death? I cannot bear this pain. I do not wish such a life for me, not even for my worst foe. It's the most wretched life. Even lesser creatures like the dogs and pigs too live comfortably within their limitations. Why is my life alone like this? They say human life is the most celebrated among all the creatures, then, what do you have to call mine . . . receiving liquid food through tubes inserted in my mouth, ejecting the waste matter? Is this life . . . is it not being said that in God's creation man's life is the most eminent . . . then what is to be said of my life . . . burden to my family . . . burden to the earth . . . a burden to my own self?*

Siddhartha gently tried pulling out the oxygen tube, but he could not. He stopped short of applying force.

He fell back upon re-thinking, 'even in countries permitting mercy killing legally, there are certain conditions governing it. If there are no medicines, even if available are ineffective . . . if death is inevitable, to escape from chronic physical pain and if a patient is in a healthy enough condition to take a free and fair decision, mercy killing could be carried out. If the patient is in no position to give a consent, as per the wish of close relatives, measures that would expedite an end to misery may be carried out . . . in which case it amounts to either disconnect the life supporting apparatus and drugs . . . or withdraw food and water, or through giving a lethal injection terminate life. In the case of Kiranmayi, however, no one gave consent for her mercy killing. Then can this killing be termed as mercy killing? It only amounts to murder. *Assuming the patient or her close relative gave the consent who am I to implement it?* Government is the only appropriate authority to carry it out and he does not represent any government.

Dr. Siddhartha's mind vacillated between opposing views . . . a situation wherein he was unable to arrive at any decision . . . as in the play *Hamlet* a 'to be or not to be' situation . . . a moment of indecision. . . .

He let go of the tube supplying oxygen and stepped back. One of the patients sat up in his bed coughing ceaselessly.

Siddhartha silently returned to his room and threw himself on to his bed. He felt weak, what he planned to do, did that amount to mercy killing or murder . . . if it were mercy killing he can excuse himself because in his opinion, it was not wrong . . . so there did not arise question of any excuse. He would even congratulate himself for doing that favour to the patient.

Siddhartha remembered Kiranmayi's father whom he had met a week ago. That was the first time he saw him after he joined the hospital. Could have been sixty years or so . . . he appeared lean as a split wood. Penury was writ large on his face . . . bent low as bearing mountainous burden on his shoulders. . . .

'You have been looking after your daughter keeping her in this hospital for the last ten years, alright, but how are you managing the expenses?' Siddhartha asked.

'We are not well off, doctor. We are not penniless either. I have inherited ancestral property of a house and ten acres of farmland from my father. I am a teacher in a government school. I raised my children lovingly and reasonably well. My son, two years older to Kiranmayi, is a software engineer in Boston. He has two children. If this had not happened to Kiranmayi, I would by now been spending my time happily with my grandchildren, but god willed it otherwise.'

'How much do you think you have spent on your daughter so far?'

'A considerable sum, doctor. A part of it went into fighting the case and sending the culprit to prison, and lakh of rupees went into her treatment and is still being spent. Having sold my house, my wife and I now stay in a rented house. My ten-acre farmland exhausted long before. Even the little money I saved in the bank is spent.'

'Then how are you managing the expenditure now?'

'I received some help from some organizations. Now I have no face to ask them for more.'

'Doesn't your son help you out?'

'If he did, why would I stretch my hand for help in front of others? He could rid himself from the burden of taking care of his sister who is in serious condition, but can my old wife and I do so? Have we not borne her? Whatever be the consequences, we will take care of her till we are alive.'

'Instead of keeping her in the hospital, won't you be saving on the expenses if you arrange a nurse to look after her at home?'

'We could not take such a step fearing the expense. We can't say when she requires medical help. At least we are assured that if she is in hospital there is someone to take care of her. Besides, Mr. Venkat Reddy, the man who owns this hospital, is my old student. He is treating her without expecting any gain. If not, we would have been begging on the roads by now.'

'How many years more, will you go on like this?'

'What is in our hands . . . it will be as many years as willed by God.'

'That was not my question, how will you meet the expense till then? You have exhausted all your resources, approached all organizations for help . . . what will you do next?'

'I will do anything . . . we are prepared to even work as daily wage laborers. I will keep my daughter going even if I have to beg for alms on the street.' Kiranmayi's father burst out weeping.

The old man's sorrow echoed in Siddhartha's ears. The words that he would keep his daughter alive even if he had to beg for alms reverberated through his mind. Now he walked up to Kiranmayi's bed determinedly. He was convinced that what he was about to do can be definitely termed 'euthanasia'. By helping her break away from mortal suffering, he would be helping three people now. He would be not only liberating her from her mortal pain, but also would be sparing her parents from turning into beggars.

Before removing the oxygen tube, he looked into her face intently one last time. *'I don't know how I can thank you enough, doctor. Had someone done this to me a few years ago, my parents could have had something left to subsist on. I have sinned. . . . I left them without shelter . . . my many thanks to you for sparing them a life of beggary.'* Siddhartha thought he heard her saying those words.

Now he pulled out the tube forcefully. He stayed for another ten minutes by her bedside to ensure that her life was snuffed out. Replacing the tube in its place, he returned to relax in his room.

Now his mind was at peace. Serenity descended on him at the end of an agitating storm of thoughts. He felt as though his grandmother was blessing him: *'you did a great job, my dear boy!'* He slipped into a deep slumber . . . a sound sleep . . . he saw a white pigeon in his sleep . . . its broken wing was in place again . . . its neck was once again moving gracefully . . . no injuries whatsoever . . . flying high in the sky . . . flying, it disappeared into the clouds transforming itself into Kiranmayi.

*   *   *

It was Saturday. Saroja suffered from stress and fatigue managing home and workplace and wished she could snatch four winks of rest, that very instant, Prasad, her son, came to her mind. Just as she cleaned and dressed him as a baby when he soiled the bed, he had now become a child all over again . . . a twenty-three-year old infant. . . . As she thought, tears welled up in her eyes. The next day was anyway Sunday, since there would not be any work at the bank, she would find some rest. Every morning, as she woke up, she would walk into Prasad's room to help him complete his chore of visiting the washroom, rest of her own work came later. She would bathe and clothe him, give him his food before leaving for the bank.

She tried rising from her bed, wondering if there would ever be a day when she could escape from her routine, but her body did not cooperate. She felt indisposed . . . body pains and headache. She might even start running temperature very soon. The symptoms that illness might strike her scared her.

Could she afford to fall sick? If she were to take ill, who will look after Prasad? Who will cater to his needs?

As an infant, what a bouncing baby boy he was! How dotingly she reared him! He used to be her entire world. Seeing that, her husband used to go into sulks. Once he quipped, 'Saroja, you forget that there is a person like me in your life . . . other than taking care of your son it seems you have no other work left in the world. Please turn your attention to me too once in a while . . . there is danger of you one day inquiring who I am and not allow me into the house.' She had laughed then aloud at his words.

Those were the only sweetness-filled days she had in life . . . the time when she felt proud as though the entire world was at her feet . . . a loving husband, a lovely son, a decent job! What else could a woman ask for!

Saroja's troubles started with the death of her husband. How he left her midway, he who promised at wedding time that he would be by her side till the end of her life! Remembering that turbulent time, made her shake in fear.

Saroja learnt to get on with life reconciling with her loss. With her husband no more, she decided to live for the sake of her son, but her son was now confined to the bed like a living corpse. She felt her entrails worn down every time she thought of him. If everything went well, he could have been by now a software engineer in a plush post. He would have got a wife too, helping her around the house. She would have had grandchildren too with whom she would while away her time back from work.

She would have been teaching her grandchildren, helping them with their homework and playing with them . . . oh . . . what sweet sensations . . . all remained now mere dreams . . . her life now a fallen tree blunted to wither away . . . with no chance of another spring in sight.

Another fresh problem had begun to trouble her mind. No doubt, she would take care of her son, as long as she lived. Who would once she left this world? The thought agitated her to no end. She would have to live as long he lived, but was it in her hands? Did she ever think that her husband would leave this world all of a sudden? What if an accident snuffed out also her life? She would hence walk with care while out on the street. More than fear of death, it was the fear of what would happen to her son if she had to die that plagued her.

As there was no one to fill in for her, a tired Saroja rose to her feet despite her illness. She looked into Prasad's bedroom. Prasad was already up and waiting for her. Seeing his mother, at first his eyes brightened with joy . . . but that was for a mere moment . . . in no time endless sadness spread in those eyes.

'Did you sleep well last night, son?'

Woefully, Prasad looked at his mother, 'How can I sleep, Mummy . . . as always I could not.'

'What did you do then all night?'

'Thoughts, Mummy . . . frightful tormenting thoughts haunted me . . . nightmares kept visiting me disturbing my sleep.'

'How many times did I tell you, son, not to entertain those wild thoughts, and that you should learn to accept what's come over you bravely?' saying, Saroja detaching the bedpan below the bed, took it to the washroom and flushed it. Washing the pan clean, she placed it back in its position.

Squirting some toothpaste on to the toothbrush, Saroja brushed Prasad's teeth and helped him gargle some water and spit out into a nearby bucket. She then wiped clean his face with a fresh towel.

It severely embarrassed Prasad to see his mother do those chores for him even at his age . . . he wished for death. Every day he died innumerable deaths . . . with hurt . . . shame . . . embarrassment . . . desperation . . . sorrowed and petrified . . . he died several times. Every time it happened, he wondered: *how long this wretched life was going to last* . . . he wondered whether his mother and he would ever find relief from this torture?

Prasad was even more vexed with life thinking about his mother's plight. His life held neither purpose nor purport for him. Then why should he continue living except to trouble his mother? His father too was not around to share her burden. She bore the entire burden all by herself. How long could she continue this way . . .

her health was not supportive and their financial position was also not good, due to which reason she could not afford to give up her job either.

How colourful were Prasad's dreams as a youngster! He dreamt of earning millions . . . see his mother settle in comfort . . . dreamt of taking her on a world tour to countries like America, Switzerland and Australia . . . but now he himself had turned a burden on her. Even now, there was a way to make her life comfortable . . . that was by inviting his death. . . . . The sooner he died, greater would be the comfort for her . . . .

As soon as she had finished her cooking, Saroja sponged Prasad's body with a towel dipped in liquid soap and warm water. She wiped him dry with a fresh towel and helped him put on a new shirt and tied a *lungi* around his waist.

Saroja made him sit propped up against two pillows for support and fed him mashed food in small morsels.

Saroja observed Prasad gained weight in recent times. The doctor had forewarned her of this, that the steroid Prednisone, though undoubtedly would slow the weakening of his muscles, would lead to weight gain and low bone density resulting in bones going brittle and might at times even break.

Before leaving for the bank, Saroja inquired, 'son, do you need anything else?'

'No, Mummy.'

'Aunty had informed that Ramya is arriving today. She may visit you this evening,' saying so Saroja pulled a chair closer to Prasad's bed, 'If she cannot make it today, she may later, after I return from work. It won't be a problem when I am around. Is it okay . . . shall I go now?' Prasad nodded his head in agreement.

That Prasad's eyes brightened with the mention of Ramya's name and that the next moment his eyes saddened, did not escape the eye of Saroja. Once Saroja left for the bank, Prasad's thoughts revolved around Ramya.

Ramya . . . a name that entwined with his life closely . . . she was the only other woman who he liked most next to his mother . . . beautiful figure . . . a name well suited to her person . . . over and above, kind and compassionate. It was when he was in his tenth standard, it occurred to him for the first time, that he was in love with Ramya . . . an age when one understood little about love . . . the time when love appeared as shown in films in all its glory and glitter. He had come to realize now that he might have taken it as love going by the way Ramya treated him because of his frequent visits to doctors. He often had to miss classes, and every time he missed classes, Ramya lent her hand-written notes to him. Where he did not understand, she used to coach him personally.

After finishing her Intermediate course, Ramya chose the electronics stream in engineering. How much Prasad begged his mother to allow him to join the same college . . . at first his mother did not want him to attempt the entrance exam itself for admission into engineering course, but on protest she agreed. Since Ramya scored a high rank, she secured a free seat in engineering. He secured a much lower rank in forty thousands. Then he pleaded with his mother. 'Becoming a software engineer is my dream; you know it Mummy, don't you? I hear there are management seats available in Ramya's college. We just have to pay four lakh for it. The same seat last year cost eight, this year it is only four. How cheap it is! Since there is a slump in the software boom, demand for the course too went down. I will study only an engineering course, Mummy.'

'No, my son. Listen to me. Join the degree college close by.'

'Why do you say that, Mummy? Do you know who does an ordinary degree course . . . dull students alone . . . or who cannot study a course in engineering. I am intelligent Mummy. If this disease had not affected me, I too could have scored a better rank. Engineering study has become common these days. It is as a degree course that was common in your time.'

'Son, after much thought I arrived at this decision. Join a degree college. Choose any combination of subjects as per your interest. For that matter, you can take computer science even here by opting for a B.C.A. course.'

'No, Mummy . . . I will study only an engineering course. Are you denying me this because it costs you four lakh? Am I not your only child? Recall how many times you said that all this money and property is to see me happy. It is just four lakh. I shall pay you back ten times over once I get into a job.' Prasad recollected that hapless look his mother gave at the time.

'It's not the question of money, my son. To see you happy, I will not hesitate to spend all that we have, but I am thinking only of you. All engineering colleges are twenty to twenty-five kilometers from our house. How will you commute that far? Everyone goes by bus or by his personal transport. Have you forgotten the doctor mentioning that you may have to use a wheelchair very soon? Can you imagine, going that distance in that condition? When that condition strikes you, can you put up with the accompanying pain? Did you calculate the time it would take to reach the college? The college I suggest is close to our house. It is in every way convenient to us.'

Prasad's eyes brimmed with tears. Thoughts of her son and his welfare alone filled the mother's mind . . . he could understand her concern for him. How to convince her? Joining an engineering course was not as important to him as staying close to Ramya. He would have argued with equal desperation to join a college graded low if she were to be in that college. How colorful as a rainbow his life would appear if the two of them walked together to the college chatting away! If he were not to be close to Ramya, life would be one filled with darkness. As Prasad sobbed going over all that, his mother took him in her arms. 'I can't bear to see you weep, Prasad. It is all right. You will study an engineering course. We can move to another house close to the college. Is that okay? Please don't weep.'

Hearing her words, Prasad felt sadder and sorrow overcame him that his mother for his sake was preparing to vacate her own house and move to a rented house.

'How will you commute to the bank, Mummy . . . won't it be far for you?'

'It is alright. I will commute by some bus to reach my bank,' she replied.

Finally, Prasad joined the degree college nearer home to do B.C.A course.

Prasad almost lost control over his legs when he was in the college. His mother bought him a wheelchair to continue going to the college. Around the time, Ramya's father bought her a *Scooty*, a two-wheeler. Whenever she saw Prasad on her way to the college, she would stop and walk with her two-wheeler.

'Why do you take that trouble . . . you go ahead . . . I will go slowly,' Prasad used to say.

'It is okay. Let us go together till your college. You too need company, don't you?'

Walking that way in the company of Ramya and hearing her laughter made Prasad forget the fact that he was actually in the wheelchair, a sweet feeling as though they were walking hand in hand through a park chatting away. On such days, he floated away in sweet dreams.

However, Prasad's heart agonized coming in the grip of fear: *does Ramya really like me . . . does she really love me? Does anyone at all love people like me? Perhaps, what Ramya is displaying is not love at all! Could it be pity for me?*

Recalling how the heroines in some films he saw loved the blind and the physically challenged, he escaped once again into a dream world . . .

Ramya called on him at least once a week. Gradually those visits came to be monthly visits. Once he even expressed his wish unable to control his thoughts. 'Please come once a week at least Ramya . . . it feels good to talk to you.'

'Sorry, Prasad! It is an engineering course, is it not? There are quite a few assignments on hand. I have the best scores in my batch since the first semester. If I have to maintain the same standard, I have to work harder. There is not enough time on hand.'

Once Prasad completed his final year of study, he became less mobile. Since confined to bed, his mother made him study privately for post graduation in Telugu.

While still studying in her final year engineering course, Ramya got a job in Wipro through a campus interview. Her company was located in Bangalore. Hearing she would be earninga salary of twenty-five thousand a month, Prasad felt elated as though it were his achievement. He felt like weeping the day she came to take leave of him. The sorrow was that the only person he knew closely beside his mother was going to a far off place leaving him.

'I am going far, but not away from you, Prasad. How far is Bangalore? Whenever I come home, I will make it a point to visit you. Is it okay with you?' He felt relaxed when Ramya consoled him with those words.

Four months after she left for Bangalore, Ramya visited Hyderabad.

Prasad felt as if he found a long lost lover . . . a joy of a lost child in a fair, finally reunited with his mother.

Ramya had gained some weight and looked fairer too than before.

'How is your job?' Prasad asked.

'It's great. I am enjoying my work. Can't you make out from my appearance that I am happy? The Working Women's Hostel where I stay is very convenient. The food too is good, like homemade food. The cab comes early to pick me up and drops me back at the hostel after work. I am very comfortable and do you know I have also put on some weight?' Ramya said spreading the wonderful cheer of her smile.

'You drew four months' salary, didn't you? What did you do with so much money?' Prasad asked.

'Keeping some for my expenses, I transferred the rest to my father's account. My father, of course refused, yet I credited the money to his account. You know how gratifying that feeling is! All these days we lived on their money. Do you know how thrilling it is to place in our parents' hand all our earnings? The thrill has to be experienced each by oneself, impossible to put in words. I brought a silk sari from Bangalore for my mother and clothes for my father. Their faces lit up with an extraordinary brightness as they received them.'

Ramya suddenly stopped as she looked into his face. She must have certainly sensed the sadness in him. Recovering quickly Prasad said, 'you know I am doing my M.A. Once I finish the course I will take up a job. Teaching profession is good, isn't it? I can teach. I shall buy a silk sari for Mummy and a dress for you with my first pay.'

Ramya smiled and said, 'Will you buy a dress for me too?'

'I shall, certainly. Besides Mummy, aren't you the one who looked after me well?'

'Oh, thanks . . . that was very sweet of you, Prasad. I got a gift for you too . . . in my hurry, I forgot to bring it along. I will just go and get it,' saying so, Ramya ran out.

As he waited for her to return, many a sweet thought sprouted in his mind. What could be the gift that Ramya had brought for him! A Titan watch . . . a ring . . . a readymade dress . . . all gifts that girls usually gift their lovers came to Prasad's mind. Soon enough, Ramya returned within ten minutes. She held in her hand a book in English. . . .

'This is an interesting book, Prasad. I thought of you as I went through this book, Thinking, it would be of use to you, I bought a copy for you as my gift.' Prasad took the book in hand. It was Dale Carnegie's *How to Stop Worrying and Start Living*. He flipped open to look at the first page. He read the words scribbled on it. 'To Prasad with love.' A wave of joy rose in him. 'Thank you, Ramya. I love this gift.'

After they chatted for a while, Ramya asked, 'When does Aunty get back from work?'

'Usually by five-thirty . . . if there is work left, at around seven.'

'Okay then . . . I will come back at seven-thirty. It has been some time since I met her. Besides, I got some good news to share with her.'

'What good news . . . won't you share with me first?'

'How eager . . . I shall share it with you together.'

'Can't you at least leave a hint for now?'

'Well . . . it is to do with what I kept to myself all these days . . . first I would like to reveal it to my parents today . . . I know for sure it would set a storm raging and I also know it is a storm that will not subside that quickly. At that time, I will come running here to your place to share that news with you and Aunty. Till then, it is going to be suspense.'

Prasad's heart went onto a flutter: the secret has to do with his love for her. Yes, that was the secret Ramya kept under wraps all these days, but who will agree to a marriage with a person afflicted with Muscular Dystrophy, physically challenged and confined to bed? Certainly, there is going to be a storm in her family. Ramya would then say, 'love knows none of this Dad. I love Prasad, my life has to go with his, he is going to be my husband. If I were to be down with such a disease after marriage, would you wish my husband left me? You won't, will you? This too is the same. Good bye,' saying so, Ramya would come to our house to share her secret with Mummy and me.

In fact, several times Prasad wished to reveal his mind to Ramya. At home and in the park the day he tripped and fell down, the days she walked with him to the college pushing her *Scooty,* when she was in her final year of study, when she announced her appointment at Wipro, and when she left for Bangalore to take up her new job.

He simply could not gather enough courage. What if her response was, 'what is there in you to love you? Education . . . looks . . . high position, none. You can't stand straight on your legs. You are incapable of even looking after yourself. What do you expect to achieve through marriage? You need only a slave to serve you. Not just I, no girl in this world will take to liking you and will not mar her life by marrying you.' Prasad feared Ramya's rejection. He suffered from an inferior feeling and at the same time an inability to face the rejection.

Prasad thanked himself for not proposing to Ramya from his end. Now she was going to propose on her own. Now he did not have to fear facing her rejection. He was very lucky. His mother and Ramya would do for his life.

For a long time since Ramya left, Prasad felt as on cloud nine. On his mother's return from work, he shared excitedly the news of Ramya's visit.

'She said she would come back soon, Mummy . . . said she wished to share some good piece of news with you.'

'Perhaps it's about her marriage.'

'Mummy, I too thought so,' Prasad said excitedly.

Prasad resisted from telling his mother that she intended marrying him. He expected his mother to swoon overjoyed on hearing the news from Ramya. How anxious he was, waiting for Ramya's return, and also irritable . . . .

Prasad may have inquired a hundred times of his mother, 'didn't she come yet?'

Prasad's mother reproached him, 'rest assured, my son, she won't leave without seeing you?'

What did mother know of the problem facing Ramya, earth may have quaked when she announced what she had on mind . . . did her parents confine her to a room . . . oh . . . how could he save her? He can't move from his place, can he? If only he possessed some magical powers! *What if I tell Mummy what is happening . . . Mummy may take help of people to rescue Ramya . . . shall I call in the police for help, otherwise?'*

'Hi Aunty, how are you? How is your health?' Ramya's words fell on his ears as music. That was Ramya's voice. Thank god! Ramya came back at last.

She entered Prasad's room and greeted him. Her face was glowing as if thousand jasmines blossomed at once . . . bright . . . he had not seen her that happy ever. Did that mean her parents gave consent to her marriage . . . did she manage to convince them . . . was it for that her face was beaming with happiness?

'Aunty! You too come in. I have to share with both of you a piece of good news!'

Saroja walked in and settled into a chair next to Prasad's bed.

Ramya too pulled a chair closer.

'Tell me, my dear girl . . . is your marriage fixed or what?' Saroja asked.

'Yes, Aunty'

'Is it fixed by your parents . . . what does the boy do?'

'It is not fixed by my parents aunty . . . I have selected the boy myself.'

In a few moments, Prasad thought, he was set to hear words that would cause a pleasurable change in his life.

'Well, who is that lucky boy?'

Ramya looked at Saroja coyly.

'It is all right. Tell me who is he?'

'Aunty, His name is Kalyan. He was my classmate from my engineering college days. Now he too is working at Wipro. He is not from our caste. I announced my decision to my parents just a while ago. To begin with, I feared my parents would be outraged hearing of it, but nothing of the sort happened. My mother just murmured a protest and my father supported my proposal. So now, the line is clear for our marriage. I am truly very happy, aunty. You know, Kalyan is a very good boy . . . he is good looking too, you know?'

Saroja laughingly said, 'how do I know unless I see him?'

'I have his picture in my cell phone. Wait, I will show you in a moment.' She pressed a few keys and displayed a photograph. Saroja took the phone from her hands and glanced at the picture closely for a minute. 'Truly he looks very handsome as a film hero . . . good selection. You are a lucky girl!'

'Why do you say that, Aunty? In fact, he is lucky to get a girl like me for a wife. Prasad! You too take a look.' She thrust the cell phone into Prasad's hands. 'Now, how is he? His hair curls. He is a six-foot handsome guy, you know,' she kept describing Kalyan to them.

The moment Prasad heard the name Kalyan, his face fell. His heart broke into thousand pieces. He was shattered. Like a black python, disappointment began to twine round him.

133

'Tell me Prasad, how is he? Doesn't he look great? You know, he is a good conversationalist and very jovial too. I will inform you of the date of our marriage once I consult him. Both of you must attend the wedding. Especially, you should not miss it. Do you know I told Kalyan you are my best friend?'

Ramya kept on excitedly without waiting for Prasad's reply. 'Your liking for that boy is very much evident from your talk,' Saroja remarked.

'Truly so, aunty . . . tell me how did you find out?' Ramya asked like a child pleading.

'Haven't you been talking about Kalyan for the past one hour? That is how I made out,' Saroja replied.

'Why an hour . . . even if I talk about him for days on end, there would still be a lot left to talk about. Such is his personality,' she said proudly.

Having chatted for another ten minutes and having had the sweet served her, Ramya had left reminding them once again to attend her wedding without fail.

Ramya walked out of Prasad's life and his dreams thus . . . but she remained forever in his thoughts.

That day . . . that black day . . . so stayed imprinted in Prasad's memory, that it remained fresh even two years later as though it happened just the other day.

Prasad looked at the clock on the wall to check time. When would Ramya come . . . would she come at all . . . would she forget to visit him? It had been a year since he last saw her when she came to say that Kalyan got a posting in Australia and that she too had plans of joining him there . . . she must be twenty-three years old now . . . his own age . . . he wanted to see how she looked now. Did she gain weight . . . and grown fairer?

Prasad remembered the 'Hero' pen she gave him years ago as a gift for his birthday . . . how he treasured it . . . how many dreams surrounding that pen . . . that he would be writing love letters to her with it. When his dreams troubled him, he slept with that pen in hand. When he first heard that she loved someone else and that she planned to marry him, he threw it into some corner in his cupboard.

How many days was it since Prasad discarded that pen! If he could show it to her now, how happy she would feel! As the thought passed his mind, there was eagerness in him, to ferret it out somehow before she arrived. He slowly moved up in bed against the pillows and pulled the wheelchair standing next to the bed. He struggled for about twenty long minutes to slide his paralyzed legs by bed's side and transfer the rest of his body into the chair. Then he wheeled himself to the cupboard and opened its doors. It was full of his things, mostly his clothes. . . .

To the best of his knowledge, Prasad flung the pen into some corner at the bottom of the cupboard. Looking for it, he bent forward a little. He could not reach. He bent down further holding the handle of the door. Even so, he failed to reach the bottom of the cupboard. He had to just bend a little more . . . a little . . . the wheelchair moving back and he falling down, both happened at once. His lip had a cut and began to bleed. More than the pain of falling down, he was anxious about Ramya's arrival. '*I wish I were not be seen by her in this hapless condition,*' *he mused*

Prasad thought at that moment, that it was more important for him to get back into the wheelchair than finding the Hero pen. Crawling, he reached for the chair. He tried to raise himself up with the support of the wheelchair, but failed. He once again gathered all his strength to lift his lower body onto the wheelchair. He fell to the floor again with a thud. At once, grief and despair seized him. He lay on the floor for some time face down and tried to gather his breath.

Prasad caught hold of the wheelchair and tried to heave his body a bit higher. The wheelchair kept sliding away from him. He held its wheel tightly and rose again to reach the seat. The wheelchair skid again. He just could not figure out how he could keep the wheelchair steady and at the same time manage to upraise himself.

As time passed, Prasad's anxiety that Ramya would be there anytime took the better of him . . . the disappointment he faced in the park was still fresh and raking as a raw wound. Ramya should not see him in a helpless state yet again.

Realizing his attempts to sit on the chair to be impossible, Prasad slowly crawled toward the cot. He assumed the cot would not slide as easily as the wheelchair, and that it would be easier to raise his body with the cot's support.

Prasad lifted his torso a little and took hold of the edge of the bed. He used all his strength to raise the rest of his body on to the cot. He could not move an inch. Since his lower part of the body gained weight, howsoever hard he tried he could not move his body an inch. Once he succeeded in getting hold and managing to lift the body, he struggled to hang on. However, in a few moments he slipped and fell to the ground. A paroxysm of despair, disappointment and debility took hold of him . . . Prasad made one last attempt to get on to the bed somehow. The cot moved to a side creaking.

With that, the bedpan detached and fell on the ground with a thud.

Saroja might have placed it loosely in a hurry to leave for her work. In an instant, foul stench rose to hang in the air heavily . . . what to do if Ramya were to arrive now? When asked, what would he say about the stench? Oh, why ever did this dreadful happen only now? Were it not better she never came visiting him? Better still, she forgot about her visit to his place. Could she not think it better she visited when his mother was around? Once his mother was back, she would clean the mess and there would be no problem then.

Prasad wondered to himself: *even so, what if she did arrive . . . please, Ramya . . . don't come . . . I can bear any disappointment but not an experience of discomfiture in your presence. I wish I were dead, instead. That is why, don't come . . . don't come. I am as a worm struggling trapped in phlegm . . . don't come visiting . . . Ramya, even if you bear to see me in this state, I cannot bear to be seen by you in my present state.*

'Hi Prasad!' Ramya was about to greet Prasad when she checked herself as she entered. Noticing him sprawled out on the floor, she quickly reached his side to help him to his feet but she could not. 'Oh God! What happened to you, Prasad . . . did you roll down the bed . . . what is this water all around?' The stink offended her nostrils. She realized Prasad was too heavy for her. 'I will be right back, won't take long!' She scurried out and returned with her mother in a few minutes. Together they held him by his arm on either side. Lifting him helped him on to the bed.

Ramya asked gently, 'How did you fall down? Didn't Aunty position you properly before she left?'

Ramya's mother guessed what exactly had happened by looking at the overturned bedpan and the contents flowing in different directions on the floor. 'I will go send our domestic help. Get the room cleaned!' she left instructing Ramya. Ramya did not utter a word until their domestic help finished cleaning the room and left the place. Ramya then pulled a chair closer to Prasad's bed. 'How are you keeping these days . . . Are you taking the medicines regularly?'

Prasad nodded his head helplessly.

'How is your postgraduate study proceeding?' No answer came from Prasad.

'Are you feeling bad for what happened? You will have to learn to treat lightly a few things in life, Prasad . . . otherwise life will turn out to be miserable.'

Prasad thought to himself that his life turned miserable long ago. Noticing tears welling up in his eyes, Ramya understood he was in no mood to talk. 'I will come back later, Prasad . . . I will come once Aunty is back from work.'

Once Ramya left, Prasad strongly felt that it was time he put an end to his life.

*   *   *

Dr. Siddhartha was on his morning duty. By the time he reached the hospital, Dr. Wali was already there. They were busy in the O.P. from ten until noon.

In ten minutes, Dr. Wali joined Dr. Siddhartha, who by then settled in his chair having scrubbed his hands clean. 'It beats me why so many people fall sick these days. Has people's immunity level waned or has their spending capacity increased making them run to the hospital even for minor ailments?' Dr. Siddhartha commented.

'Both arguments are right . . . the immunity of people has nosedived . . . the air we breathe is polluted . . . lack of vitamins and mineral nutrients in the junk food we took a liking to . . . due to all these man's capacity to resist diseases has come down. I stayed in my village up to my Intermediate. I don't recall if I ever consulted a doctor regarding my health for any complaint whatsoever. When sick, all I had was plain simple food like rice with pepper *Rasam* with coriander to go with it, or better still barley water. That was all! All sickness vanished in two or three days. As you just said, today people's awareness of health is on the increase and alongside their earning capacity too has gone up,' Dr. Wali replied.

'It is good to be aware of one's health, but what we see today is all due to needless fear leading to paranoia.'

'The corporate hospitals are creating a phantom of fear, and unleashing it into the market to cash in on man's paranoia about sickness. Added to that, interviews with doctors, who specialize in treating various ailments on the TV frighten people into believing that it is essential to visit a hospital even for any minor ailment, lest they fall prey to a major ailment.'

'That is right. I heard a doctor mention recently over the TV, that every woman who crossed twenty years of age should get the Pap smear test done. Can there be anything more nonsensical . . . meaning from the age of twenty itself every woman coming under the fear of cancer, has to keep undergoing tests. Earlier we used to hear that women over fifty have to undergo that test. Now that age has declined to twenty. In the coming days, they might say every new born baby needs to undergo tests.'

'Yes, children too are prone to cancers these days, is it not so? What reason can we give . . . everything is in the hands of Allah.'

"I don't believe it. Everything is in our hands . . . in our genes . . . in our diet and in our habits.'

'The mention of food reminds me. I am hungry, Dr. Siddhartha,' saying Dr. Wali looked to consult time. 'It is past one. No wonder the alarm bell rang inside.'

Over lunch, their conversation veered to mercy killing.

'Have you seen this morning's newspaper? A girl by name Seema Sood from Himachal Pradesh wrote a letter to the President . . . seeking permission to commit suicide,' Dr. Wali opened the subject.

'Yea . . . It was heart-breaking reading about her . . . what a brilliant student . . . see how her life took a turn for the worse due to illness . . . she was a gold medalist from BITS Pilani in Engineering. Now for the past thirteen years she has confined herself to her bedroom due to Arthritis. Her joint bones have degenerated so badly that she cannot move her limbs. Her mother is a seventy-five-year old woman. Ten years back she underwent surgery for knee replacement. Her knees need replacement once again. How many diseases are there which modern medicine cannot cure! Is it not better to die than lead a horrible life?' Dr. Siddhartha remarked.

'I don't agree. Mercy killing is as good as killing. An old person in America by name, Gilbert shot his wife dead who was suffering from Alzheimer's disease. The court convicted him to twenty-five years of imprisonment. The accused said in the court, 'I love my wife very ardently, for which reason, unable to bear the sight of her suffering, I killed her. My impulse that drove me to kill her was love and kindness. I don't deserve punishment,' he argued. All these people appear to me as psychic patients. What is this killing out of kindness? It is nothing but a cover-up of their psychological problems and inhuman behaviour.'

'In Switzerland there is a charitable trust called *Dignitas*. There is need for such an institution in our country too.'

'*Dignitas* . . . I never heard of it . . . what does it do?'

'That institution is termed 'Euthanasia Charity'. They help in executing 'Death on Wheels', assist those who wish to die. They take those with intense death wish to a place of their choice and by making them sit in a car, offer a chemical mixed decoction. The said client willingly takes it. For assisting in that client's death, the 'Euthanasia Charity' collects from each client three thousand dollars as fee. They call that assisted suicide,' Dr. Siddhartha explained.

'Is it not considered a crime in Switzerland?'

'No, it is not. When a person intending to die drinks that decoction willingly, it does not come under crime, unless he is forced to drink.'

'In the first place, it's a crime to allow such an organization to operate. As it is, suicides are on the rise in our country with one taking place every ten minutes. If there were to be an institution such as 'Death on Wheels' or mercy killing, deaths such as these will see a phenomenal rise. If all terminally ill patients who wish to end their lives ask for assistance, what about those suffering from inexplicable mental illnesses? Don't they also look to death as a release from their suffering? Then people will begin to prefer death on frivolous grounds. Have you ever given a thought to the harm it would cause to the society?'

Dr. Siddhartha did not agree with him. 'Why so many restrictions preventing those who wish to die? Only the person suffering knows how horrendous it is to live on, how does a government or judicial courts sense that suffering in their lives? How justified is it to compel a person to live who does not wish to live? If the government cannot provide opportunity to live happily, free of suffering, it also cannot take away man's right to die. It is violation of human rights.'

'I am getting scared hearing your views, Dr. Siddhartha. Are these the views of a doctor who has to try hard until the end to save life of a patient? You are not holding human life in respect that it deserves. Who are we to take life . . . for that matter who gave man the right to take his own life?'

Before Siddhartha could answer, his cell phone rang. It was a call from Venkat Reddy, the hospital owner.

From the other side the voice said, 'do you remember, today we have to operate upon that Income Tax Officer? You have to remove the steel rod placed in his left shoulder. I have talked to him. He said he would come to the hospital at four o'clock. Keep the operation theatre ready by three-thirty. I have already alerted the anesthesiologist too. He will be there in time. You remind the surgeon too. This patient of ours is looking into our income tax case . . . so you have to take some special care of him. Nothing should go wrong . . . you will look into the case personally.'

'Yes, sir . . . I remember, you need not worry. I will take care. Dr. Wali too is with me,' Dr. Siddhartha hung up.

Leaving the room, Siddhartha said to Dr. Wali, 'I will go and instruct the head nurse to get the operation theatre ready. You give a call to Dr. Sridhar and remind him about the operation. I will alert the rest of our staff.'

By three-thirty, the hospital staff readied everything for the surgery. The surgeon arrived. The anesthesiologist had also come. The nurses and the other attendants were ready. What remained was the arrival of the patient . . . .

Dr. Siddhartha looked at his watch . . . three-forty . . . .

'It gets on my nerves to wait for these VIPs . . . are those coming really VIPs? In our country, everyone takes himself to be a VIP . . . and each has an ego as high as a palm tree. Just because he looks into cases of our hospital, do we have to spread a red carpet welcome? Doesn't this fall under misuse of power? I wish we could slap cases against such persons . . . only then will they learn a lesson or two,' he quipped to Dr. Wali

'What is the use of filing complaints . . . when justice is not rendered even if one waits for years on end . . . who knows how many principles were compromised in running this hospital! Venkat Reddy alone knows how much he is making while running this hospital . . . both meet a match in each other . . . a mutual service to each other.' The time was three fifty-five . . . the patient had not arrived yet.

In the meantime, a fifty-year old man rushed in. '*Ayya* . . . please save the life of my wife. I touch your feet, *Ayya* . . . she is dying . . . if she dies my kids and I will be ruined, *Ayya*!' Behind him appeared three youngsters carrying a woman in hands. She had blood all over her . . . a sickle appeared stuck in her head. Her hair matted as though bathed in blood . . . .

The stranger continued. 'She angered me, *Ayya* . . . I was heavily drunk. I had the sickle in my hand. In one move, I hit her with it . . . she fell to the ground writhing in pain as a hen with its throat slit . . . immediately my stupor came down. I cannot live without her. I brought whatever money I had in the house to pay your fee . . . if you want more, I am prepared to pledge my house too . . . please save my wife, *Ayya*.' The laborer fell at Dr. Siddhartha's feet. Without waiting, he fell at the feet of the nurses and attendants there.

'Look, this is a medico-legal case . . . meaning a police case . . . it is not possible to treat her here,' Dr. Wali said.

'*Ayya* . . . but by that time, she will die. We live right behind your hospital. Please attend on her quickly . . . I will fall at your feet. I am not asking you to treat her free of charge. I will pay for her treatment . . . as much as you want.'

'Don't you understand when I say it is a police case?' Wali shouted angrily.

'You first attend to my wife and save her life . . . I am ready to go to jail later. If she dies I too will die.' He again fell at the feet of Dr. Wali and wailed.

'See, the operation theatre is not free. Take her fast to a different hospital. Why don't you understand . . . she has already lost a lot of blood . . . she may die due to your delay. Attend to her at once, please.'

'*Ayya* . . . please show some mercy . . . I am greatly indebted to you and I will never be able to repay my debt of gratitude. Please save my wife.'

He was so full of tears that he appeared to be washing Dr. Wali's feet with his tears.

Dr. Siddhartha's phone rang. Venkat Reddy came on line. 'The ITO says he has some urgent work to attend to. The operation is postponed to tomorrow.' Dr. Siddhartha conveyed the message to Dr. Wali. For a second, both exchanged glances. Dr. Wali telephoned the nearest police station informing them about the medico-legal case that they had on hand. They rushed the unconscious woman into the operation theatre on a stretcher. In another hour, the operated patient came out into the general ward.

'The operation has been successful. There is no danger to her life. You and your wife are lucky. You escaped the hangman's noose,' Dr. Wali patted on the shoulder of the patient's husband. The man wailed falling at the feet of Dr. Wali and Dr. Siddhartha.

On returning to the room, relaxing, Dr. Wali said, 'did you see, Dr. Siddhartha . . . how it is proved in this patient's case, that there is God above? We readied the operation theatre for someone else. We all were ready with nurses and attendants including the surgeon. Allah did all this only to save her life. Otherwise, she would have been dead by the time the theatre readied and surgeon sent for. How else can you explain all this, except as Allah's miracle?'

'All trash, Dr.Wali. It was neither God's greatness nor a miracle. Whatever happens in life is due to chance. There is nothing like luck and ill luck. To say there is God because she survived implies she would have died had that Income Tax Officer arrived. Would that have proved that there was no God? A person called God should exist or should not. It is meaningless to say that he exists when good happens to us, and does not if the contrary happens.'

'Because you are an atheist, you support the inhuman horrific killings such as mercy killing. Don't Hindus too say that even an ant cannot bite except under Lord Siva's command? Even our religion says the same . . . nothing takes place without Allah's consent, Allah alone decides whom to give life to and whose life to take.'

'Dr. Wali, you know how many abortions take place every day in our hospital, don't you? If mercy killing is wrong, abortion is equally wrong.'

'Dr. Siddhartha, your argument is contentious . . . are not abortions legally permitted here?'

'That is what I too am saying. If mercy killing is legally permitted, it will not be considered as wrong, isn't it? Why doesn't the government legalize it as in Netherlands?'

'How can the two be the same? Mercy killing means you take away the life of someone . . . that is, to kill a person. Abortion is not that, is it . . . it is just termination of a pregnancy wherein life has not taken any form or birth . . . and we are allowing abortions of fetuses not more than twenty weeks old. There is nothing wrong in it, is there?'

'What a self-deception, Dr. Wali! It is a mere jugglery of words . . . this too is killing, is it not? This too is to take away life. In mercy killing, death takes place with patient's consent. The case of abortion is not the same . . . the fetus in the womb which is eagerly looking forward to seeing the light of the world is mercilessly killed without its consent. Doesn't that killing appear as unjust to you? A film showing the movements of a twelve week fetus is available on the Internet. Haven't you seen that? I saw that three-month fetus moving its limbs and throbbing with life inside its mother's womb.It is no crime in America to terminate a pregnancy during the first twenty-four week gestation, but think how many cases there are where a twenty-four week's baby survived after being born prematurely. What is a crime and what is not keeps shifting according to vicissitude of changing times. At one time performing an abortion was a punishable offence in our country . . . now it is legally tenable.'

'You legalize mercy killing when you become the President or Prime Minister of our country Dr. Siddhartha, except putting forward our pointless arguments, is there any other use?' Dr. Wali said jokingly.

Next day happened to be Dr. Wali's wedding anniversary. His idea was to make Dr. Siddhartha accept to take on night duty somehow in his place. He was afraid of arguing any further, lest he offended Dr. Siddhartha. That reason made him laugh away and close the argument.

Next day Dr. Siddhartha took on the night duty in Dr. Wali's place.

Dr. Siddhartha too had plans of putting an end to a conflict within him that had been raging for the past ten days. The reason for the conflict was a cancer patient who came to that hospital. He was seventy years old. He ruined his life due to addiction to alcohol. Chemotherapy and removal of cancerous organ, all were complete, but of no avail. Cancer had spread to the rest of the organs. He was a terminally ill patient . . . a situation where doctors too had given up. The patient was undergoing terrible pain. His sons, who had admitted him, vanished from the scene. Except bearing the expenses, they appeared to have left him to

147

his fate. The patient did not have even a wife to be by his side and the daughters-in-law had neither the time nor patience to serve him. Dr. Siddhartha, therefore, thought it was his responsibility to relieve the patient from that suffering. He decided that the time had arrived for him to cause another mercy killing.

*   *   *

Every day by evening, Saroja started to suffer body pains and felt weak. She had been putting off a visit to the doctor for no apparent reason. Since it was Sunday, she thought of seeing a doctor. Once she gave Prasad his food, she left to see their family doctor Dr. Raja Rao in the neighborhood.

'How are you? How is your son doing? It has been a long time since you came to me,' the doctor inquired.

'Fine, except that my son has been recently finding it difficult to speak due to weakening of throat muscles. His doctors have advised me to feed him only soft food. They fear that he may in future find it difficult to breathe, at which time he may need life support system. I am frightened of that prospect.'

'The disease is such, deadly, it kills the patient in a slow process. You have to be strong and be ready to face every change to the worse.'

Once the doctor heard to Saroja's own complaints of recent illness, he responded, 'age is catching up on you, isn't it . . . what with heavy work at the bank and taking care of your son . . . how much stress you should be facing besides physical strain! It is common for people in your position to develop body pains and minor illnesses . . . even so, I recommend blood test and urine test . . . get them done. Did you any time lately undergo Pap Smear test?'

'No, doctor'

'Every woman crossing fifty has to undergo the Pap Smear Test every year. I am suggesting also that test. Get back once the reports are ready . . . I shall suggest other medicines once I see the reports.'

The next day on her way to the bank, Saroja stopped by at the Vijaya Diagnostic Centre and gave the samples for the various tests recommended.

Two days later, she thought of collecting the reports while on her way home, but postponed wondering in what state Prasad could be . . . a constant haunting fear . . . she was apprehensive of something happening to him. Problems such as of breathing had begun to surface only lately. As the doctors had cautioned her, instead of a gradual deterioration, he might have problems aggravating in spurts. Since hearing of it, every day she hurried home in fear of something happening. She even requested Ramya's mother to drop in two three times to check on Prasad's health while she was at work. Prasad was always on her mind even at work. Whenever the phone rang, her heart skipped a beat . . . she wondered if the call was from Ramya's mother . . . a fear that she might have to hear of something untoward happening to Prasad.

Saroja noticed a change in Prasad since the time of Ramya's visit. His throat muscles have so weakened that even mashed food was difficult to swallow and his speech slurred accompanied by strange sounds escaping from his mouth. He became more restless and in place of pain, bitterness surfaced. At times, he looked at his mother in anger, but when observed from close she noticed that his anger was not toward her . . . he looked beyond into nothingness . . . into empty space. At whom was he angry? Was he angry with himself . . . with the kind of life he was leading? Saroja came under lot of stress due to perturbation and added to it her own waning strength. . . .

As she entered the house, Saroja first looked into Prasad's room. He looked at her for a brief moment and shifted his gaze to the ceiling. Carrying the bedpan to the washroom, she was lost in thought: what is the meaning of that gaze? At one time, he used to wait eagerly for my return and welcomed it with a glimmer of joy on his face. He used to insist on sitting by his bedside and chat with him. 'Mummy, I have been all alone since ten in the morning . . . I feel I will die of boredom. Please talk something, won't you?'

'What new things are there to share every day, my boy . . . it is routine work at the bank . . . and now I have to get into the kitchen to cook, as such it is late. Aren't you feeling hungry?'

'I am not hungry, Mummy . . . I am not hungry for food, but . . . I am hungry for some company. It is hard to bear this loneliness, Mummy. The disease has ceased to frighten me long back, not so this loneliness. You just sit by my side for some time. Say something. I would like to just hear your voice . . . be it any voice that can assure me that I am not alone,' Prasad used to say.

For the last one week, Prasad had not been asking her to sit by his side. He remained disinterested and unrelated to the world around him. 'I have a small job to attend to. I have to go to Himayatnagar. Shall I go?' Saroja asked Prasad as she has to collect her reports from the Diagnostic centre.

'How long will it be Mom?'

'It may take an hour and a half. Do you need something?'

'Yes, Mummy . . . will you give me anything that I ask for?'

Though clarity was lacking in his speech, Saroja could understand well. 'Try . . . you will know if I can give or not.'

'You can't give, Mummy.'

'Son, I am living for your sake . . . so tell me what you want. I will definitely get it for you. If it is beyond me, even if I have to pledge my head I will get you what you asked."

'Mummy, can you get me poison?' Prasad asked with tenacity in his eyes.

'Oh, what words are they? Don't let such thoughts enter your mind. Don't you know that it would sadden me to hear such words?' Intense sadness surged beyond words.

'Mummy, it is better to die than to face all this suffering . . . I have no patience . . . I don't wish to live. Why should I live a wasteful life . . . a miserable life . . . of no use to anyone? Please release me from this wretchedness, Mummy.'

Tears clouded his eyes as he said those words.

'It is wrong, my son . . . don't say that. Why do you consider your life to be wretched?'

'Then for whose sake am I living, Mummy?'

'Son, you are living for me . . . I am living for your sake. If you think of taking any such drastic step, there is no meaning to my life . . . I too will have to take my life.'

'Mummy, don't say that . . . I can't stand the very thought of it.'

'Then, can I hear you say that, as your mother?'

'I feel like dying every time you do certain jobs for me. You have to clean me when I dirty myself, bathe me, towel and clothe me. I shrink with shame. How many times I die on a day with shame and embarrassment!'

'Son, though you are a grown up, you appear to me a child. Don't allow such thoughts to enter your mind. Who is doing all that for you? Only your mother, isn't it?'

'I feel more ashamed exactly for the same reason. When I should be seeing you happy and comfortable in life, I am troubling you throwing my burden on you.'

'How can my son be a burden to me? Even if I had four more sons like you, I will not take them as burden. For the sake of my children I shall take on gladly any drudgery.'

For a long time, hugging Prasad, Saroja stayed weeping.

'Didn't you say you wanted to go somewhere, Mummy? Go and come back fast.'

'Before I leave, promise me that you won't harm yourself,' Saroja stretched her hand toward Prasad.

'I promise, Mummy . . . .' Prasad said, looking at his mother with devotion.

Saroja went first to the diagnostic centre and collected her reports. From there she visited her family doctor to show him the reports.

The doctor examined the reports carefully. 'It appears you have some major problem. I cannot confirm it until you undergo some more tests. It is better you take these reports to Dr. Raghu. I will write a referral to him. He is well experienced in this field.' Consulting his watch he said, 'he should be in Apollo Hospital now. Why delay? Go there immediately.'

Saroja reached Apollo hospital. She asked at the reception, 'Is Dr. Raghu in?'

'He is in, madam . . . first floor, fourth room. He will be leaving in another ten minutes. Please go there quickly. I will call him to tell him that you are coming,' the receptionist said.

Saroja took the stairs. She paused before knocking on the door. The nameplate on the door read, 'Dr. RAGHU, ONCOLOGIST'.

Was it to an oncologist that Dr. Raja Rao sent her to consult? She took him to be some reputed doctor. An oncologist meant one who specialized in cancer related diseases . . . why did her family doctor recommend that I consult him. A sudden fear gripped her.

She was healthy, was she not? She had been only feeling a little weak lately. Her body merely felt some pains. Could be some viral fever . . . of low intensity . . . that was all . . . did she have to consult an oncologist for that? Just as those thoughts flit past her mind, she tapped on the door and entered. The doctor might just be around seventy years of age. He appeared fair-complexioned as a ripe mango fruit and his hair flowed silvery gray.

'You have to undergo some more tests, Madam, which I am prescribing. Get the tests done at the earliest.'

'Is it necessary to undergo all those tests, doctor? Is there any problem?' Saroja asked with trepidation.

'Yes, I have some doubt . . . to clear that, it is necessary you go through those tests.'

'What is that doubt, doctor?'

'I am afraid you have uterus cancer . . . it looks it is in its advanced stage. Let's see, if it is God's blessing or curse, we have to accept it as His gift, haven't we? What is in our hands? We are mere instruments in His hands.'

She gave him no reply. She paid the fee due to him and got back home.

Saroja finished her cooking and helped Prasad have his dinner. She did not feel like having anything at all. Once she retired for the day, she recalled the words of the doctor: '*I am afraid you have Uterus cancer.*' When she heard that, she neither feared the disease nor the approaching death, but worried about Prasad's future.

Thoughts kept coming back to Saroja: *who will take care of Prasad in my absence? Who will serve him as I do? Maybe someone will, if I transferred my house to favour that person, but will that someone look after Prasad wholeheartedly without a whimper . . . will that person render service that only a mother can . . . Oh God, let not even my worst enemy pass through this kind of predicament. How would it be if I asked the family doctor to help engage a nurse . . . deposit money in a bank and arrange payment every month as salary, how would that be?*

Saroja's thoughts continued in the same vein, 'my brother's family lives in America. What if I sold the house and made him the trustee of the sale proceeds and my son a beneficiary? Better still send for my mother who is staying in an ashram. Saroja however did not want to disturb her mother at her age who was leading a life of peace. Is it better, if I sold the house and enter into an agreement with a charity home to extend medical assistance to Prasad?' Saroja could not arrive at any decision. No single proposition seemed to offer a satisfactory solution.

Could there be any replacement for a mother's service . . . except coming to a compromise regarding one of the choices, there seemed to be no viable alternative ahead.

Saroja kept undergoing various tests for the next one week. The doctors finally confirmed her illness to be uterus cancer.

'Doctor, please tell me without any hesitation, at what stage is my cancer now? I have to settle a few things before my end approaches. So kindly tell me how much time is left for me,' Saroja asked.

'It appears you have been neglecting your health for some time now, madam . . . when there is an illness in us, the body keeps sending out signals. At such a time, we should not ignore those signals. You have been having cancer for quite some time now. Right now, it is in the second stage. At best, we can extend your life to another two to three years.'

At a time when Saroja was thinking hard recently about finding a solution to the problem that cropped up of her illness, for the first time, an idea flashed across her mind as a bolt from the blue. The thought sent shock waves shaking her. Was she indeed a mother to foster such a wishful thought? Why did she get such a merciless thought? How could she think so at all? It is said circumstances change a person to become a monster . . . her thought was such perhaps.

How could she think that it was better if Prasad died?

Saroja tried to erase that thought from her mind, but she did not entirely succeed. Hiding beneath the layers of her mind, the thought resurfaced off and on to agitate her. Had not somebody said that even bitter *neem* leaves would taste sweet when chewed several times over . . . thought over, that same idea seemed acceptable. If her son died before her, she would then leave this world in peace.

However, that was not in her hands . . . everything happened according to God's will. What else could she do except pray God to take her son ahead of her? Oh, how treacherous of her to expect her son's condition to worsen so he might die soon, when as a mother, she should be praying for his speedy recovery! It was her helplessness. He should go before her, for better or for worse!

* * *

By the time Akshara woke up, she saw Kiran reading the newspaper.

She yawned snapping her fingers against her mouth. 'Oh, you woke up before me today!'

'You haven't put it right. Today you woke up late since you did not sleep well last night.'

Akshara smiled. 'Today is the judgment day in Pranavi's case. Understandably, won't I be tense?'

'There's some meaning if it were to be your first case. You have argued a good number of cases until now. It makes me laugh to see you feel tense even now.'

'Well, I can't help it even if it makes you laugh or angers you, Kiran. Each case seems new to me. I can't sleep until the judgment is given favouring my client.'

'Haven't you heard what is said in the *Gita, 'Karmanye vadhikaraste ma phaleshu kadachana*'? It is our duty to try doing things to the best of our ability, but the end result is not in our hands.'

'Why indulge in this pointless debate? I can't leave any issue taking it to be the cause of man's actions, fruits of our karma and as fated to happen . . . all are trash. I am not a supporter of corrupt and unjust ways as some lawyers are. It is more important for me to see that justice and *dharma* triumph rather than earn money. Since my stand is for justice, I cannot take any adverse judgment. I get intensely agitated to see justice lose out to injustice as though fire is stricken with pestilence,' Akshara replied.

'Success is going to be yours even in this case. You have argued vehemently. I have heard you, haven't I? First get ready . . . it is time to go to the court.' As Akshara struggled to shift her legs to hang by the bedside, Kiran in a quick move lifted her and seated her in the wheelchair.

'Kiran, won't you allow me to do the jobs that I am habituated to doing by myself?' Akshara looked at her husband fondly.

'Akshara, you have other important matters to attend to . . . you have already earned a name as a leading activist fighting for the cause of women. You are now proving to be a first rank lawyer in the eyes of all judges. When invited by organizations to give talks on women's issues or in support of the physically challenged, you gather praise as an eloquent speaker. When you can handle so many activities multi-tasking without respite, let me be of help to you so to prove that I too had a role to play in your success.' As he said these words, he pushed the wheelchair into the washroom.

'My parents were at one time cause for my success, but in the present you alone are the cause. Without your moral support . . . your love and affection . . . where would I be? Your love is the force driving me from behind as life support.' Akshara's eyes turned moist as she said the words.

Once Akshara finished brushing her teeth, Kiran offered to bathe her, which she gently forbade. 'No, Kiran. I feel terribly shy. Call my mother . . .' she said.

'You are making fuss every day. Do you feel shy in front of your mother?'

'I don't, for my mother treats me like a baby.'

'You are a crazy woman . . . you are a baby for me too . . . when I bathe you, you appear an infant to me. When I feed you morsels, you seem a baby to me. Why do you ever have to trouble your mother when I am there . . . while I bathe you, I remain your mother. Don't make fuss. Make it fast. Already we are late.'

Once ready, they both reached the dining table for breakfast. Akshara called out to her mother. 'Mom . . . hurry! We are getting late to the court. What is for breakfast today?'

Akshara's mother replied from the kitchen, '*Dosa* and peanut chutney to go with it! I am waiting to serve them hot. Two minutes . . . .'

'Kiran . . . will the verdict today be in our favour as we are expecting?'

'Definitely . . . I believe it would be. First of all, why did you get that doubt?'

'These are days when justice is sold in the open market, is it not so? There are innumerable temptations . . . pulls and pressures . . . economic, political and caste related compulsions. If we analyze the cases I lost, most fall under these categories. I am skeptical for that reason.'

'That way our opponent has the capacity to indulge in such unethical activities, indeed. Unless he is depraved how can he being a Sub-Inspector, duty bound to safeguard the lives of the helpless and the innocent, deceive an innocent girl?'

'Yes, Kiran. Do you remember that day . . . the day when Pranavi, the slim and innocent girl, visited our office? How could he think of deceiving such a girl . . . chasing her in the name of love . . . cheating her with deceptive words . . . promising to marry her . . . satisfying his carnal pleasure . . . if he readies in the end to marry another girl from his caste for a ten-lakh dowry . . . he should not be pardoned. He has to receive punishment most certainly.'

'There is another angle to it which you missed, Akshara. In spite of getting to know and hear of such incidents, girls continue to fall into traps set by these deceivers! Take Pranavi's case, for instance. She gave up her education after seventh class. Her parents are employees in private sector in odd jobs. How did she believe when an SI followed her with a promise of love? With what conviction did she surrender to him? How did she fail to notice that what he sought in her was her looks and not a share in her life?'

'Where does that girl have the necessary age and maturity? One look at this society gives you an idea of the extent to which films have a baneful influence on today's youth. Look how films are glorifying love . . . as though meaning and fulfillment for life lie in physical gratification alone . . . and that to achieve it, however many men are killed or blood streamed, all that is considered heroism and not to be taken as evil. The films are projecting it adding all spice to it. Teenaged girls too fall for the very word 'love', without even understanding the true essence of it,' Akshara said.

'Where is true love these days, Akshara? Love to them merely means visiting *Coffee Days*, seeing movies and going round parks and indulge in forbidden pleasures, dance in drunken stupor in pubs . . . that is all. What can it be but infatuation? It is hard to find true love today even if one were to look out for it far and wide.'

'Still I can see it, Kiran.'

'Don't joke. Where is true love? Everything is infatuation . . . selfishness . . . a desire to realize carnal pleasures . . . girls too have turned unmanageable. They do not hesitate to have an affair with two or three boys at a time. They do not take love seriously either, thinking that if not this boy, another will do. Casual sex is so common these days. Do you see the economic perspective in Pranavi's case? She required money for her needs and pleasures. That money she found with the SI. The SI found in her the beauty he needed. I suspect even in her insistence that the SI should marry her, money seems to be the clinching factor.'

'Wow . . . how well you explained the whole case? I too knew all that, but when I said I could see real love in front of me, I was referring to the one true lover, named Kiran, sitting by my side,' Akshara said smiling, 'I consider myself lucky sometimes when I think of the many sacrifices you made for me. And at other times, I even wonder if I deserved such noble love.'

Just then, Akshara's mother entered with *dosas* for breakfast and chutney in bowls to go with it. While spreading the plates in front of them she asked Kiran, 'has she started referring to merits and sacrifices again?'

'Aren't we used to hearing such talk from her, Aunty, as we keep listing out her merits and tell her that she deserved more. From all this, I understand one thing. Akshara loves flattery,' Kiran said to tease Akshara.

'Stop there. Both mother and son-in-law are out to rib me . . . yes, I agree. Praise is magical. I mean honest praise . . . such praise can make possible those given up as impossible. It gives immense strength when praise comes from people close to us. The love showered by my parents and the interest you evince in me . . . the sacrifices . . . I tell you two the truth. At one time I used to grieve over my crippled state and take my life to be meaningless, but now my life is a fulfilled one and blissful. It is as though a hundred rainbows have burst upon the horizon all at once . . . how do I repay for giving me such a blissful life?' Tears swirled in the eyes as Akshara said these words.

'You are at it again . . . first achieve whatever you set out to achieve . . . that would be as good as repayment,' Akshara's mother replied.

Wiping her tears away Akshara started having her breakfast. As a torrent of rain, thoughts surrounded Akshara . . . memories stirring, crowded agitating her. What distress and pain prevailed in matters leading to her marriage all came back to haunt her.

The instant Akshara communicated her acceptance to marry Kiran, unable to control his emotion of joy he kept repeating the words, 'thank you, thank you' shaking her by her shoulders. He could have repeated those words atleast a hundred times. In fact, she has to thank him for the boon showered on her. How strange! God granting wishes was thanking the receiver, as though that alone gave him immense joy!

'Come, let's go and break this news to my mother first,' Kiran said.

'As a deer leaping the very moment of getting on to its feet, why this great hurry? Think again with a calm mind. Will your mother accept our plans for marriage? Just in case she doesn't approve, shouldn't we be thinking of what next?'

'There is no need for that. You are saying this without knowing my mother intimately. She is a very fine person. She never disapproves of what I desire. Can you guess how overjoyed she would be hearing my decision to marry you?'

'I do not even slightly doubt your mother's goodness, but she can brook a hundred doubts to counter your idea of having a girl confined to a wheelchair for her daughter-in-law. She may have her own ideas regarding who and how her daughter-in-law should be.'

'Don't argue as you would in the court of law. I am assuring you, my mother would welcome you as her daughter-in-law. Do you recall the day you visited us the first time, how happy she was to have met you? She even appreciated your good looks and intelligence.'

'Kiran, there is a lot of difference between showering praise on an unknown girl and approving the same girl coming to know that she is going to be her daughter-in-law.'

'No more arguments please . . . you are insulting my mother!' Kiran said slightly angered.

'Sorry . . . that was not my intention. I am only cautioning you that calculations shift with changing situations. Okay . . . let us proceed as per your plan,' Akshara remained silent noticing Kiran taking her words amiss.

'Let us go then.'

She protested. 'Why me? You first announce the news to her. Once I get to know how she received the news, I will visit her another day.'

'I know what she is going to say. You just come along without another word. My mother will be very happy to see you and at the same time it would be like breaking the news of our marriage together,' Kiran pressed on. Akshara could not help accompanying him. She went along with Kiran with one sole reason that Kiran should not feel offended, although a doubt lurked somewhere inside her.

Kiran's mother received Akshara with lot of affection. 'How are you doing, Akshara? You have visited us after many days. I hear your practice has picked up, Kiran keeps telling me of you.' Hearing her words, Akshara wondered if she doubted her unnecessarily. As Kiran's mother got up to enter the kitchen to scramble up something for Akshara to eat, Kiran stopped her. 'We don't need anything now, *Amma*. First, come and sit here with us. I have to tell you something important.' He brought her a chair and made her sit.

'What is that important thing?' As Kiran's mother said those words, her eyebrows twitched, which Akshara did not fail to notice.

'Akshara is getting married, *Amma*.'

'Oh! What a good news!' Kiran's mother turned towards Akshara and asked. 'What does the boy do . . . where is he from? Is he from a known family?'

Not knowing what to say, Akshara looked to Kiran. 'The boy is from this place only, *Amma*. He is from a known family,' Kiran told his mother.

'Since you came to give me good news I must treat you with a sweet. You haven't said as yet what he does.'

'He too is a lawyer,' Kiran replied.

Akshara noticed the smile disappearing from her face.

'Why are you answering all the questions, when I am asking her? Do you happen to know the boy?'

'You also know him, *Amma*,' Kiran continued without noticing the change in his mother's expression.

'Do I know him . . . tell me the name and I will tell you if I know him.'

'He is Kiran. You know him since the time of his birth,' Kiran said with a smile.

For a little while, Kiran's mother failed to get what Kiran was trying to say. Once she did, her face paled. Even so, to clear her doubt, she asked, 'I don't get what you are trying to say.'

'Didn't you say once before . . . whichever house Akshara may set foot in, that family would be lucky? I wish that lucky family should be ours. It took six years for me to bring Akshara round to accept my proposal. Akshara is going to be your daughter-in-law.'

Kiran's mother rose suddenly and retired into her room shutting the door behind her.

Kiran looked at Akshara as though shocked. By then, Akshara had already gone stiff with fear.

Kiran rose in a swift move and followed his mother into the room.

'What is that *Amma*? Why did you come away? Are you not for this wedding?'

Akshara could overhear their conversation.

'Have you lost your head? I only thought you were merely showing pity on her. I never entertained the thought even in my dreams that you would marry her. How can you be happy marrying a girl with a severe physical disability?'

'*Amma* . . . what are those words? If Akshara were to hear you, she would be hurt.'

'Let her. Why should she feel hurt if I call a cripple a cripple? I am just telling the truth. What happened to you? Here, I am aging fast. I cannot hope to possess the same strength after a few years. When I am expecting you to bring a smart girl for my daughter-in-law who would give me some rest, why did you choose this girl? Are you off your mind? If that is so, I am not getting a girl who could help me, but one who expects her mother-in-law to serve her.'

'You don't need to do anything. I will do everything myself instead of her.'

'What will you do? Will you do the cooking? Clean the utensils and do the washing? Do you plan to stay home and serve as a woman does? Are you going to eke out your living serving her as a slave, instead of being a husband? Oh God! Why have you given me such an innocent boy for a son?' Kiran's mother burst into a wail.

'*Amma*, one marries to share one's life. Life for a wife is no longer limited to cooking, washing utensils etc. Times have changed. We both are practicing lawyers and we both are earning well. If it is for jobs that you just mentioned, I do not have to stay home to do those chores. I just have to engage servants. If it comes to serving you, I will serve.'

His mother replied tersely, 'It is okay for me, but, don't you have to serve your wife too?'

'Yes, I will, *Amma* . . . and willingly. I like Akshara. I have been in love with her for the past six years. She is an extraordinary person, reminding me of Jhansi Lakshmi Bai who fought battles with her infant boy tied to her back. She is a fighter who never retreats . . . and never gives in to pressure. She is a brave woman. I never saw her disability. She is an activist. She will undoubtedly create history as a brave woman. I intend staying by her side lending her necessary support. There won't be any change in my decision.'

'I will not agree to this as long as there is life in me. If you insist and bring her as daughter-in-law to this house, I threaten to hang myself.'

'I won't allow such sorrow to befall you. I am leaving this house for you. I will go with Akshara to her place. I am not prepared to leave Akshara for you. I am sorry.'

'Isn't your birth that of a man? How can you go against the conventional norms of the society and stay in your in-law's place? Are you not ashamed to go as a member of the household of your father-in-law?'

'I don't know all that. I stay wherever Akshara is going to be.'

'It is your fate and my misfortune . . . you are spoiling your life with your own hands. Are you going to abandon me in my old age and be the cause of my misery?'

'No *Amma* . . . you may come to us unhesitatingly anytime if ever you change your mind. That is your right. Akshara is not petty-minded to take to heart all that happened today to take it out on you. Her heart is soft as butter . . . her person is gold. You don't seem to understand her clearly.'

'Yes . . . at your age, your wife will always seem sugar candy, but she is not candy, she is an unworthy stone.'

'Please *Amma* . . . don't say another word about her. I am leaving. I will provide for your subsistence every month to meet your needs,' saying, Kiran came out.

'Don't be in haste, Kiran . . . tarry a while,' Akshara cautioned him.

'This is a decision I arrived at after many years of thinking. Come let us go. If your parents too don't approve of our marriage, we will rent out a new house,' saying so, he began to push Akshara's wheelchair and walked out.

Akshara finished having her breakfast. Recovering from her thoughts, Akshara looked at Kiran with affection and devotion. She would not have agreed if anyone told her of a person like Kiran. Now she believed because she had lived with him and had known him from close. If she came across any writing that mentioned such a person, she would have dismissed the whole thing as unnatural and wondered, 'where are such persons these days so selfless and honest? No chance.'

'Why are you looking at me that way?' Kiran asked Akshara as he wiped his hands with a napkin.

'What do you mean?'

'How do I know? You women alone know all about glances.'

'Kiran, I won't say now that there is no god. There is god.'

'My God! You have changed.'

'Yes. In my own house, there are three gods. That is why,' Akashara said wholeheartedly.

*   *   *

Prasad was bored and restless. There was little to do for him and that was more fatiguing. To stay confined

167

to bed having had nothing to do for hours on end, made life seem miserable. When he told his mother of it she said, 'I will get you a TV arranged in your room, you can then watch the channel that interests you. You just have to have the remote in hand to have plenty of entertainment.'

'No, Mummy. I don't like those soaps . . . I feel bored watching those serials that are abound in hatred and revenge. They are all repeat programs. Watching TV is to kill time in the most wasteful manner. If one were to sit sticking one's eyes to the TV screen alone, in due course mind is sure to go rusty and dull.'

'Then what do you want me to do, Prasad?'

'Buy me a computer, Mummy. Having it is like having the entire world before me. I can e-mail my friends and chat with them too. I can watch movies that interest me and download movies of my choice. Besides, I can listen to good music.'

Prasad's proposal appeared most reasonable and suitable. Saroja therefore, immediately bought a laptop with an internet connection for Prasad. From then on it became a pastime for Prasad to browse the Net.

That day Prasad's mother left for work early at nine.

Prasad watched music videos from films for some time inserting a CD in the Drive. Every song dealt with some aspect of love alone . . . a boy and a girl . . . the hero dancing with a heroine wearing skimpy clothing in a park in some distant land . . . romantic love given pre-eminence over true love . . . and some vulgar songs . . . watching them all Prasad's agony only increased. Hopelessness as python coiled round him . . . with one tired move of his hand, he removed the music CD.

Why should he not browse the Internet regarding his own disease? Would that not be informative and knowledgeable, Prasad wondered. It would be wiser too, he thought, to use the Internet that opens up a whole world of knowledge, instead of using it for listening to music or watching videos alone.

Adjusting the pillows a little high to support his head, Prasad googled for information on Muscular Dystrophy. From among few hundreds of websites, ten sites appeared on the screen. Moving the cursor to the Wikipedia site, he clicked on it gently. He saw the information he was looking for a click away in front of him on the screen. His eye began scroll down the page slowly.

'Muscular Dystrophy is a congenital disease. Due to the disease the muscles in the body weaken.'

Prasad knew all this. He went to the next page. It read, 'Muscular Dystrophy — Types'. He knew that his disease was termed Muscular Dystrophy and that it was also called M.D. but he did not know that there were many types under it. He began to read to know with which type he was afflicted with.

'Duschen Muscular Dystrophy (DMD) is the most common of all types and is also the most severe. Its symptoms normally appear in the patient's fifth year, beginning with weakening of muscles surrounding the pelvis. When a patient reaches the twelfth year, the patient may need to use a wheelchair. He may require a ventilator due to weakening of muscles of the windpipe. Chances of him dying by the twentieth year are very high.

'Another type under this is 'Becker Muscular Dystrophy'. This type is very rare. The symptoms show up very slowly. They may appear as early as in teens. The symptoms start showing weakening of muscles around the pelvis but move upward to the back and to the shoulders.

'Limb-girdle Muscular Dystrophy' affects male and female patients alike around fifteen years of age. This type too progresses in a slow process.

The type that starts to show signs in the weakening of facial muscles is termed 'Facios capulohumeral Muscular Dystrophy.' Under this type, there is difficulty in closing the eyelids. It then spreads to the shoulders and finally down to the pelvis.'

Instinctively, Prasad ran his fingers over his face: *Oh my! I am lucky . . . mine is not that type. How difficult it would be if I cannot close even my eyelids . . . nor can speak! Won't I go mad, if I cannot speak the few words I exchange with Mummy?* Prasad then wondered to what type his disease then belonged? Was it Duschen Muscular Dystrophy . . . that meant he should have been dead by now . . . who knows . . . it may mean one may die around that age . . . he was now aged twenty-four years . . . did that mean his time was approaching?

Prasad got very scared.

Prasad quickly shut down the laptop and lay back closing his eyes, '*what kind of life is mine? To die achieving nothing, experiencing no pleasure . . . what is the purpose of this life?'*

A worthless life . . . can my life be termed respectable? I am not destined to experience even the most normal and ordinary happiness and pleasure accessible to the poorest of the poor. I cannot look after myself . . . . have to depend on my mother for everything. Just as my father died before his time, if anything happened to my mother, what will happen to me? Who will take care of me then?

That very thought made Prasad's body to tremble.

Prasad tried to shut out all thoughts from his mind and tried to snatch some sleep, but could not. Sleep that did not approach during nights, would it during daytime? Where is place for peaceful sleep in a sorrow-filled life?

The mind cluttered up with thorny bushes as it were!

Prasad switched on the laptop and went to the Net once again. Reluctantly he opened the website on Muscular Dystrophy. A particular site attracted his eye as a magnet.

'A wonderful drug for Muscular Dystrophy . . . you will get back to normal life within just six months . . . if wished, you may also run. Guaranteed . . . if not your money will be returned!'

Hope as a wave sprang in Prasad's bosom . . .

How could he have missed that website all these days? Oh, had he seen that site six months back, by now he would have been walking normal. At least he would have been in a position to manage his own affairs!

All right, he was lucky to have seen that site at least that day!

Filling his whole heart with hope and all eyes, Prasad read the information given in that website. 'Wonderful results assured if tablets made of cow's urine mixed with certain herbs are taken thrice daily for six months! The disease showed signs of complete recovery in sixty among a hundred patients! The rest of the forty patients showed partial recovery! All of them are now doing their own chores. A hundred-pill bottle would cost a mere ten thousand rupees! If the desired results are not realized, refund of the entire amount assured!'

Alongside, pictures of people who used the medicine followed by interviews of recovered patients . . . all found mention. As a boxed item, there were also mentioned in detail, significance of cow's urine and *slokas* detailing its medicinal value, and information gleaned from various extant texts . . . all, all were given.

Having finished going through it all, Prasad's heart sank. He went to another site. Another patient enumerated that by taking a decoction prepared of various herbs helped in his triumph over Muscular Dystrophy. The site also gave the names of persons to consult and how much money to mail if anyone desired a cure.

Even in his sorrow, Prasad wanted to laugh.

Prasad felt sad that when thousands were suffering from the disease, there were fraudsters who wished to cash in to make a quick buck. Just as he decided to come out of the website, another site caught his eye. The title of the site attracted him immensely. It read, 'I have Muscular Dystrophy, do you?'

Prasad visited the site immediately. Close to twenty-five persons who were suffering from Muscular Dystrophy, shared their experience on that site. Their pictures with their name, age and the region to which they belonged . . . all were there. Following that information, was the experience of each of them . . . their opinion . . . tears and hardships they faced . . . the empathy displayed by others . . . encouraging words and that the membership to the site was free were all mentioned. Anyone was welcome to seek membership and share his experience with others or reading others' mail may give his opinion.

Most members in that site happened to be foreigners. Prasad came across one Telugu name. He set down to reading it immediately.

'My name is Sundaram. I am twenty-two years old. For the last fifteen years, I have been suffering from McArdle's Disease. The doctors diagnosed that among all the types under Muscular Dystrophy, the one that affected me was very rare. Remembering one of my early experiences when this disease first affected me, I decided to share it with you all.

'That was Sunday . . . we all sat for lunch at the dining table. After I finished having my food, I was about to get on to my feet to go to the sink to wash, when I suddenly discovered I could not get up. Thinking that I may have developed cramps having sat for long, I rose with the support of the wall. I even took two steps toward the sink. As I took the third step forward, I fell down with a thud.

'My mother came running to help me to my feet. She could not. I looked up to *Nanna* and *Anna* expecting one of them to come to my help, but they were laughing.

'My mother got angry, 'why are you two laughing instead of helping him? Is it a matter for teasing?

'Hearing my mother's reprimands they further laughed. I felt peeved . . . I felt ashamed . . . mother trying once again, succeeded in helping me to my feet.

'Are you hurt?' She asked. I nodded my head in the negative. By then tears were welling up in my eyes. As my mother looked at my legs, she noticed that I was bleeding. I looked down at my legs. The big toe was hurt with an injury, with the toenail yanked out completely. Watching them laugh, I did not feel the pain, I think.

'My mother got agitated. She got some cotton and *Dettol* from inside and cleaned the wound.

'She yelled at my father, 'first, will you take him to the doctor or not?' The same night, sorrow filled our house. The same night, the doctor expressed his doubt regarding my disease. Since then, there have been only new moons in my house, no full moon. After that, *Nanna* never smiled. I feel he could not excuse himself for laughing the night I fell down.

'Will he ever excuse himself? I am not angry that he laughed. I love my Dad. Now I want to see him laugh.'

Once Prasad finished reading, he felt like crying. A pall of gloom overcame him as a cloud. He remembered his fall in front of Ramya in the park. Ramya did not laugh, but that hurt was still raw festering. He felt he found a companion who underwent the same pain . . . he felt that he was not alone and felt encouraged that there were many others like him.

Others like him who read it, had recorded their response below. Prasad read them all. If someone wrote, 'you are lucky to have such a father', another wrote, 'tears came to my eyes reading your post.'

Prasad felt, he too should record his experience on that site. He joined the site as a member. From then onwards it became a routine for him to read the other members' experiences and thoughts. Besides, he too wrote what he felt.

*   *   *

It was eight in the night . . . . Kiran and Akshara were seriously discussing a court case seated in their office. They had recently converted one of the rooms in the house to conduct their official work.

'You two have worked enough for the day. Wind up your work for now and come for dinner,' Akshara's mother called out from the kitchen.

'Set the table . . . we are coming!' Akshara replied loudly for her mother to hear.

Just then, a woman appeared at the entrance to their office. '*Namaste*! You are the lawyer, Akshara, aren't you?'

'Yes I am. Please sit down,' Akshara said and gestured through one look to Kiran. Kiran went in to inform Akshara's mother that they would be late for dinner.

'My name is Anita. I have come to seek your help,' the woman said. Akshara looked at the woman intently. She could not have been more than twenty, but looked as though she entered her forties. A certain sadness settled on her face . . . dark circles around her eyes indicating that she had not slept for many nights . . . her manner of dress did not fail to reveal that she belonged to a lower middle class family.

'Tell me what your problem is,' Akshara asked Anita.

'*Amma*, I was married off soon after I finished my tenth class exams. My people felt I had enough education and did not heed to my wish of studying further. My husband works as a peon in a government school. He is also a blood relative. He took two lakh as dowry at the time of marriage. He looked after me well *Amma* for some time, but lately he has begun to beat me on some pretext or the other as though I were an animal. These days he is causing me a lot of trouble.'

'Is he demanding additional money towards dowry?'

'No *Amma*, he says he wants to leave me. He is asking for a divorce.'

'But why? Has he given any reason?'

'Yes *Amma*. I haven't borne him a child in spite of being married for three years. That is it . . . he wants to have children, so wishes to remarry. What can I do *Amma* if I cannot bear a child for him? Is it in my hands?' Anita began to weep.

'The problem could be with him.'

'No *Amma* . . . we underwent all tests required. The doctors said it is difficult for me to conceive. There is something wrong with my uterus.'

'You can take some treatment for it, can't you?'

'They said it cannot be rectified either with medicine or surgery.'

'Okay, what do you plan to do then?'

'I want him *Amma*, he is my life. I cannot bear to live without him. At the same time, I cannot see him taking another woman as wife. Call him and tell him whatever you think is right and proper. Do the needful. If he refuses to abide by your words, threaten to take him to the court, but tell him that I am not prepared to divorce him.'

'Even if he had a fraction of love that you have for him, he would not be asking for divorce, nor would he be eager for another marriage. Why do you still go after such a man?'

'No *Amma*, don't say that. He does like me very much. He can't stay without me even for a minute *Amma*.'

'If so, why is he asking for a divorce?'

'He thinks that if he threatened to divorce me, I would agree to his wish of marrying another woman. He loves to have children. It is proper for a man to want a child of his own, isn't it?'

Akshara did not get exactly what Anita was driving at. On one hand, she was refusing to give divorce and threatening to take him to court if he remarried. On another, she considered it natural for him to want a child of his own.

'Okay, leave behind his name, the name of the school where he is working and his address,' saying so Akshara looked in the direction of Kiran. Kiran took down the details Anita gave.

'I will send for your husband tomorrow, and talk to him, but how do I communicate to you? When do you plan to visit me again?'

'I will *Amma* whenever you want me to. It is enough if you call me on my phone, I will see you immediately.'

'Do you own a cell phone?'

'Yes, *Amma*. He bought me one,' Anita said shyly. Kiran took down also her number.

Long after Anita left, her words kept echoing through the room. The words echoed in Akshara's heart too, 'it is proper for a man to want a child of his own, isn't it?' Then, is Kiran too entertaining such a wish within him too? Why not . . . is he not a man? Is he suppressing that desire of his for her sake?

Before their marriage, Akshara had expressed a wish to Kiran, 'Once we are married, let us not go in for children, Kiran. Think well before giving me your decision.' She agreed for their marriage only after he gave his consent.

Akshara wondered, 'is Kiran coming under stress for not having children . . . is he concealing his sorrow . . . is he regretting for not listening to his mother's words of caution . . . .'

The cankerworm of doubt vexed Akshara to no end leaving her restless. Unknown fears swarmed her mind . . . her heart came under a blaze of that anxiety. . . .

Akshara did not relish the food before her.

When Kiran inquired, she merely dismissed his query that she was not hungry.

Kiran had the habit of reading a book or a magazine before going to bed.

Akshara tried snatching some sleep, but of no avail.

Akshara turned her head to look at Kiran. She saw him immersed in the book he was reading.

Observing that Akshara was staring at him, Kiran put the book aside and queried, 'what is the matter Akshara? Aren't you feeling sleepy? Shall I hand you a magazine? Have you read the article that lauded you in glowing terms in the latest issue of *Bhoomika*?'

'Yes. I read that,' Akshara replied. Kiran was alarmed noticing at once the turmoil that was obvious on her face.

'Why do you say that in so feeble a tone . . . how well they praised you as a gem and a beacon to womankind?'

'Kiran! I don't want their praise . . . I want the truth.'

'Is that not true . . . I don't see any exaggeration in that article on you.'

'It is not that . . . I am referring to issues related to us two.'

'Our issues . . . I don't get you.'

'Okay . . . I will come to the point without beating around the bush . . . Kiran, tell me the truth. Don't you feel like having children?'

Caught off-guard, Kiran looked at Akshara not knowing what to make of it.

'Suddenly, why this query?'

'You have heard what Anita said, haven't you? Didn't she say that it is natural for every man to desire for children, and that for it a man wouldn't hesitate to even go in for another marriage . . .'

Kiran laughed until his sides split.

'This is no laughing matter. It is a serious matter.'

'Akshara . . . you are a successful lawyer. Don't you know that there is an exception to every rule . . . I am one such exception.'

'Do you mean . . .'

'Akshara, I remember the condition you laid for our marriage regarding children. I agreed for our marriage after much deliberation over the matter. My mind is not so weak as to change within a few years. I am still the same Kiran . . . it is you who is needlessly troubling your mind with unnecessary apprehensions and fears.'

'Tell me the truth, Kiran. I will not take you amiss or get perturbed . . . didn't you ever get a thought of having a girl or a boy?'

'I just wanted you, Akshara . . . and to gain you I was prepared to give up on anyone . . . including children.'

'Doesn't that thought bother you even once? Don't you feel sad for the lack of children?'

'You are cross-examining me as though I am a witness in the court, but my answer is the same, it will not change. Till you reminded me a little while ago, that thought did not occur to me.'

'Even if you don't have children . . .'

Kiran interrupted Akshara. 'Don't keep harping on that subject. Who says I don't have children?'

'What? Do you have children?' Akshara asked, her eyes widening in wonder.

'Yes . . . here . . . this is my daughter,' saying, Kiran pulled her close to him. 'Why do we need children, Akshara . . . we are children to each other.'

Akshara, delighted, shed tears of joy.

How sweet it was to hear those words . . . as though pouring ambrosia into her ears . . . something sweet coursed through her blood vessels as it were . . . she understood from where she received the courage to defy even death. Could there be any better cure for a disease than others' love and concern? No disease could dare approach where there is true love, not even death. Death has to take to its heels in fear showing its back.

That moment, a truth dawned on Akshara . . .

True love is a veritable *Sanjeevani* . . . a medicinal herb that could bring back to life a person from his deathbed.

*   *   *

That morning Prasad woke up crusty and feeling low . . . cross at being a dependent on others . . . upset to be stuck to bed forever . . . tetchy over life such as his . . . shaken for having had a nightmarish dream the previous night. It was still haunting and troubling . . . taking form before his eyes closed or open even now . . . he had woken up in the dream and looked at his mother still asleep on the bed next to his. She had never slept so long. He had called out, '*Amma*'. No answer came. He called louder, this time. He saw no movement in her . . . the truth that she was no more, struck him as a thunderbolt. He burst into a long wail repeating the word, '*Amma* . . . *Amma.*' He screamed out aloud. No one heard him . . . no one came. One . . . two . . . three days had passed . . . the decomposing corpse lay beside his bed . . . the stench spread all over hanging heavy in the air . . . his tears shed, streamed the room. . . . He, soaking as a worm in his own urine and feaces . . . rank with the stink and rotting . . . the corpse of his mother next to him . . . very close to his bed, he who was soon going to turn a corpse himself . . . each atom in his body sorrow-worn longing for death to reduce him quick to a corpse . . .

Prasad woke up with a start. The familiar sounds from the kitchen indicated that his mother had woken up long before him. Those sounds assured him that his mother was active and alive . . . the freedom from fear those sounds offered . . . that the horrific experience had only been part of a dream . . . at the same time he was petrified to recall the nightmare. What if it were to happen in life . . . oh God . . . before such a thing happened, he should leave this world long before his mother.

Prasad's mother left for work. Despair re-entered to fill the room full . . . melancholy pervaded his mind as his desire for death gained strength.

Prasad opened the Internet. He tried giving expression to the forlorn hope in words. He rounded it off saying, 'death seems to offer a better prospect than this wretched life.'

Soon, Prasad received a bulk mail in response reacting to his words. While some said, 'man should put up a brave front in times of crisis. He should fight until the end. You are a coward' . . . some others wrote disparaging: 'aren't you aware how your mail would demoralize other patients? How is it fair to cause them more despair through your words?'

From among all the mail Prasad received, one particular mail that came from a twenty-year old girl by name Ragini from Nakrekal attracted his attention and pleased him immensely. There were two reasons for it to have pleased him . . . while the rest of the other mail he received came from patients suffering from Muscular Dystrophy, from outside the country and outside his state, Ragini's was the only mail that came from within the state of Andhra Pradesh. . . . Secondly, Prasad saw in it a soothing temper that hitherto he had not seen in mail received from any source.

How many times did Prasad not go over the mail! He even saved it on his desktop. He began going over it again.

'Hi, Prasad! I am Ragini. Is it not a pleasant name . . . how much I love my name! Do you know how much I thank my parents each day for giving me such a sweet-sounding name?

'Do you recall how many times you watched the rising sun . . . I watch it every day. What charm and grace the sky wears as a beautiful woman in a colourful sari draped round her! The sun as a crimson dot on the forehead of the horizon in the east . . . it appears anew as many times as I watch it. You unfortunate souls, city-dwellers, where is the good fortune for you to see the beauteous sight of the setting sun in the urban sprawl? I have not told you yet the name of my village, have I? It is Nakrekal.

'The last house in the village is ours. There is a yard outspread in front of our house . . . you just have to plunk yourself down in the yard, to watch the wonderful rising of the sun . . . so also trees in our yard, how many there are! My mother loves to grow trees . . . so too I. . . . Butterflies of variegated colours come visiting us as guests . . . the melodic chirping of birds when heard as auspicious instruments waking you in the morning from sleep, oh, it is a great experience . . .

'I studied up to my tenth standard in the local Zilla Parishad High School. Thereafter I completed my undergraduate course studying privately from home. School life was wonderful, is it not . . . how many sweet memories!

'I wish to enjoy life to the full. I wish to fill each minute in each hour of each day with delight . . . to pack in a bundle of endless joys . . . do you know one thing . . . there are so many joys lying in heaps before our eyes, if only we gather them up in handfuls . . . everyone thinks joys are for the moneyed alone. How wrong they are . . . nature has preserved for us several small pleasures aplenty . . . if many fail to notice these, it is their ill luck.

'If we cannot fill out all our moments with laughter, I feel life is a waste . . . if life is a gift from God it is in your hands to see that gift coming to fruition. . . .

'Shall I tell you a joke . . . ?

'Why does a girl suffering from Muscular Dystrophy take only light beer? Don't you know? Shall I tell you . . . because she cannot carry heavy beer. Do you feel like laughing . . . have you laughed or not . . . laugh heartily, you won't lose anything!

'I forgot to share with you an important thing . . . guess who told me that I look as beautiful as my name . . . who else? My mirror . . . The mirror never lies . . . true.

'Having read your mail, I felt I should make friends with you, so this mail. If anyone asks me how far I studied, I say unhesitatingly without batting my eyelid that I studied up to M.D. Do you know how great I feel saying that? When that person reacts to it saying, M.D? At such

an young age? Great. I laugh about . . . innocent lives . . .
they take M.D. to be Doctor of Medicine. Aren't we both
M.D.s? Aren't you feeling glad that we two are M.D.s
without having to study M.B.B.S.? Are you laughing at
least now? You are thinking that it is a cruel joke, aren't
you?

'Life is itself a cruel joke . . . if we run away from it
in fear it will chase us around like a bloodhound. If we
look straight in its face and laugh sneering in defiance . . .
defeated, it will fall at your feet . . . then tears, torment
and trouble all vanish taking to their heels with their tails
between their legs. You are taking view of one side of the
coin alone, look on the other side. An entire new world will
present itself to you.

'Walking through a dark tunnel . . . pausing . . . in
self-deceit, you are taking the path and its darkness to be
endless. Try walking a little more distance. Walk with
a belief that there is going to be light at the end of the
tunnel . . . walk with a heart full of hope . . . an unending
light is awaiting you at the tunnel's end.

'You may be thinking saying is easier . . . but I am
saying as one who saw that light. Let me know if you find
the going tough . . . I can lead you by hand toward that
light . . .

Looking forward to your friendship

Ragini'

Prasad sent his reply immediately . . .

'How relaxing it was to have read your mail . . . as an oasis
to a thirsty traveler tired walking through a desert . . . to a

184

parched tongue thirsting for ambrosia . . . I am in doubt reading your mail. Are you really a victim of Muscular Dystrophy? Sorry . . . I am expressing my doubt because your mail did not seem to have come from a person suffering from M.D. but from a healthy spirited girl. Whatever, please continue to send mail . . . your words are as supply of oxygen to a person gasping for breath . . . I now crave for life . . . at least to read the wonderful mail from you. . . .'

The next day Ragini sent reply to Prasad's mail. *'Hi! You are also going poetic . . . you have employed good similes. Do you know something . . . oh, how will you, unless I tell you? I too write poetry . . . I have been writing for the past four years and they appeared off and on in a few magazines too. Some magazines paid me some remuneration. I am excited the day I receive that, walking on clouds as it were . . . after all my earning, is it not . . . even a meager amount seems a fortune. Who said I am not a live wire? I am very mischievous . . . my people at home say that it is difficult to put up with my mischief . . . I was worse as a child . . . they wondered if I was a child or a thunderbolt!*

'You wonder if I have M.D., is it not . . . yes, beyond a shadow of doubt I don't have M.D. That is because I pay no attention to it. As though I were not afflicted with the disease, I enjoy life. . . . As a person knowing he would die the next day yearns to slurp up all delights offered him on that day, I too heartily take life as it comes and all the joys it brings along, as though I were to die the next day. Do you still doubt me? Then come to check for yourself . . . when do you plan to come? It is very easy to find my address . . . my house is the last on the east of the stadium

in Isaykunta . . . with the mention of my name anyone will lead you to my house . . . I am that popular in these parts! As I mention this, you can see me lifting my collar high. . . . Shall I relate another joke to you?

'Why does a girl suffering from M.D. go to a restaurant where sea-food is available? Guess . . . think hard . . .

'You do not know, do you? I know you cannot be more intelligent than I am . . . here is my answer, take it!

'She went there thinking that mussels were available in that restaurant. That girl took mussels to be muscles . . . foolish girl. Just spelling difference . . . mussels mean a certain edible sea animal that lives inside a shell . . . like prawns . . . believed to be very tasty to eat. Restaurants in America serve them as a delicacy . . . do you get the pun at least now?

'It hasn't provoked you to laughter, has it? If you have to understand the joke, you should know enough English, my friend! I have it in plenty, but please don't ask me to loan it to you . . . I cannot.

'Doctors diagnosed that I was suffering from Muscular Dystrophy. I was then four. They even informed my parents that I would not live beyond my ninth year. I am now twenty, that means I have outlived by eleven years escaping death sentence pronounced by the doctors. Don't be afraid. Death will not dare come anywhere near me. I believe, I will live many more years to come, I have many wishes to fulfill . . . have to get married, bear children, rear them . . . oh my . . . so many more tasks . . . do you take me to be overambitious?

'Have you read Sri Vidya Prakasanandagiri Swami's Gitasaram?

'He says: whatever is ordained by fate will certainly happen. Do not come under stress going over it for too

long. Anxiety is the root cause of ill health. Try getting over anxiety without letting up on your attempts. Accept the result of your actions as a gift of God. Do not rue over for not possessing riches. Be happy you have enough for your subsistence. Do not sorrow over the thorn that pricked your foot . . . be happy that it didnot pierce your eye. . . .

'This is my philosophy of life. I do not regret over what I do not have. I take great satisfaction over what I have. I am excited that I have eyes to behold the nature's beautys around me to go into raptures . . . derive pleasure for having ears to listen to melodious music . . . thrilled that my tongue can relish a variety of tastes . . . thankful I have a father blessed with enough money to keep me away from hunger. I take delight in feeling the evening breeze blowing against my body . . . for having a heart that can dwell for long on these beauteous forms and for possessing a mind that is wonderfully active . . . I revel in all these. Why should I grieve when so much beauty is mine to own to feast on?

'Have you caught on to what I just said? You too start to think in peace. Then you will agree with me that what I say is right. When there is Ragini by your side offering hand of friendship, why bother . . . my dear silly Prasad? (I did not say foolish Prasad, lest you get hurt. I suppose, you will understand)

That is it . . .

Ragini'

The mail from Ragini started to work as tonic on Prasad. He was no longer bored of the time on hand in the absence of his mother and of late, his face too gained a strange glow. . . . Once his mother left for work, he spent his time chatting with Ragini . . . or read mail from her . . . sent replies . . . and on the return of his mother from work, shared with her the day's activities . . . all these helped him to overcome his physical pain.

* * *

It was close to a year since Ragini came to be a friend of Prasad. These twelve months saw many sweet moments. Prasad longed to meet Ragini . . . very strongly.

Prasad once wrote to her. 'Can I come to see you . . . my mother and I plan to visit you. Do you have any objection? Will your family members agree to our visit? We will start once you let us know of their opinion.'

Ragini replied promptly. *'Hi! I was thrilled to read what you wrote . . . coming to see your future bride, as it were . . . I felt terribly shy going over the mail. Come to think of it, why didn't the thought occur to us all these days . . . you are a M.D. and I too am . . . made for each other . . . how will it be if we both decide to marry . . . think of it. Colourful rainbows start to dance in front of our eyes. I do not know how you appear, but in my imagination you are a handsome man (you will not disappoint me, will you?) I for one told you earlier that I am good-looking, didn't I? I am mailing you my picture. I am confident you will like my picture unless you lack vision . . . I am sorry, you must be having large eyes.*

'Oh, the very idea of marriage makes me go into raptures treading on air as it were. Why don't our elders realize we both have come of age to marry . . . Prasad, these elders are such. I forgot . . . there is a character in some Telugu film

nicknamed Bachelor Prasad . . . from now on I will address you by that name, Bachelor Prasad. If you wish to get away from that nickname, you come soon to marry me. If my parents do not agree to our marriage, no problem . . . I am ready to elope with you . . . are you also ready?'

As Prasad read the mail, both joy and sorrow overwhelmed him at once. How well Ragini wrote the mail full of humour . . . in playful banter . . . how does an individual manage to be so cheerful? She not only remains happy but drowns the other person also in happiness . . . what an exquisite quality for one to emulate? Determination grew in Prasad that he should somehow make it to Nakrekal to see Ragini.

Nonetheless, fear engulfed Prasad from all sides . . . a fear that his beautiful dream might melt away . . . a doubt that on reaching Nakrekal, he might fail to find any girl by name Ragini. . . . Even if there was one, she might not be from Nakrekal . . . didn't he read in newspapers that many who come on to chat on social network sites sport fake profiles? Yet another, could Ragini be a boy claiming to be a girl . . . even if there was a girl by name Ragini, could she be suffering from a disease at all . . . could she be merely pretending to give him courage . . . how many doubts . . . how many apprehensions? It did not matter, even if Ragini proved to be unreal. She was a charming illusion . . . Prasad desired to exist in that illusion but not attempt to erase it.

Thinking hard over his doubts and apprehensions, Prasad decided not to visit Nakrekal. Prasad received three mails after that from Ragini to find out when he was visiting Nakrekal.

Ragini wrote in one mail. *'Are you coming . . . when . . . didn't you like me in the picture? I look better when seen in real life than in the picture. True . . . I swear in your name!*

'When shall we marry? I hear there are auspicious dates falling next month for marriages. I heard my parents discussing. Couples getting married during those days are supposed to live happily ever after. If so, our M.D. will then fail to have any impact on our lives and death will not dare approach us, is it not? Oh . . . doesn't it sound exciting? Where doctors fail, auspicious dates succeed, it looks. Will you get a suit stitched for the wedding? A black one will look nice, a blue one will also do for me. Which sari shall I choose? I will take a colour of your choice, but I find a silk sari heavy to wear, I don't like it. I will leave the selection to my sister. She has a fine taste. She is an expert at the selection, do you know . . . no sooner money falls in her hands than she will spend it in no time going to the market.

'She is worth gold, lest you take her to be frivolous . . . . I have a tremendous love for her. She is in the final year of her Intermediate. Until it is time for her to leave for the college and since the time she returned, she attends to all my work. Anything I ask she does with a smile and never complains. More, she gets what all I need from the market.

'I have already told her everything about you. She even teased me if ours is an e-mail love. She is keen on seeing her future brother-in-law, but you have not mailed me your picture. She expressed her apprehension: he may not be as handsome as you imagined. So to disprove her, send your picture immediately in your next mail. She insists that her approval is required if we are to get married. I don't get this equation, I should like you, not my sister, isn't it . . .

but I have taken a liking for you even without seeing your picture. Your looks don't matter to me . . . are you dark . . . snub-nosed . . . are your two front teeth missing . . . bald-headed . . . small-eyed . . . will you trouble me in my dreams if seen during the day . . . didn't I assure you it is okay with me whatever your looks are . . . send me your picture at once . . . .'

Prasad mailed his picture.

'Oh, how handsome you are. You are just as I imagined. Your eyes are beautiful . . . as a girl's, wide-eyed . . . filled with ardour . . . as for my sister she took an instant liking for you. Now, you only have to come deciding on the wedding dates. Your Ragini will stand waiting with garland in hand. Sorry . . . sorry, I cannot stand, can I? I will remain seated with garland in hand . . . okay . . . . The delay is yours.'

Prasad sent mail immediately, but no reply came despite waiting for two days. It agitated him . . . Ragini was never so late . . . on a day, she mailed at least once, and if she was in a pleasant mood, she wrote even three four times.

Ragini always remained in a good mood. *'What happened to you? Why are you not responding? Aren't you keeping well . . . are you running temperature . . . did you consult a doctor . . . send reply soon,'* Prasad wrote.

Even for the above mail, he did not hear from her. Prasad sent several letters in quick succession. Even so, he did not hear from her. A certain fear started to take control of him. What could have happened to Ragini? Ragini . . . his close friend and confident . . . one who entered his life with a soft touch as a gentle fragrant breeze . . . a melodious song . . . Four days . . . five days passed . . . but no mail arrived.

Anxiety grew in Prasad . . . grief extended as vast as the sky . . . and unusually once or twice, he even displayed his irksomeness in the presence of his mother, but regretted seeing tears welling up in her eyes. 'I am sorry Mummy . . . I am not feeling up to doing anything.'

'It is alright, my son . . . I can understand you . . . or else how can I be your mother?'

After a weeklong wait, finally, Ragini sent mail . . . the long awaited mail. Prasad's life springs revived refreshing. Had she not sent mail, he planned to go to Nakrekal the week next. Eagerly, for now, he went over her mail.

'You were worried, were you not . . . and could have expected that I took ill . . . never . . . didn't I tell you all illnesses seeing me in fear, will have to take to their heel . . . I am a demon . . .

'On opening my mail box, letters from you in heaps came down tumbling to fall at my feet. You like me a lot, don't you . . . I know it . . . I too like you.

'Sorry, I did not give reason for the delay. My laptop came in for repair. Virus . . . I don't get to understand what this virus means, as virus attacking men. I came to understand that computers too come under the threat of viruses only after mine crashed.

'Ours is a small village, and the laptop did not come back from repair. It was said my computer did not just go mute . . . it crashed. The Mother Board went quite out of gear, and we had to send it to Hyderabad, or else I had to go in for a new laptop.

'I insisted on having only my old laptop, whatever the cost may be. The shop owner said laptop had gone very old, and it was hard to get its spare hardware parts. My father asked me to go in for a new one that would work well. How does he know that all your mails are stored in the old laptop? Won't the mail be available in any laptop, you may wonder. That is what sets apart women from men. You don't understand sensitive feelings of women. I am sentimental about that laptop since I first came to know you through that laptop. I insisted hence on having it repaired.

It took so long to send the Mother Board to Hyderabad and get it back repaired. Have I been cause for much anxiety? I understand your concern. Sorry for that. What can I do . . . I cannot go out to send you mail. Even so, my sister offered to write on my behalf, but I refused for fear that she will come to see the mail exchanged between us. She is still a young girl. It is a week since I chatted with you and there is much to share with you, but all that in my next mail.'

Prasad sent reply immediately.

*   *   *

As something stirred inside the womb, Sunita gave a pause to the work on hand and concentrated on her bulging tummy holding her breath to feel the sensation. No such sensation repeated. Is it a mere imagination? Even so, why is she so crazy about children? Can there be women who do not crave for children, that too when they conceive the first time? As for her, she is fond of them. Kishore won't agree, but she wouldn't mind having a dozen of them. A whole lot of them . . . prancing about the house . . . chattering away sweetly . . . and causing adorable trouble . . . oh, that sweet clamour.

That very thought brought a smile to dance about on Sunita's lips. Remembering the country's population problem, she reconciled to limiting to two children, 'I was merely joking. Two adorable children are enough, a girl like you and a boy like me will do . . . okay, Kishore!' She said to herself.

Since her marriage to Kishore . . . whenever he was not next to her, Sunita got into the habit of holding imaginary dialogue with him. A feeling as though he was in her presence . . . as conversing with her . . .

'Is this, this talking to myself, any kind of madness . . . you are a doctor, aren't you . . . tell me the truth,' One day Sunita confronted Kishore with the question.

He only burst out laughing. How nice he looked! 'Why play it so soft . . . it is madness of mammoth proportion,' he replied.

'Hey, tell me the truth without resorting to leg-pulling. Am I resorting to this little imaginary dialogue with you, just to divert my mind from the loneliness once you leave for the hospital?'

'I am just as you are . . . at times when I am left alone in my hospital room, I too indulge in small self talk with you, when you appear in front of my eyes . . . I as a Schizophrenic patient . . . chattering . . . teasing . . . this is love sickness, a thickening syruppy sugar.'

As Kishore said those words, Sunita joyfully fell in an embrace of Kishore. 'To escape from it, I will have a baby fast . . . he will give me company when you are not around,' Sunita said.

'Do you want to have a baby fast . . . no, you have to wait for nine months, otherwise you will have a premature baby. Then the baby has to be kept in an incubator,' Kishore said teasingly.

Sunita was very angry at those words . . . also had tears.

'I never believed when my friends said doctors lack sense of humour. What are those words . . . ominous!'

Once again, Sunita felt as though something moved within her . . . running its tiny hands along the walls of the womb. . . . She went into rapture as though an electric wave ran through her body . . . she was now five months pregnant . . . the baby was declaring its presence . . . it was sending signals: *just another four months . . . that is all . . . then I am going to be in your hands all swaddled!*

Sunita decided to ask Kishore on his return. She was eager to know how a twenty-week fetus would appear . . . do hands and legs take shape . . . the rest of the organs . . . is it possible to know the gender . . . if she talked this way, Kishore would make fun of her.

'It is my mistake being a doctor myself to have married a commerce graduate . . . it is my fate . . . you don't possess even basic knowledge.' She would not take those words lying down . . . she was well versed in giving repartees. 'Oh, how wrong I was to have married a doctor? How is it I have got a learned man who talks of human anatomy even in time of romance!' One had to see Kishore's face then . . . face turned crimson . . . anger showing in his eyes, he would chase her around with raised hand, 'Hey . . . you . . .'

Sunita was startled to hear the doorbell ring. Lately, she woke with a start by even a slightest sound.

Would have to ask Kishore the reason . . . perhaps he would want to check her blood pressure . . . there were advantages in marrying a doctor. When taken ill, there was no need to go looking for a doctor. Similarly, hearing often of medicines and diseases, there would be gain of some medical knowledge.

Having had dinner, and having cleared the table, she came and sat next to Kishore. 'I am now five months pregnant. I am eager to see how developed our baby is.'

A mischievous glint showed in the eyes of Kishore. 'You are wondering if you can have the baby in nine days instead of nine months, aren't you?'

'Wow . . . how well you read my mind . . . you would come up better as a psychologist instead of a general physician.'

'Even now no regrets. Am I not excelling in my profession due to your companionship? Come, I will show you pictures of the fetus on the Internet,' saying, he opened the laptop. 'At twenty weeks, the fetus develops to a length of eight to ten inches. The head . . . hands and legs take form. Look at the picture on the screen, when scanned the baby will appear like this.'

Sunita watched the picture keenly with eyes wide open. 'If I undergo scanning now, will our baby too appear the same?' Sunita said as a child excitedly.

'Sure' Kishore said.

'Then I too will go in for scanning . . . please . . . please . . . on request the hospital will give us the copy of the picture, wouldn't they? I am going to get it framed and gift it to our son when he grows up, so that I can tell him how he looked at five months inside the womb.'

Without reacting, Kishore remained silent.

'Why aren't you saying anything? Let us go tomorrow . . . is that alright?' Sunita asked running her hand along his hair affectionately.

'I am also thinking of it, if it is better to have an Anomaly test done. It is a scanning that every twenty-week pregnant woman has to undergo.'

'Look . . . although I am just a commerce graduate, how I reminded you of it in time? First, educate me regarding Anomaly test,' Sunita said.

'In an Anomaly test, one can know if all the limbs and organs of a baby have grown in form . . . or if any abnormalities have taken place.'

Sunita was frightened hearing those words . . . as though acid poured to sour a pleasurable moment. 'What words are they Kishore . . . why will our baby have any abnormalities?'

'I didn't mean to say so. What can go wrong with our baby . . . he will be a bonny baby worth a mountain of gold . . . we are the manufacturers, aren't we . . . no chance of defects . . . I have only informed you as to what an Anomaly test is.'

Sunita's mind calmed a little. 'If it is only for that, I don't wish to have any scanning done.'

'Weren't you curious to know how a twenty-week old fetus looked? Let us get the scanning done only for that.'

'Tomorrow is *Ashtami* . . . day after is *Navami* . . . no . . . let us have it done on *Dasami* day.'

Kishore laughed aloud. 'I am a doctor . . . If I wait for auspicious days the patient will kick the bucket by then.'

'I do not know about you. It is my sentiment . . . that is all . . . no arguments.'

As decided, on the *Dasami* day, Kishore took Sunita to the hospital where he worked. As he introduced her to the duty doctor, he said, 'meet my colleague Dr. Siddhartha, famous general physician' and turning to Sunita he introduced, 'she is my wife . . . Sunita.' Sunita greeted him with folded hands. Although she had been coming to that hospital for regular check up, she had never met him. He too greeted reciprocating. 'You are doing a good thing doctor . . . our people do not know enough about Anomaly test and the government too ignores it. We can avoid birth disorders and deformities up to fifty percent, if every pregnant woman gets herself scanned,' saying he turned towards Sunita. 'Look how many advantages are there in marrying a doctor, sister. You are lucky . . . Dr. Kishore is an ideal husband.' As he left, he wished Kishore shaking his hand, 'all the best.'

Although Sunita felt a little unnerved while entering the scanning room, she composed herself that it was a familiar hospital and need no fear. Before the scanning, they were made to sign on some documents by way of an undertaking that they would not attempt to know the gender of the baby . . . and that they would not raise the matter with the sonographer regarding the gender of the child.

'Do you know that any attempt to know the gender is a punishable offence and since 2002 the punishment has come to be applied more stringently?' Kishore said.

'I know . . . one need not study medicine to know such things,' Sunita said a little in anger to which Kishore laughed teasingly. What a beautiful smile . . .

isn't it seeing that smile that she fell for that magic when he came to see her the first time!

'Isn't it horrible to have an abortion done knowing that it is going to be a baby girl? In my opinion, abortion in itself is horrible . . . who has given the right to take someone's right to life?' Sunita spoke in an emotion that left her choking with tears.

Kishore remained silent. Although he wanted to tell her the various circumstances that made an abortion inevitable, seeing the sonographer calling them in, placing his hand round Sunita's shoulder he led her in.

'Relax Mrs. Kishore . . . just fifteen minutes . . . that is all,' the sonographer said. A little while later, 'there . . . you can see your baby on the screen . . . there is the head . . . here are the hands . . . here the legs.' As she showed the baby on the screen, Sunita watched in bated breath overtaken by joy and surprise.

'You can also see the internal organs . . . see . . . what you see here in white are the bones . . . the area in black is the fluid . . . the grey areas there are the soft tissues . . . what you see here is the heart.' The sonographer, who till then had been showing everything enthusiastically, suddenly stopped . . . her eyebrows knotted.

Sunita looked at Kishore in alarm. His eyes focused on the screen. Turning now to the sonographer she asked in trepidation, 'what happened? Any problem?'

'Nothing . . . relax . . . we have to look closely for some details . . . that is all.' Throwing a glance at Sunita the sonographer once again immersed herself seriously in her work.

Once scanning was over, Kishore walked Sunita out and went back in. As time stretched and his arrival delayed, Sunita's anxiety grew. Finally, when he did come out, she saw an unfamiliar gloom on his face.

Sunita understood that instant that something unforeseen was in the offing. However much she pressed the matter Kishore did not come out with the details. She had nightmares the whole night . . . blabbering in sleep . . . the next day Kishore made her undergo Amniocentesis test. As he saw the report, Kishore was heart-broken. As though someone erased all the dreams related to his child . . . disregarding the curious queries of Sunita, he brought her home.

Sunita who till then observed control and patience, let out the steam and broke down. 'Tell me the truth . . . what is happening . . . what did you see in the scan report? What did the Amniocentesis test reveal? Please tell everything without concealing anything from me,' Sunita said shaking Kishore by his shoulders.

'You can't bear to hear it, Sunita,' Kishore said in a tearful tone . . . noticing his eyes moisten, Sunita became more worried. 'I can, tell me. I am his mother. Is it not occurring to you that I need to know everything about him? What happened to our baby?'

'Toughen yourself . . . our baby has a genetic disorder.'

'What does that mean? Is it a minor problem . . . what is it?"

'It is called Edward Syndrome.'

'Not in your medical parlance . . . put it in my language,' Sunita screamed impatiently.

'If it has to be put in simple terms, where single chromosome has to double itself, it divides itself into three. To take it further, you know there are twenty-three pairs of chromosomes in man. Of them twenty-two are ordinary, and the twenty-third carrying XX or XY chromosome pair determines the sex of the child. In Edward Syndrome, the eighteenth pair of chromosome has an additional chromosome, so much so where there have to be two there are three chromosomes.'

Sunita intervened, 'I didn't ask you to teach me a lesson. I wanted to know, due to that, what will happen to our child? What complications may arise? Is the problem major or minor?' Her eyes by then turned tear springs.

Kishore was lost for words. After a few silent moments, he continued, 'This is not a minor problem. It is a serious problem. It occurs very rarely, may be one in three thousand. In many cases, chances of the baby dying in the womb are very high. Even among those born, most babies die within the first one month after birth. No matter what, even in the rarest cases, there is no record of anyone living beyond the first one year'

Sunita stayed sorrow-stricken for a long time. After a while, she asked, 'can't the doctors do something? Is there no medicine at all for this?'

'There is no medicine available for this, Sunita. Apart from various deformities, our baby will also be afflicted with various diseases. Except for giving compassionate care going by the existing complications, the doctors too cannot do anything further.'

'Then what is to become of our baby? Why did God punish us this way? What sin have I committed . . . Oh God . . . how many dreams I dreamt about our first issue! How excited I was . . . why did my life take this turn?'

Kishore did not know how to pacify Sunita who was disconsolate.

'There is only one way out for this problem, Sunita . . . it has to be abortion . . . let us not take a risk. Although there are chances of a miscarriage before completion of a full term, there are also chances of you delivering the baby. That is why . . . I will talk to the gynecologist tomorrow itself. Since you crossed twenty weeks of pregnancy, the law will not permit you to go in for an abortion. Since I know the hospital, I will take care to see that it is carried out covertly.'

Sunita did not become herself until another week. Overcome with grief, she starved herself going without food and water.

'Sunita, why don't you understand? If you keep delaying, complications might arise,' Kishore tried convincing her.

'I don't want to abort the child. Let whatever happens as per my baby's fate. I will deliver the baby and I will bring him up, I shall look after him as my life with love and care, but will not kill him even before he is born. I will not agree to that.'

'It is a punishment and pain to live each minute looking after a baby born with Edward Syndrome. I pray God that no one, not even an enemy should face such a punishment. Listen to me. You are talking not knowing what is Edward Syndrome. I can understand you and your words as a woman, but as a mother, you will not be able to bear the pain of seeing our child suffer. Complications may visit our child in innumerable ways . . . his heart and kidneys may not function properly . . . his growth may retard . . . his body from below the waist may not work . . . he may develop problems of sight and hearing. . . .'

'I can't hear. Please stop!' Sunita screamed plugging her ears.

'I will call the doctor to arrange for the abortion tomorrow,' Kishore said pressing a number on his cell.

'Do you think I will agree if you scare me? No. I am going to deliver the child. Not only that I shall bring him up lovingly as any other child.'

'Are you mad? He will not live long even if you give birth.'

'Do you want to kill him therefore before he is born? Who gave us the right to kill? Even if we had not gone in for scanning we would not have come to know of this, is it not? Wouldn't I have then given birth to him?'

'Sunita . . . don't talk like an educated brute. Do not forego the advantage of an advanced knowledge offering a better life. Do not stand on sentiment . . . think practically. Can you remain happy seeing our son suffering due to ill health?'

'Do you think I will remain happy if you kill him showing his ill health as a reason? Can't disease afflict us . . . if either of us is down with ill health, are we then going to give up on each other . . . or kill each other?'

'How can the two be the same?'

'Why not? Even his is life . . . ours too is life . . . we are looking into our comfort. Since he is not born yet and since he is not in a position to inform of his likes and dislikes we are for our comfort thinking of killing him. How horrific and cruel it is!'

'Sunita . . . think in peace. Think the whole day. I will not force you. If your decision is to carry him to the full term, as a husband I am ready to face any consequence standing by you, but I have only one request. Arrive at a decision going over what is good and what is not for our lives,' saying, Kishore left the decision to Sunita.

For another week, Sunita did not give any decision. Having looked at the problem from various angles, she analyzed, sorrowed, feared, distressed, shed tears and in the end, she agreed for an abortion.

Without further delay, Kishore discussed the matter with Dr. Geeta, the hospital gynecologist.

'Do you want me to terminate a twenty-four week old pregnancy, doctor? Are you the one who is asking for it? I can understand if any ordinary person were to ask me this. Being a doctor, is it fair to ask for it? Don't you know that an abortion is legal only when the fetus is less than twenty weeks?

'How can you knowing everything talk like this . . . you know the baby has the problem of Edward Syndrome, knowing how dangerous the disease is, why do you talk of the legality of the case?'

'The government has made abortion legal recommending it only in cases of genetic disorders or physical deformities, but such abortions have to take place within twenty weeks of pregnancy. If done after that, it is illegal and a punishable offence. Knowing that well, I cannot abort the child.'

'Think from a humanitarian angle, doctor . . . how can this be considered a crime? Is it wrong to stop the birth of a baby who is going to be born with various deformities and critical health problems . . . you also know such a child will not survive long . . . what is the advantage of bringing life into this world knowing fully well that it is going to be short-lived? Did you think of the agony of those parents . . . even for the baby, what physical torment! A problem that has an easy solution, do you want us to complicate it? We are doctors working in the same hospital . . . tell me how can we not help each other out?'

'Are you into sentimental blackmailing? Sorry. I shall not do this. You tell me, since we are working at the same place, I should do happily what you intended me to do. If it is so, I will never agree to it. You are at fault if you have not gone in for the test before twenty weeks to know if the baby had a genetic disorder. For being so careless, in spite of being a doctor, you cannot help but pay the price for it.'

'Okay, if that is so, I will get Venkat Reddy, our hospital M.D. to recommend the abortion. Will you at least then agree to perform the abortion?'

'Not Venkat Reddy, not even if God were to come down. I shall not. If required, I will not hesitate to give up my job here and go else where to work.'

'How can you talk so irrationally, doctor?'

'How dare you talk to me like that? You are arguing irrationally. You are bringing pressure on me to commit a crime. It is not just commitment of crime, but abetting someone to commit a crime is also criminal. Mind it. If you argue further, I may have to lodge a complaint with the police against you,' Dr. Geeta said furiously.

'Do you take yourself to be the only gynecologist in city? There are over a hundred hospitals in Hyderabad city . . . and gynecologists in hundreds. Anyone will perform an abortion for profit,' saying so, Kishore stood up.

'I am going to lodge a complaint wherever you get the abortion done. I will send you and that doctor to jail. Remember that,' Dr. Geeta said in a rage.

Kishore stood up rashly. 'I will see to that too!' He stormed out of the room seething.

Reaching home, he continued feeling harrowed. He felt quite hurtful and sore in mind.

Though Kishore had earlier heard stories of Dr. Geeta's stubbornness and obstinacy, he didn't quite imagine her to behave the way she did. When he shared what transpired with Sunita, she concurred with her. 'Isn't what she said also true? Why should we as educated people commit a crime? Even so, the question of whether or not the baby should be given birth is a mother's prerogative. Where is place for a government or its laws to interfere in it? Let us go to the court. We cannot leave this matter here.'

'Laws have been formulated keeping in mind a pregnant woman's health. The medical world feels strongly that if an abortion takes place after twenty weeks, there is going to be danger to mother's life. Therefore, chances of getting a judgment in our favour are very remote,' Kishore reasoned.

'Since the time you left for the hospital, I have been browsing the Internet for information. In America, abortion can take place up to twenty-four weeks. Then, how can there be danger to a mother's life only in India? Anyway, ours is a special case. We take pride over the fact of our advancement in the fields of science and technology. When a woman decides to terminate her pregnancy, instead of developing medical science to help that woman whatever the stage of pregnancy she is in, how just is it to stop her from terminating her pregnancy? Will the government take care of our child? Will it take his responsibility for life? Let us meet a good lawyer,' Sunita said with a firm mind.

Kishore filed a case in the High Court. His lawyer argued that the case needed urgent attention and a judgment given expeditiously, since any delay in the case meant narrowing chances of abortion. Hence, the court took up the case immediately. The arguments commenced the next day.

Hearing the arguments on both sides for full four days, the court gave the verdict against abortion. Sunita had no option but to carry the baby to its full term.

It was ten days since Sunita delivered the baby. Since Dr. Geeta resigned her job, another gynecologist attended to Sunita's delivery.

Everyone watched the baby curiously the day he was born. Until then there was no delivery with Edward Syndrome in that hospital. Except seeing pictures of babies born with Edward Syndrome in medical books, it was the first time even for Dr. Siddhartha to see such a baby with genetic disorder.

The baby appeared fragile and weak with a small abnormally shaped head. His ears were low set and he had a cleft palate. The heart carried defects . . . kidneys were malformed. The pelvic section was smaller than it had to be. One of the ribs was missing . . . the toes were an indistinct mass of flesh. The baby was underweight . . . a kilo and a half. Soon after birth, the baby was shifted to the I.C.U.

'The baby appears like a phantom child!' Dr. Siddhartha overheard a cleaner of washrooms commenting.

*   *   *

It was twelve-thirty midnight. Siddhartha walked slowly into the I.C.U. and stood beside the baby born with Edward Syndrome. He observed the ten-day old baby's chest expanding as struggling for breath. He was on artificial respiration . . .

Dr. Siddhartha thought to himself watching the baby: *Thinking you would die a natural death, I gave you ten days time. Why didn't your end arrive? How many more days will you go on with this torture?*

'*How many medicines per day . . . and how many more, injected through the drip . . . do they allow me to die . . . I too would like to die. You are all making me live under force . . . please, will you do me a favour . . . I am unable to see my mother's tears. I won't live long anyway. However many medicines you give, I will not last for more than another twenty days . . . do I have to undergo this torture for a life of thirty days? Please relieve me of this pain!*' Dr. Siddhartha thought he heard a fervent plea reaching him from the baby.

Dr. Siddhartha was pained. A tide of endless pity overtook him.

Why do people deliver such babies? They could go in for abortion, is it not . . . even Kishore, how stupidly he behaved . . . why did he get into that argument with Dr. Geeta? Couldn't he have easily got the abortion done silently in another hospital . . . his adamant approach made him knock the doors of law courts . . . what happened in the end?

Why are the laws too so blind? When someone cries out for death, why does it force anyone to live? Even when that mother cried and pleaded with the court, why didn't it show mercy on her? Why don't these people understand that instead of allowing the baby to live a month or two, putting him through torture, is it not better to kill him before birth?

How many loopholes in these laws . . . murderers and rapists move around with impunity! But in the case of women, the laws are stringent. The reason is the victims here are not anti-social elements such as black marketers, ruffians, rowdy elements or politicians. How cheap common man's life is before law . . . no guarantee of food, shelter and clothing . . . not even an opportunity to lead a life of dignity . . . if he desires to die, considering it a crime, is put behind bars! What kind of justice is this?

It was for that reason that Dr. Siddhartha was doing his bit for justice. He might have until now granted release from mortal pain to fourteen patients. This child was the fifteenth. This case was the youngest among all those to whom he gave relief . . . a ten-day old infant babe. His hand that was just about to pull off the oxygen tube, pulled back. Only patients past their prime or their extreme old age were worthy of his benevolence until then. The life to which he was going to present relief now was ignorant of what life meant. It was unaware the pain it was putting up with was hell and that it had to find an escape from it . . .

Dr. Siddhartha's mind was in a state of rebellion as though someone was pulling away his hand.

The infant would anyway die, until then he was a source of immense mental pain to his parents. In addition, he would leave behind a financial burden on Dr. Kishore. Had not the baby's parents plan to kill him while he was still in his mother's womb? They had stopped in their tracks because the court came in their way. He was merely completing the task that they left undone.

Setting his mind at rest of all its doubts, Dr. Siddhartha in one final move of his hand tried pulling off the tube.

*   *   *

Dr. Wali was jolted out of his sleep. He heard to somebody crying in pain. The sound came from the room next to his. His two sons slept in there. One was ten years old and the second was eight. Not finding his wife on the bed beside him, he walked into the hall. He heard his wife's voice from the sons' room trying to pacify one of his sons.

Pushing the door open, Dr. Wali went in. The elder son was crying in his mother's lap. She was patting his stomach. 'You will be all right . . . indigestion perhaps . . . haven't you taken some warm water just now . . . even gas problem if any will let up,' she was consoling.

'When he is complaining of stomach pain, why didn't you wake me up? Couldn't I have given him some medicine?' Dr. Wali said.

'That is why I didn't wake you up. What will happen to their health if you make them pop in medicines for simple ailments? As children it is common for them to develop stomach pain . . . if it doesn't subside it is enough if I give him some *ajwain* and salt mixed in water!'

Ignoring the words of his wife, Wali felt the stomach of his son. The child writhed in pain when he laid his hand on the left side of lower part of his abdomen. He knew it immediately . . . pain due to appendicitis . . . no doubt.

Without any delay, Wali reached the hospital with his son. It was midnight, twelve thirty-five then. Waking up the nurse resting on the table, he instructed her to ready the operation theatre and made his son lie down on a vacant bed.

Dr. Wali remembered Dr. Siddhartha to be the duty doctor, but was surprised that he did not care to come out of his room despite the sound of voices outside. Perhaps he was in deep sleep. Even Dr. Wali could perform the surgery for appendicitis, but his own son after all . . . could he apply the knife to him . . . make an acute cut with the knife on his stomach! Siddhartha was an expert at performing laparoscopic surgery. He had to first wake him up. Later find out if the anesthesiologist was on call.

Dr. Wali went to the room of the duty doctor. Siddhartha was not present there. Not finding him even in the ward, thinking him to be in the I.C.U. Wali began to climb the stairs swiftly and entered the I.C.U.

Dr. Wali found Dr. Siddhartha standing beside the bed of the child with Edward Syndrome. In his hand was the oxygen tube . . . Wali looked at the child. There was a few moments' stir inside that small body . . . a movement that normally was seen in patients suffering pangs of death . . . he swiftly moved and reached the patient's bed. 'Dr.Siddhartha! What are you doing?' saying, he pulled the oxygen tube from the hand of Dr. Siddhartha and tried re-fixing it to the patient, and pressed the patient's heart softly. There was no stir of life in the child. He was dead by then.

Dr. Wali turned furiously to Dr. Siddhartha. 'Do you know what you have done? You have taken the life of an innocent patient, mercilessly . . . a cold-blooded murder . . .'

'I have granted this child relief from agonizing pain,' Dr. Siddhartha replied.

'What a mistake you have committed, doctor!'

'I don't think I did anything wrong. You too know that this child will not live for more than a month . . . what is the use of compelling him to live . . . a burden to the earth . . . a burden to his parents . . . a burden to himself . . . so I did what I could.'

'Who are you to do that? You are not God, are you . . . no living organism is a burden to the earth. If you were right, God wouldn't have them in this world. The sin you committed is inexcusable. We have been working here since many years. You are my friend, but I cannot stand guilty in the eyes of Allah. I am sorry doctor. I am calling the police. I will tell everyone the bitter truth I was witness to,' saying so he walked out briskly.

As an honest and upright employee, Dr. Wali initially called to inform Venkat Reddy before calling in the police. Venkat Reddy normally went to bed taking two pegs. Hearing what had happened through Dr. Wali, Venkat Reddy's tipsiness came down immediately.

'You don't inform the police in a hurry. Please wait until morning. I will be there by six. Let us convene an emergency meeting. We will call the rest of the staff too for the meeting. After holding discussions, we will implement a decision. Until then, please don't inform anyone of this.'

'Impossible, it is murder that has taken place here . . . right in front of my eyes. There is no question of suppressing the facts. Allah will not approve of it.'

'I am not asking you to keep it under wraps. I am merely asking you to wait for a few hours. What is involved is our hospital's reputation. What is at stake is the years of hard earned good will.'

'*Maaf karna saab*! You are thinking of saving the reputation of the hospital, I am thinking of my moral responsibility as a human being. Dr. Siddhartha many times earlier argued with me the necessity for mercy killing. He used to argue that it was not wrong to kill terminally ill patients and that it was a good deed done in kindness and pity. Going over the whole thing, my suspicion is gaining strength that his hand might have been there behind many of the deaths that had taken place in recent times in our hospital. You remember Kiranmayi, don't you . . . the patient who we had taken care of for ten long years . . . when she died, I went through lot of stress. Dr. Siddhartha's hand of mercy must have been there behind her sudden death too. Those doctors who take lives of their patients are not worthy of pardon. Dr. Siddhartha has to face punishment.'

Venkat Reddy's heart sank hearing that Dr. Siddhartha was cause for many deaths in the hospital. Future for him appeared bleak and dark. Will there be anything left, if the news spread? Like vultures, the TV channels with their cameras would arrive on the scene in hordes. Set aside punishment for Dr. Siddhartha, he would, as head of the hospital receive punishment first . . . a punishment that would see the permanent closure of the hospital.

'I am coming right away. Please wait till I come,' Venkat Reddy pleaded.

'Sorry . . . I cannot make any promises to you. You may fire me for taking this to the police. I won't give you that chance. I have decided to resign and look for another job. I cannot commit anything wrong to stand before Allah as the guilty after *Khayamat,* on the Day of Judgment.'

'Are you going to betray the institution which offered you a job immediately after you finished your course in medicine? Just think it over.'

'I am not being treacherous to the hospital. I am only disclosing Siddhartha's murderous intentions. I am unable to see a doctor who supposed to take care of his patients, turns a god of death and takes their lives . . . that doctor's betrayal . . . his breach of trust.' Without leaving room for further discussion, Dr. Wali hung up the phone.

Dr. Siddhartha, who by then had come down from the I.C.U. walked into his room without a word. Dr. Wali was surprised further by Dr. Siddhartha's silence.

Dr. Wali expected to see Dr. Siddhartha accept his mistake and plead with him not to inform the police. Dr. Wali was stunned and felt an intense disgust to see no trace of remorse or fear in his face. The police arrived within fifteen minutes.

Within ten minutes of arrival of the police, Venkat Reddy collapsed into a chair as he came holding his head in hands.

Coming to know that a doctor working in the same hospital had killed her child disconnecting oxygen supply, Sunita began to wail collapsing on the lifeless body of her child. Kishore was shocked to know what had happened. Keeping in check his own sorrow, however hard he tried to console Sunita, the heart-rending loud wails of her reverberated through the hospital.

Siddhartha continued answering coolly to the questions of the police. He did not seem even a wee bit concerned about his arrest charging him with killing. He supported his act of disconnecting oxygen supply to the child as in a surgery a doctor excised the appendix from the body.

'Your colleague Dr. Wali complained that you had killed a child in the I.C.U. of your hospital on purpose by disconnecting the oxygen supply to the child, what do you say to that?' It was the fourth time that the Inspector of police had posed the question without losing his cool.

'It is not true.'

"Does it mean then that you had not murdered him?"

'No'

'Dr. Wali claims to have seen you pulling out the oxygen tube and that you held it in hand till the child breathed his last. Is it not right?'

'Yes. It is true.'

The inspector looked irritated. 'In spite of being educated how can you be so careless with your answers, doctor? On one hand, you claim to have not killed the child and on another you accept to have pulled off the tube. Don't you know that disconnecting oxygen supply would kill a patient who is on ventilator? Give a clear reply,' he asked in a harsh voice.

'That I had pulled out the oxygen tube is true. I had done that to help the child. I have merely lent my support to relieve him of acute pain when he anyway would die very soon.'

"That means you are accepting to committing the crime.'

'What I have done is no crime. It is a mercy killing. My weakness is I cannot see anyone suffer. As a doctor, I do my best to reduce that pain. I pity the patients who have to suffer from diseases that doctors have given up as incurable and no medicine can relieve them of pain. I pity them more if they have to await their end suffering intense physical pain. As doctors, except extending the pain of that child, we are not helping him in any way.

Dr. Kishore is fully aware of this. The child's parents themselves sought legal help and permission to put an end to that pain through an abortion. I have merely fulfilled their wish though late. I am sure they will feel happy for what I have done.'

Hardly were those words out from Dr. Siddhartha, than Sunita who had just then entered the room, hearing those words lunged forward in a frenzy rising like a goddess of fury on Siddhartha and holding his shirt began to slap him hard.

'You monster! You have taken life of my child! How could you bring yourself to killing that infant . . . cursed be those hands . . . are you a man or a beast?' Sunita kept madly slapping him.

Kishore pulled her away with force. As one possessed, Sunita swayed . . . her hair all disheveled . . . eyes turned red and fiery . . . she gave a frightening picture of herself.

'Let go of me . . . I will kill him. He is a savage who had done away with my child. I will not spare him. I will go to jail killing him.' Freeing herself from her husband's hold, as a lioness, she leaped on Dr. Siddhartha.

The police, who till then ignored her initial anger, now stopped her. Despite two constables holding her back, she kept trying hard to free herself.

'Hang him. Don't leave him. Bury him in a pit. I wish to see him writhe in pain dying,' she continued screaming . . . wailing.

Not only did Kishore feel mournful but also extremely angry. His good breeding held him back from raising his hand at Siddhartha. He could not overlook the fact that they had worked together in the same hospital as colleagues for some years.

With a penetrating eye Kishore could only bring himself to saying, 'why did you do this doctor?'

Dr. Siddhartha who by then was in a state of confusion regarding Sunita's behavior said, 'what do you mean Kishore . . . aren't you also a doctor . . . don't you know that a baby born with Edward Syndrome does not live long? Is it necessary to torture him in hundred different ways to keep him alive for a few days in the name of medical treatment? I arranged to facilitate an easy and peaceful end for him. I thought you would appreciate me for doing it. Even you and your wife thought of killing him while he was still a fetus, didn't you? Didn't I do the same? I don't understand why she is coming under so much perturbation.'

'Yes, it is true that we wanted to go in for abortion, but once he took birth he has become my life, he is everything to me, you brute! Did we tell you that we would be happy if he is gone? We are not murderous like you . . . I gave birth to him. I am his mother who is prepared to give her life to see him live,' Sunita said shouting in furor.

For Dr. Siddhartha her conduct seemed strange. She, who went round the courts to have the fetus aborted, why was she abusing him now?

'Have you seen that baby . . . how he is born as a phantom child with how many deformities and diseases? Don't you think it is better for him to die than live? Why are you making an issue of a minor problem?' Siddhartha said angrily.

The moment Sunita heard those words, she went into a towering rage. With one jerk, freed herself from Kishore's hold and fell on Siddhartha like a lioness. With that force, Dr. Siddhartha lost his balance and fell down.

'Do you call my child a phantom child . . . you are the phantom . . . you are the spectral ghost . . . my child is my delight. If you cannot see him, shut your eyes tight. No . . . no, didn't you say my child appeared a phantom child to you? I will pluck out those eyes of yours!' Sunita who till then was kicking Dr. Siddhartha, now started to tear his face with her nails. Two police constables pulled her aside with force.

'It is not safe for the accused to stay here. We will take him to the station for inquiry. You also come to the station and give your statement,' telling Dr. Wali and Kishore, the Inspector left the place with Dr. Siddhartha.

'Hang him. Don't leave him! Kill him!' Sunita kept yelling from behind.

*　　*　　*

As each day passed, the feeling that he was nearing his end came to dawn upon Prasad. Recently, his throat muscles too began to weaken. He had been swallowing food with much effort. Even speech had slurred, and he was struggling to express in words.

As a proof that his heart muscles weakened, his breathing slowed. His lungs were not taking in enough oxygen. Breathing through the mouth had not been of much help. When Saroja consulted Dr. Rao, he said, 'very soon, he may need to be put on a ventilator.'

Prasad wished to meet Ragini before his death. It was a year and a half since he came to know Ragini . . . he was now scared that he would die without meeting her.

Prasad wished to talk to Ragini for some time at least. He wished to thank her for making his life delightfully rejoicing. Lucky his mother was able to understand his speech. Even if Ragini did not get him right, there was a chance of his mother communicating his thoughts to her. If he were to wait longer, a time might come when he would be in no position to communicate even this much.

That day on his mother's return from work, when she settled down with a cup of coffee, he expressed his desire to meet Ragini. 'Let us go to Nakrekal Mummy. I just want to meet Ragini once.'

'Why hurry . . . we will go at leisure when time permits,' Saroja said.

'Why do you mislead me Mummy . . . you are aware I don't have that much time before me. There is no guarantee that I would survive even for another year. My speech has developed a slur . . . breathing has turned wheezy. I remained happy over the past one year and a half despite my deteriorating health, mainly due to the mails from Ragini. Since many days, I have been thinking of meeting her and talking to her once who gave me mental resolve and enlarged my desire to live, Mummy. If delayed, I may not be in a position to talk to her. Delayed more, I may not remain myself. I should go when still my throat muscles are co-operating and in a position to communicate my thanks to her. Please understand my anxiety.'

'Please don't talk that way. I feel like weeping. I am living only for you. Nothing will happen to you. By talking about death, don't make me feel sad,' tears rolled down Saroja's cheeks.

'Be practical Mummy . . . why run away from the truth? Let us accept the truth.'

Unwilling to talk about that topic, Saroja talked about the journey to Nakrekal.

'Can you withstand the rigour of a long journey?' Saroja asked.

'To see Ragini, I shall put up with any pain the travel may involve, Mummy. As Ramya's friendship gave me infinite joy during my adolescent years, so also is Ragini's during my confinement to bed. It motivated me adding sweetness to my life. Her words and her essential goodness pervaded my life leaving no time to rue over my misfortune. What can I give to such a great friend, except looking at her to my eyes' content and expressing my heartfelt thanks . . . don't refuse this, Mummy!'

It had begun to dawn on Saroja too gradually that Prasad's days were numbered . . . she also observed in his eyes a strange glow since the time Ragini came into contact with him. Where she failed to give courage and bring about a change in his attitude, despite all her sincere efforts, a girl with her kind words succeeded. Ragini's words worked like magic. She too was keen on meeting the girl who over-powered her son so infinitely.

Saroja took off from work and hired an *Innova* car. Making Prasad lie down comfortably in the back seat, and loading the wheel chair in the car's boot, they started for Nakrekal.

Though Prasad was lying in the back seat of the car, his mind was going over in detail the mail exchanged between him and Ragini.

'If you ever come to our Nakrekal, I shall first take you to the Saibaba temple close to our house. Do you know it is a very famous temple! My mother visits that temple every Thursday to pray for my recovery. My poor mother! I don't understand the propriety of asking the same God who gave me this affliction to also help me recover from it. After all a mother, is it not? Probably all mothers are such.

'There is 'Chayasomeswaralayam' temple twenty-five kilometers from our place. I visited that temple when our school took us there. Do you know the uniqueness of that temple . . . the shadow of the two pillars in that temple through the day remains only at one place! What a unique scientific knowledge it is . . . I am amazed recalling the intelligence and understanding of our sculptors in optics who built our temples and their spires!'

'It is indeed difficult to accompany you to that temple, but for your sake, I will certainly come. I will show you around remaining by your side, okay?' Ragini wrote once. Since anyway there was a car in hand, Prasad decided to visit that temple with Ragini.

Since Ragini wrote him in English, Prasad could not make out which dialect of Telugu Ragini's family spoke, so once he tried finding it out from her. 'I wish to hear you speak . . .' he wrote. For that, she wrote back her entire mail in Telugu but in English script. 'The dialect we speak here in our parts is the Telangana dialect of Telugu close to the language of the common man. I love my language, my dialect and our culture. I used to play Batukamma energetically as a child. Even today, we celebrate Batukamma festival grandly. We address children here in these parts as 'bidda' in all affection.'

Prasad's heart was yearning to hearing Ragini speak in her favourite Telangana dialect. She who wrote long mails, did she chatter when she spoke?

How mature and mellow were her views and responses . . . so mature as to make him wonder if she really was only twenty-two years of age.

Two months of getting to know Ragini, sending his mobile number Prasad asked her to call him back. No call came, however a mail arrived instead.

Ragini wrote, '*Is it necessary to use cell phones knowing they harm us . . . they have to be used during emergency situations when important messages have to be sent. We should not use them for casual talk and for saying sweet nothings. This is my policy. Hence, let us while away our time by exchanging mails. Since I have your cell number, I will call when required.*'

In one mail, Ragini gave her opinion on present day filmy music, '*Do you hear to old film songs, how melodious those are . . . as you hear those songs, you feel floating away lightly in the air, how elegant and sensitive especially the romantic songs! The songs in new films are so cacophonic . . . but don't take my taste in music to be in any way orthodox. I too like music with good beat and rhythm. It is only that the lyrics of some songs put me off entirely. In a recent song, the lover says—'let us both turn beetles!' There is so much difference between longing to turn into butterflies than into beetles. Isn't it? If I meet that lyricist I will push him into a swarm of beetles!*

'*Did you hear to another song . . . the lyric says, the lover experiences 'the sound of sky collapsing within him' when he sees his girl friend. Isn't that comparison suited to denote danger and fear? Should not temple bells ring when a lover meets his girl friend . . . if not, soft tinkling of ankle bells . . . the gurgling waters of a running brook?*

'*Prasad, in today's songs, the drift and tenor of love is shifting . . . the ardour among people . . . humanity . . . all are missing. As stones lacking in ardour, minds are turning lump. Can you call love won through swords and blood baths as love? How wrongly they are depicting girls, as treacherous and violent . . . as with intent of slaughter and free from all control . . . are the censor board members asleep?*

'Have you noticed the quality of voices we hear in these songs . . . is there any sweetness anywhere . . . or melody for that matter . . . a Ghantasala . . . a Balu . . . a PB Srinivas . . . a AM Raja! How sad I feel hearing to this music!' The car approached Nakrekal.

'Ragini's house is the last in the row of houses facing the east next to the stadium in Isaykunta' Saroja told the driver.

Inquiring from persons on the way, they reached the stadium near Isaykunta. When asked, a few people expressed their ignorance of who Ragini was. Some others asked what her father's name was and what he did for living.

'You said the mention of Ragini's name was enough to take us to her place!' Saroja said smiling.

Prasad felt discomfited by that comment.

Passing another four five houses, they asked a twelve-year old boy playing in that vicinity.

'Oh, Ragini *Akka*'s house . . . the last house there!' he pointed.

As the car driver pulled up outside Ragini's house, a young girl of sixteen or seventeen looked out from the veranda curious and a bit surprised.

Getting off the car, Saroja asked the girl, 'Is this the house of Ragini?'

'Yes Aunty . . . may I know who you are?' the girl inquired.

'Are you Ragini's sister? What is your name?'

'I am Subhashini. Do you know Ragini . . . how do you know her? I am sorry, the reason why I am asking is I don't recall meeting you any time earlier Aunty.'

'Are you going to ask questions at the doorstep itself? Won't you allow us inside?' Saroja said amused. Meantime, Subhashini's mother also came out.

'Oh, sorry Aunty . . . please come inside!' saying Subhashini brought out two chairs and placed them in the veranda.

As Saroja seated herself, she said, 'I am Saroja . . . my son Prasad and your sister Ragini are e-mail mates!' saying, Saroja wore a broad smile.

Noticing that neither Subhashini nor her mother smiled in return, Saroja was surprised. She felt they were not welcome there. They were showing that displeasure on their faces. How cultureless! Mused Saroja.

'I am sorry for coming all of a sudden . . . my son said he didn't have your phone numbers. He said Ragini did not provide them in spite of his request. He did not agree to my suggestion that he should inform you of our coming through e-mail. He wished to surprise her with his visit. I accompanied him unable to ignore his affection for Ragini . . . sorry . . . we will not be cause for inconvenience to you. We will leave within ten minutes,' Saroja said disconcerted.

'It is all right Aunty. Where is Mr. Prasad?' That girl asked but her face did not reflect even semblance of a smile. Her mother seemed not to evince any interest nor bother to show even slightest of hospitality of indulging in some small talk with visitors. She just disappeared inside.

Saroja regretted coming over to that place. Yet, having had come, she told herself why back out now fearing the blows of the pounding pestle. Didn't Prasad commend Ragini several times that she was superbly noble-natured? Why were her family members then behaving strangely . . . her mother went in without even offering a glass of water and the sister though talking, was conversing in a matter of fact manner. Had she been misled by Prasad's words . . . if she were to linger there a little longer, they might miss retaining their dignity. Meeting Ragini for a few minutes, should clear out of the place fast. . . .

Unloading the wheelchair from the car and placing it on the ground, the driver asked, 'shall I help the youngster into the chair?'

Saroja recovered from her disconcerting thoughts. She realized that the reason she was there was to fulfill the wish of her son. It did not matter if she had to face insults or if anyone talked to her or not. It was enough if Prasad could meet Ragini just once and talk to her. Once she made up her mind to leave that house only after fulfilling the wish of Prasad, she experienced a new enthusiasm seeping into her.

Saroja helped the driver to shift Prasad into the wheelchair. Once the driver placed the wheelchair in the veranda, she pulled her chair next to him.

Prasad smiled at Subhashini by way of greeting her. She did not smile in return. She went and fetched two glasses of water. *'Thank god, at least they are offering us a glass of water. Seeing the way they conducted themselves, I didn't expect even this,'* Saroja thought to herself. Taking the glass of water in hand, she drank the water in one go. Prasad declined.

Taking back the glasses inside, Subhashini returned to settle silently in another chair.

For the next five minutes, no one talked. Unable to take that silence any longer, Saroja attempted to break the silence. 'Where is Ragini? Is she resting . . . sleeping . . . did you tell her that Prasad and I have come?'

Prasad waited all ears for an answer from Subhashini. His eyes fixed to the door, he eagerly waited for Ragini to come out in her wheelchair any time.

Subhashini remained silent . . .

'Thanks to the mails your sister sent, my son recovered from despair and dejection to some extent at least. If he had been happy these last one and a half years, it was all due to your sister's efforts. Not just he, I am also eager to meet her.I too came only to thank her from within my heart. Could you please bring her out once?' Saroja said.

'It is not possible, Aunty.'

Saroja at once understood she did not put it right. 'Oh sorry . . . is it difficult for her to come out . . . in that case can we come in to talk to her?'

'Okay . . . come in,' saying, Subhashini led Prasad and his mother in.

'*How long you took and what anxiety you caused for such a simple thing!*' Saroja muttered to herself, slowly pushing Prasad's wheelchair inside following Subhashini.

It was a small hall inside. Saroja looked around for Subhashini's mother. 'Where is your mother?' Saroja asked.

'She went in to lie down. She has headache.'

'Oh, is that so . . . is Ragini too in that room?'

'No, Aunty. She is right here in this hall.'

'Where in this hall . . . .' Saroja asked, looking around once again.

It was then that Saroja heard Subhashini weeping . . . Saroja suspected something. She quickly raised her head to look on the wall. There was a portrait of about twenty two years old girl on the wall . . . garlanded with an electric lamp glowing beneath it.

Saroja put her hands around Subhashini to console her. 'When did this happen?'

'It is close to six months since my sister passed away,' Subhashini answered between her sobs.

Saroja was stunned to hear that . . . six months . . . she did not quite get it.

Prasad burst out crying as one insane. That cry of pain struggling to find expression seemed an animal struggling caught in the throes of death.

Saroja tried hard to console him, on failing, gave it up.

For quarter of an hour, Prasad lamented . . . he sorrowed trying to cross the ocean of grief . . . in endless woe . . . in deep anguish . . . he knew death was frightful . . . but he came to experience only now how much more frightful and how much more agonizing death could be of the near and dear.

Saroja asked once she regained her composure, 'is it six months since she died?'

'Yes . . . Aunty.'

'Then how is it Prasad has been getting mail, yesterday too he told me he received a mail.'

The same doubt had been swirling in circles within Prasad too for some time now. It was a doubt that until now sorrow had eclipsed. When the same question his mother asked, Prasad waited anxiously for an answer.

At that point, Subhashini's mother came out of the bedroom.

'Before her death, my daughter requested Subhashini to continue sending mail to Prasad on her behalf as though nothing happened. She took a promise that under any circumstance Prasad would not come to know of her death,' Subhashini's mother dabbed her tears with her sari end.

'I would like to share with you Aunty what my sister said to me before she died, '*it was for giving him strength to live that I continued my friendship with him. I resolved to make him overcome his disability and face life with courage. I am leaving before fulfilling my intended task. It is now yours to complete it, my sister. Write letters to brighten him up. Write as though hope is beckoning him. Write as one enjoying life to the brim. Write giving him utmost courage.'* She took a promise from me Aunty to that effect. It was for that I have been sending mails on her behalf since six months.' Turning to Prasad, Subhashini said with tears in her eyes, 'I am sorry Prasad . . . please excuse me. I had to do it to fulfill my sister's last wish.'

As Subhashini completed, Saroja in an impulse, folded her hands as to pay her respects to Ragini.

Prasad kept on grieving as one bedeviled, looking at the picture on the wall lovingly and adoringly. From time to time, he pulled at his hair. Saliva dribbled from corners of his mouth as his facial muscles had weakened. His heart-rending wail seemed to stir anyone to sadness.

Saroja brought Prasad out forcibly from that room.

How mistaken she was about those people! How great were all the members of that family! What nobility! Saroja paid her respects to them all within her mind.

Saroja drew Ragini's mother into her embrace. 'I can understand your sorrow. Your sorrow and mine are no different. I share your grief at Ragini's passing away. I regret leaving this place with the knowledge that I could not fulfill my son's one ardent wish and along with it my grief that Ragini is no more.'

* * *

The court hall . . .

Siddhartha was standing in the witness box.

As Akshara moved forward to give details of the case, Siddhartha remembered what his lawyer said of her.

'It is your ill luck the case is going to be handled by the Public Prosecutor, Akshara. Most of the cases she took up until now she won.'

'What is that . . . you are accepting defeat even before the arguments began,' Siddhartha said.

'She is a very skilled lawyer. There is no doubt about it. Having said that, I am not saying I am less capable than Akshara. I am only apprehensive of her strong convictions.'

'What is the relation between her convictions and this case?'

'There is a lot of relation, Dr. Siddhartha. You are supporting your action on grounds of mercy killing. You know that Akshara is widely canvassing against mercy killing, don't you know . . . she is a social activist who started Association for Muscular Dystrophy patients and is trying to give them strength and courage to stand up to the disease. I attended one or two of her meetings where she spoke about mercy killing. She came off as a staunch opponent of mercy killing. That is why I am telling you at the very outset. Don't have too many hopes.'

Those words of his lawyer influenced in shaping a picture of Akshara in mind. He took her to be tall with elegant personality . . . fiery—eyed . . . razor-sharp speech etc. Siddhartha was however shocked to see Akshara before him seated in a wheelchair. The lawyer, who told so much about her, did not tell Siddhartha that she was confined to a wheelchair.

Soon the arguments commenced.

The judge asked Siddhartha, 'do you accept the crime you committed?'

'No, Your Honour. That child was born with a disease known as 'Edward Syndrome'. Children born with that disease do not survive for more than a month. Even during that period, they suffer from various illnesses, deformities and experience excruciating pain each moment of their life. It is a wretched and miserable life. Whenever I saw that child, my heart bled for him with pity. You may think that doctors are trying to extend the patient's life, but what they extended was only his agonizing pain. He was to die anyway . . . I had only hastened that process. I did that only to release him from that physical pain. I don't consider my action as an offence.'

Akshara moved her wheelchair close to the seat of the judge and commenced her argument.

'Your Honour, the accused being educated and occupying a respectful position as a doctor in the society, committed a gruesome act of killing an innocent infant. He is attempting to cover up his dastardly act, unsuccessfully though, in the name of mercy killing . . . this is a cold blooded murder . . . it is a murder committed on purpose. Even if Dr. Siddhartha argues that it is a case of mercy killing, as per our country's laws it is a punishable crime.

'Taking a unilateral decision, coming under the mistaken perception that the patient desired such a measure, and kill the said patient and later call it mercy killing is a meaningless, unethical, barbaric act. Even in countries such as Netherlands, there are definite and clear rules and laws in place for carrying out mercy killing. It is only when mercy killing is carried out keeping within the limits of those laws can it be termed mercy killing.

'Even if a terminally ill patient desires death due to reasons of intense pain, he has to seek voluntarily mercy killing. He has to express that wish not once but several times. It is for a government recommended body of doctors to determine that no amount of medical treatment will be of help and that the patient is really 'terminally ill'. The committee of expert doctors has to arrive at a decision after due deliberation that there is no relief from pain for the patient other than through mercy killing and inform by way of writing. Carry out mercy killing only after this under the supervision of two doctors. The same is also termed 'physician assisted suicide'.

'However, please think how barbaric and brutal the action of this doctor is Your Honour! The patient he killed was a voiceless vulnerable infant who could not express that life for him was a burden or that he wished to die. Some countries permit mercy killing with the approval of close relatives when the patient is in a state where he cannot express his wish or had slipped into coma, but this child's parents have not expressed that wish either directly or indirectly. Even if we set aside temporarily that mercy killing is a punishable offence, in no way can we consider the action of the accused as mercy killing. Look at it any way you please!Since what the accused did comes under murder, I request the court to sentence him to death under Section 302 of IPC,' saying so, Akshara concluded her argument.

Siddhartha's lawyer prepared to counter argue.

'Your Honour, we have to look into the case to see if the killing was a vindictive act or with what intention or evil motive the accused disconnected oxygen supply or if it was purely to help a child in intense physical pain who lacks expression.'

Akshara interrupted the defense lawyer, at this point.

'Francis Inglis too killed her son Thomas Inglis in November 2008 by administering a lethal injection. Her son had fallen earlier from a running vehicle and suffered grievous injuries in the head and the rest of the body. She had argued in the English court that she only administered the lethal injection unable to see her son's physical pain. She received a sentence of imprisonment for nine years, Your Honour. I will here quote the words of the judge in that case: *the law books have not drawn any difference between killings with ill-intentions and that motivated by relationships and affections.* Therefore, whatever the motive, taking the life of a person is definitely a crime.'

Once Akshara said, 'that is all Your Honour', the defense lawyer continued his argument.

'Your Honour, allow me to submit an article on Edward Syndrome that appeared in a medical journal. The diseased was born with a defective heart and a cleft lip. He also had problems in breathing. This was certainly a terminally ill case. Since anyway the patient was dying, my client being a doctor having full knowledge of the pain that subsequently would follow . . . believing the life of that child as meaningless and worthless, as a gesture of kindness resorted to that act.'

Akshara responded instantly, 'Respectful defense lawyer terms this case as a terminally ill case, but, Your Honour . . . there is no clear definition for the phrase 'terminally ill'. Under certain laws, 'terminally ill' means comparably less time within which the patient may die.

Again, there is no clarity on what is 'less time'. Does the 'less time' mean a month . . . six months . . . or a year? I need to state here yet another aspect. It is an indisputable fact that even experts in the medical field cannot decidedly determine how long a terminally ill patient would last. If that is so, by which measure can anyone determine someone as 'terminally ill'?

'The defense lawyer has used another term, that the child went through excruciating physical pain. Even this is incorrect, because the degree of pain varies from person to person. It is only in relative terms one can explain how much physical or mental pain a man can bear. These are determined in comparable terms. For one individual, even slight pain may appear unbearable, while in another individual it may appear tolerable. One individual may feel death to be better even for the slightest pain, while another may want to live despite going through great pain.

'We are getting into unnecessary arguments regarding mercy killing and wasting the invaluable time of the court, Your Honour! When laws in our country do not support mercy killing, it is meaningless . . . irrelevant to argue whether the killing took place in kindness or pity!

'Recently, Hon'ble Supreme Court judge commenting about mercy killing had said: *mercy killing is a very complex issue. Each time a discussion comes up regarding this matter, our situation is akin to a boat sailing in turbulent waters.*

'Your Honour, there is yet another important issue that this court cannot afford to overlook. The accused is a doctor. He has an ethical responsibility and duty to look after patients who approach him with a faith that he would safeguard their life. Here, we have to recall the oath of Hippocrates laid down in four hundred B.C. I quote '*I will not administer any lethal medicine to any patient even if asked. I shall not suggest the use of such medicine to anyone* . . . unquote'

'What can it be, except a crime if one forgetting that Hippocrates oath taken before entering the medical profession kills an innocent infant?

'Isn't the defense lawyer's argument irrational to term the killing as a mercy killing? The phrases used to support such argument such as hopelessly ill, desperately ill, purposeless life etc. are all terms that signify nothing . . . meant only to mislead those present here. I wish to recall, in this context, the judgment given by the highest court in the case of Naresh Marotrao Sakhre: *Euthanasia or mercy killing is nothing but homicide whatever the circumstances in which it is performed.*

'I request Your Honour to consider all these issues before awarding severe punishment to the accused. Going by the way the accused argued his case, and the manner in which he supported his action and since there is a strong suspicion that his hand could have been there behind many other deaths that happened in that hospital in recent times, I request the court to order a thorough inquiry from this angle. That is all, Your Honour!' Akshara concluded her argument.

The judge adjourned the case to the sixteenth of the coming month. At the same time, the judge also ordered the police department to undertake an inquiry and submit a report regarding similar deaths that had taken place in the past in Life Line Hospital and determine how far and in which cases the accused had a hand in them.

*   *   *

Saroja observed Prasad's health deteriorating fast since their return from Nakrekal. However much she tried to revive his spirits and keep him happy and rejoicing, there was not much success.

The fact is Prasad lost interest in life. The desire that he should sooner die gained strength day by day. Before coming to know of Ragini's death, although his muscles resisted, his spirit rejoiced with her thoughts. Now, he felt as though all life cells that for the past one and a half year stayed active, now were gone dead all of a sudden . . . a body left empty of its soul, as it were . . . only one single wish prevailed . . . the desire for death.

The doorbell rang very early that morning. Saroja wondered who could be ringing the bell at such an hour. She opened the door and was astonished to see her mother, Jayamma, standing before her at the doorstep.

'*Amma*! Is that you?' Saroja said elated.

'Yes . . . It is me . . . why are you so surprised? Do I need permission to come to my daughter's house?' Jayamma exclaimed stepping into the house.

'What is that . . . I didn't mean it . . . you are happily leading a peaceful life in the Ashram, aren't you? When you arrived this way without any prior information, I became a little concerned about your health.'

'What of my health . . . I am hale and healthy. Don't have any fears. I have no worry for another ten years . . . okay?' Jayamma said softly smiling.

Jayamma settled in the sofa comfortably. 'Journey by bus is tedious, isn't it? Aches and pains . . . Set aside your concern for me, Saroja . . . what has happened to you? Do you know how much weight you have lost . . .

I can see bones jutting out. Why are you looking so aged? Do you know I did not recognize you initially?' Jayamma said anxious for her daughter's health.

'Nothing . . . all my worry is about Prasad, *Amma*.'

'Do you have to spoil your health for that? Agreed, you will have worry, but you have to stand up to it bravely. I saw you last three years ago and so much change over this time! Did you consult a doctor . . . I hear they help you with a complete check-up these days . . . You could have undergone such check-up?' Jayamma said having a close look of her daughter.

'I am all right, *Amma*, but not so your grandson. I am unable to see him go down day after day.' Jayamma watched mournfully her daughter's anguish.

Jayamma quickly moved to hug Saroja. As she took her daughter lovingly into her embrace, Saroja melting into her mother's embrace, gave vent to her anguish suppressed so long in a flood of tears, as though waiting only for such a moment.

Saroja after a while calmed herself. 'First, you freshen up, *Amma*. The hot water is ready. I will prepare *upma* that you so much like for breakfast. We can talk later at a more leisurely time.'

'Let me first have a look at Prasad . . . isn't he in that room . . . is he moving about in that wheelchair . . . is he taking his medicines on time?' As she talked, Jayamma walked into Prasad's room led by Saroja.

Prasad lay in bed with closed eyes. The ventilator by his side was helping him breath.

Prasad opened his eyes to see hearing the voices.

As he saw his grandmother before him, Prasad was pleasantly surprised. '*Ammamma!*' he called aloud, but instead of words, only strange sounds emerged from his throat. No sooner, he burst into tears in utter helplessness looking at his grandmother.

Jayamma sat next to him on the bed and ran her fingers through his hair. 'How are you? You were speaking coherently when I saw you last . . . what a strange disease . . . it is dreadfully troubling my grandson.'

Prasad struggled to say something. Turning to his mother, gestured to move the laptop close to him.

Saroja placed the laptop close to his right side. Moving his fingers slowly along the keyboard, he typed a message for his grandmother. 'I am happy you are here, *Ammamma*. I was afraid *if I would see you* at all before my end.'

As she read the message, Jayamma felt sorrow surging up from within. However, realizing it was not proper to shed tears in his presence, she controlled her pain. 'Lie down for some time. Once I bathe, I will sit with you. Okay?'

Prasad's face lit up hearing those words. 'Thanks, *Ammamma*! Do you know, I am terribly bored not having anyone around to talk to once *Amma* left for work? I won't accept if you say you came only to stay for a day or two,' Prasad typed.

Jayamma smiled at her grandson who despite his illness expressed his wish as a child.'Okay . . . I will stay. Tell me how many days?'

'For many . . . many days!' Prasad typed.

'Okay . . . I will stay as long as you want till you ask me to leave. We will chat once your mother leaves for work. Are you happy?'

For a brief moment, a bright smile flashed to dance on Prasad's lips . . . yet soon he fell into a sullen mood.

'I can't chat with you. *Ammamma* . . . I will only type this way . . . is it okay with you?'

Jayamma disturbed Prasad's hair playfully. 'My crazy lad! It is okay . . . double okay!' Saroja saw a happy smile on Prasad's face after many days.

Once she came out of the room, Jayamma exclaimed to Saroja, 'How has his condition deteriorated in these three years?'

Jayamma was amazed at the turn Prasad's health had taken. 'What can I say *Amma*? It is a disease that worsens over time, does not help to get better, is it not?'

'Does he communicate with you too this way typing?'

'No . . . he communicates normally with me. Although his speech lacks coherence, by following his lip movement I manage to understand him. For the rest the sounds appear strange. He typed only to make it easy for you.'

'How intelligent . . . but of what use? God has only granted him a short life. What do the doctors say?'

'They say, the organs within are gradually deteriorating in their functioning. The muscles weakening, the organs are coming under infection . . . I hear he will not survive for more than three months,' Saroja once again sobbed.

'All is written in our fate. We are merely instruments in the hand of God. My concern is all about you, Saroja . . . how many blows of life can you take . . . did we ever imagine your husband to die so early . . . or did we ever dream this ill-fated disease to afflict this boy . . . we have to live out whatever is written in our fate,' Jayamma said in a philosophical vein.

Once Jayamma left to have her bath, Saroja got down to cooking.

Saroja failed to understand why her mother arrived that morning as a bolt from the blue. She was now seventy years of age . . . ten years since she lost her husband . . . she did not show any inclination at the time to spend the rest of her days with either her son or daughter. She left for the Ashram of Raghunath Baba whose devotee she was. She donated the pension she received after her husband's demise, to the Ashram and planned to spend her remaining days in peace participating in community worship, meditation and devotional singing.

That was why, Saroja did not wish to disturb her mother in any way, and decided to bear any sorrow silently. Even when writing her a letter now and then, she merely wrote of inane matters like, 'how are you Amma . . . take care of your health, etc. Saroja never wrote of her woes. Three years ago, her mother came on a visit, that too because Saroja expressed her desire to see her once. Jayamma voiced her concern for Prasad's health. Even at that time, she stayed for a couple of days and went back that Baba appeared in her dream.

After that, Jayamma came visiting only now . . . that she came without any prior information or indication, was raising a doubt . . . had she been unwell . . . was it for that reason, that she came away . . . was it for that she was not voicing her intention for return . . . that thought had made Saroja feel weak and infirm at once. Looking after Prasad and instance of her own ill health in recent times, had been causing immense pressure on her. At times, when she came under extreme stress, even depressing, unwise and unsound thoughts were coming to mind if it were better, Prasad met his end sooner. At such a time, can she also take on the responsibility of her mother . . . no, she could not.

She lacked the required strength. Saroja contemplated, if Amma came to stay with her in a state of ill health, she would have to tell her at the very outset, of her inability by sharing her health problems and send her to some retirement home. Perhaps all her fears were unfounded . . . she might go back after a two-day stay with her, as she did on her last visit! Saroja's conscience kept cautioning her all through that she might have misconstrued. Saroja thought over what her mother said to Prasad a little while ago. She seemed to have come with a plan to stay on and might not go back in the near future, if one were to go by the tenor of what she said to Prasad, that she would stay as long as Prasad wished her to stay.

Saroja felt at once a sense of frustration come over her, '*is life just this . . . where relationships are so fragile . . . as to snap like a thread? Are all affections . . . attachments . . . all a pretension . . . hollow . . . are all these emotional bonds meant to deceive each other? Am I right in thinking of sending my mother back, who was visiting me in her old age, when I should be extending a helping hand? How did I develop this selfishness as to take my mother to be a burden? Is it selfishness . . . no, not at all. It is just my frustrating situation . . . a situation, wherein instead of welcoming my mother, I am letting out a despairing cry of why she had come at all! Oh God . . . What cruel thoughts are visiting me even in the case of my son! Where has gone all that affection . . . where did it go flying? Why is my heart longing for my son's death? Am I a true mother at all . . . have I turned to stone . . . have troubles reduced me to an inert matter . . . has cancer consuming my body little by little, nibbling away at my soft nature and my affections too? Am I acting as a true daughter to my mother . . . God, let not such a curse befall even my enemy.*

Noticing her mother come out of the bathroom, refreshed and changed into a fresh sari, Saroja wiped her tears with her sari end. She looked at her mother, examining so to speak. Jayamma was in a white cotton sari with a blue border . . . she had a slim body . . . and how briskly she walked . . . as active as she was a decade ago . . . what radiance in that face . . . as though a splendorous aura revolved around her person . . . perhaps, due to a life spent in an Ashram, her face wore an unexplainable calm.

Thoughts came crowding to Saroja's mind once again, *'is my mother feeling sad looking at her grandson . . . does she feel sorrowful that her daughter's life had come to this pass? Is it possible for one to carry such glow in the eyes if one was sorrowful . . . I know Amma well . . . she is a goddess of love . . . how well she brought us children up . . . however much we troubled her, she never uttered a harsh word against us. I don't recall a single instance of my mother ever spanking us. How can such a mother not feel sorrow? She must have surely undergone pain . . . only that having stayed for long in an Ashram, that spiritual influence may have led her to gain equanimity, to treat happiness and unhappiness as water drops on a lotus leaf!'*

Jayamma entered the kitchen. 'Now you relax . . . haven't I come . . . from now on I shall cook for you.'

'It is all right, *Amma.* Haven't you come just now? Relax for a while. Tell me about Baba and his Ashram.'

'What to say about the Ashram! As long as Baba was around, the life of the devotees as mine was satisfactory. It is only after his demise that things changed.'

241

'I too thought so, when I saw news of his demise over the TV, that you might have faced lot of agitation . . . you came to my mind often when I heard of Baba's ill health.'

'Didn't I go to the Ashram taking Baba to be a god? He too proved to be an ordinary man. He didn't appear as having godliness or god-ordained. Like us, he too suffered physical pain and breathed his last having stayed in a hospital for a month. It was one thing that the illusion cleared, truth stood revealed. The other was the disgust that gave way with rotten politics surfacing soon after his passing away. It was a struggle for domination and authority . . . there were so many vultures that alighted hearing of his demise, all for a share in his amassed wealth . . . what more proof than this, that we were not staying in a holy place?'

'It is all right if there was no holiness, let there be peace at least.'

'Where is peace? Not a day passed without some controversy showing its ugly head . . . each claiming the Ashram to be his . . . arguments . . . the arrival of the police on the scene . . . it was a problem with no solution, is it not . . . believe it or not, it was as the funeral fires of Ravana, burning years on end unappeased. That is why I came away . . . permanently . . . you don't worry! I will not be a burden on you. I am keeping good health and I still have energy. You don't have to do anything. I will work and cook for you. You just look after your son . . . and your job . . . that is enough.'

Saroja felt a guilty feeling seizing her all of a sudden hearing her mother speaking that way. She felt miserable recalling what she thought of her mother. Her mother did not come to trouble her. That she came to share her daughter's woes moved Saroja to tears.

'Oh, do not use such words, *Amma*? How can you be a burden on me? Stay with me without any hesitation. I will take care of you without causing any discomfort to you.'

'I came with the confidence that you will not refuse me, except that I came in a state of utter financial bankruptcy. I feel sad that I cannot be of monetary help to you . . . now that I donated my entire pension to the Ashram. Still I can help you with the housework . . . I cannot do anything else other than that.'

'It's okay, even if you don't. Do not worry yourself about money. The banks are paying us fat salaries. Besides, your presence will be a great source of strength to me. All these days, I felt miserable leaving Prasad to the mercy of servants and their whim and fancy. My mind was always anxious for him, as to what he was doing, or if he received proper care. Now the thought of you being here, gives me infinite strength,' Saroja said in all sincerity.

Truly, Saroja began to feel light as if someone removed a huge burden off her chest. Just a few minutes earlier, she feared if her mother was going to be a burden on her. Now that she offered to share her burden, Saroja's heart eased up assuaging her fears. Had she not been ill herself, she would not have hesitated even for a moment's time. She was a slave of circumstances . . . especially her fear of death . . . her fear that she might meet her end before Prasad . . . and a fear as to who would look after her mother if she too fell ill. . . . Winding up all her work, Saroja served breakfast to her mother and had a little herself.

'I will go to the bank now. You take rest.'

'How long are you going to look after your son, as looking after a baby? I am saddened to see you battle alone,' Jayamma said.

'If only God gives me physical strength, I can work any number of years happily. However, these days I observed a change in Prasad's attitude . . . talk of any instance, says he wishes to die . . . pleads he be allowed to die. It is heartbreaking to see him pitiably plead that way. I am unable to take it.'

'He is in a state where he cannot articulate his physical pain and how grievous he feels . . . wonder how unbearable his condition is . . . he might be considering death a better option to living. We need to understand such a person's desire for death sympathetically.'

'Don't say that *Amma* . . . he is my child. I am a mother who is prepared to tax my energies to see him live. Even if I had desired death for him as release from pain, it was only in a moment of weakness and despair. How then can I lend credence to that idea? You at least try bringing him round . . . tell him not to hurt me with such frivolous talk, *Amma*.'

'Oh God . . . Saroja, did you bear this much agony alone all these days . . . where was I . . . I would have come here had you written a line about him . . . nevertheless, don't worry, I shall have a talk with him,' Jayamma said in a tone of regret for having had left her daughter alone until then to fend for herself.

'I didn't wish to trouble you when you were leading a peaceful life in your own way at some secluded place in your old age. I may have strongly wished to have you by my side . . . so strongly that it had to pull at your heartstrings, so that you had to come to stand by me in

244

my hour of need as though someone sent for you. Please tell your grandson in a manner he understands it. Tell him not to talk of his death in my presence,' Saroja fell into her mother's embrace and wept.

'I have been seeing you since the time I arrived . . . how long will you cry . . . and how many times . . . look at your eyes that have gone sore . . . I shall talk to him . . . you first go to the bank.'

Having seen off Saroja, shutting the door, Jayamma walked into Prasad's room and sat by his bed pulling a chair. Prasad, who till then was lying, softly smiled seeing his grandmother.

'Your mother loves you dearly, Prasad. I have been observing her since the time I arrived,' Jayamma said by way of a prelude.

Prasad typed slowly on his laptop. Once he finished typing the message, he gestured her to read it. Adjusting her glasses, Jayamma read the message on the screen.

'That is the reason, for which I wish to die.'

'How can you say that . . . don't you know how much your mother feels hurt hearing those words . . . don't you think it to be wrong to hurt her when she is already worked up?' Jayamma said as if to chide him.

Prasad typed again.

'I wish to die only to relieve her from all the pain and trouble I am subjecting her to.'

'How can you talk like that? Can any mother bear to see her child die before her eyes? We have to fight to live . . . only cowards wish for death. Aren't we all there for you . . . you are not alone . . . don't forget that.'

Prasad smiled weakly. He wrote, 'no one accompanies a person in death.'

'Oh . . . what are those words?'

'I alone know what pain I am going through. If I have pain, I have to bear it, there is none to share it with me. What can even *Amma* do . . . except agonizing over it . . . it is much better to die than to live a wretched life putting up with pain each moment *Ammamma* . . . I don't want this life that is a mockery of it. Death is respectable. Please kill me . . . I wish to die, *Ammamma*!' Jayamma saw Prasad's eyes brim with tears.

'Is there reason in what you are asking for? Do we appear so merciless to you? Do you think my daughter is so barbaric as to kill her own child?' Jayamma said in a tone slightly angry.

Prasad typed once again. 'I am only asking you to kill me out of pity . . . out of love and sympathy. It is a crime to kill me out of anger or revenge. What is required to kill me is a sensitive heart . . . soft as butter . . . . That, you and *Amma* have. That is why I pray you . . . please kill me.'

'What a horrible wish you are asking for Prasad . . . . Is it not monstrous to kill the one who you love most?'

'No . . . it is humanity . . . because you love me, I am asking you to kill me. I don't have strength left in me to face it any more, *Ammamma* . . . I pray for mercy killing!'

Jayamma did not get what mercy killing meant. 'Stop thinking crazy . . . take rest . . . life is a God-given gift!'

'For me it is a curse!' Prasad typed.

Jayamma walked out of the room helplessly. Prasad too felt helpless . . . that there was none to understand him. A frustrating anger grew out of it . . . more, helplessness for not finding an opportunity to give an exclusive expression to that wish. A weird sound escaped his throat . . . as an arrow-hit bird trembling in fear . . . a heart-rending . . . a frightful shriek.

As Saroja got back from work, she walked into Prasad's room.

'How are you, my son?' She inquired. Without an answer, he looked pitiably into his mother's face.

'Do you need anything?' Saroja asked again.

Prasad signaled to her to look at the laptop screen next to him. Turning the laptop to her side, Saroja read the message. The words 'mercy killing' appeared there. Prasad looked at his mother intently as she read the words. Saroja walked out of the room in silence without a word.

By then Saroja's mother was cutting vegetables for dinner.

'*Amma* . . . did you talk to him?'

'Yes, I did . . . he wrote something to the effect 'mercy killing' . . . those words I didn't quite understand.'

'Mercy killing means patients suffering from incurable diseases who when approached, the government grants permission to die. Such a death allowed or permitted under the supervision of doctors, is not a crime. It is a legally assisted death . . . it is death caused, based on pity.'

'It is strange Saroja . . . I am hearing only now that government gives permission to die or for causing death. Perhaps Prasad is asking for it for that reason. When he kept repeating that he wished to die, I asked angrily if we appeared to him so heartless . . . to which he wrote those words.'

'I don't see any difference . . . between suicide, to killing him going by his wish and killing him with permission from the government. Whichever way we give him death, it is terrible and barbaric.' As Saroja said those words, somewhere inside her, in her inner consciousness there was a caution. She too had been praying that he die sooner . . . how dual-natured . . . what a self-delusion . . . somewhere a feeling that what Prasad wished was right . . . and outwardly telling her mother that mercy killing was hideous and horrible.

Yet she knew how trying and punishing it was to see her son who she brought up with care and love, move closer to death before her eyes. She would pray that not even her worst enemy should face such severe a punishment.

It didn't matter if others took her to be ruthless . . . not a mother but a monster! It was better for her to see him die once for all than die a slow death. That she desired death for him because she so endlessly loved him, it did not matter if others did not know of it. It was enough if her conscience knew of the fact.

Why was she not able to bring herself to saying it openly? Was she scared what the society would say of her . . . was it important for her to worry about what people would be saying or pray her son finds a quick release from his wretched condition? Why wasn't she able to tell her son, 'what you long for is right, it was better to see you die once and for all' . . . who was she trying to deceive . . . who . . . society . . . Prasad . . . . *Amma* . . . no . . . she was deceiving herself. A fear what society might say . . . diffidence . . . why was she unable to confide her painfully agitating thoughts even in her mother?

'I wish to share with you a secret Saroja . . . I gave much thought to what Prasad wanted after my talk with

248

him this morning. I will tell you the secret that has been within me as blazing fire for the last ten years. At the end of it, you think carefully and come to your own decision.'

'Secret . . . what secrets can you keep . . . haven't you led your entire life laying it bare as an open book?'

'What you see of a person from outside is different, Saroja. Within him lies another . . . altogether different . . . hiding within him are thoughts contrary to what he declares to outside world . . . how many masks . . . great and eminent men alone can manage to remain same. What do you think of me . . . what is your opinion?'

'You are an ideal mother . . . a good mother . . . we are lucky to have you as our mother. You are a great woman embodying love, sympathy and kindness.'

Jayamma laughed at those words. 'I knew you would say that. You marked me very high. Will you tell me where you place me as wife to your father?'

'Haven't we watched you two since our childhood? As far as I know, I never saw you contradicting my father. His word was yours. We did see him at times being harsh with you but I don't recall any occasion when you even grumbled. Remember the two years when he was bed-ridden in his old age . . . those two years we saw you serving him . . . and with such devotion . . . I heard many in our place complimenting father for having a wife like you to serve him in his old age.'

'Yes . . . those were our relatives and extended family . . . and people in society . . . I too know of it. Shall I now tell you the truth . . . I only behaved in a way for them to talk that way . . . I pretended . . . for the sake of the world,' Jayamma said.

'What is that *Amma* . . . you are stating strange things!'

'Yes, Saroja . . . I am telling you today the secret. I would like to unburden myself today with the truth that has been source of much mental distress and remorse.'

'*Amma*, I can't believe that you acted in a manner that you have to feel remorse.'

'Because I committed a gruesome act while pretending to be good, I feel intense distress. Metaphors such as a leopard in lamb's clothing or honey—smeared-dagger may not serve much to describe me.'

'*Amma,* don't say such words. I can't bear to hear it. You don't stand such comparisons . . . you are so full of nectar. I consider you as one of the world's greatest mothers.'

'No Saroja . . . within the nectar you all saw I hid unseen from others' eye in some nook a drop of poison. When your father came to be bedridden, I did serve him initially willingly. After that, gradually despair began to build up within me, a feeling of hopelessness that however much I served him, that it was of no use . . . and to match that despair, I experienced an inability to see him suffer . . . a weakness often overtook me. Seeing your father laid up in bed, love on one hand and pity on another used to overwhelm me. My heart used to sorrow over his condition. At one such weak and inauspicious moment, one day an idea took seed. An idea that it would be better for him to die . . . don't think I had no love for him . . . that idea dawned only because I had love for him. Just as you are serving Prasad now, I served your father too then that way. He used to relieve himself on the bed . . . from cleaning his bedclothes . . . tidy him up . . . serve him food . . .

giving medicines on time . . . . I took upon myself all those tasks . . . willingly . . . but somewhere in some corner, a feeling that it would be better he died soon.

'Perhaps as a result of that thought . . . I missed on purpose giving him medicine for blood pressure, not that I forgot . . . even if remembered, a certain weakness . . . I know the cause for his death was my negligence in giving him his medicine. In one way, I killed him myself.

'As long as he lived, he lived his life as a king. He was as majestic as a lion when he stepped into the house. Such a man when he took ill and was confined to bed, I could not bear to see him, so I wished his death.'

Jayamma cried inconsolably.

'Still if you misunderstand me . . . or take me to be wicked, I have to tell you one thing Saroja . . . I did not weep when your father died, nor did I feel sorrow. I felt as though a heavy burden was off me . . . I felt a relief . . . for sparing me that drudgery . . . and spared him that excruciating pain . . . we both were relieved at the same time.'

'*Amma* . . . I too was there when *Nanna* died . . . didn't you lament his death tossing from side to side?'

'Yes, I did . . . I wailed that I killed my husband with my own hands. I bewailed regretting that I felt a relief at his passing away. If you insist I sobbed lest you children may take me amiss . . . I wept that society may mistake me if I did not.'

Saroja sat stunned as a statue. She was at a loss for words . . . seeing a new person standing revealed in her mother . . . a mother she did not know . . . a mother who did what she did beyond her imagination.

'Saroja, listen to me . . . I wished his suffering would end if your father died, but that wish lingered in me only vaguely. In Prasad's case, I have no ambiguity. He wishes to die. He knows better of his physical suffering than us.

'Ten years back, when your father was laid up in bed and suffering, I did not know then that there was something called mercy killing . . . that the government would by itself permit a mercy killing. Had I known, I would definitely have knocked at the doors of the government. I would have pleaded with the government to relieve my husband of his pain.'

'Does it mean that you support Prasad's plea for mercy killing?'

'Yes, Saroja . . . it is our responsibility to fulfill his wish . . . be tough Saroja . . . if he is your son, he is also my grandson. Even I bear a lot of love for him. Since I love him, I say there is justice in his asking for death. You have already delayed. Look into what that mercy killing is . . . set about making arrangements for it.'

Saroja sat stunned for a long time after her mother ended her conversation.

Yet, nothing seemed strange to Saroja in those words of her mother. They were all ideas that remained repressed within her unconscious . . . now gaining life had come out through her mouth. That was all. How well *Amma* had expressed same thoughts! If she petitioned to the court asking for mercy killing for her son, the society might say something untoward . . . that she was murderous . . . wicked . . . that she was resorting to mercy killing to escape from serving her son . . . let it be . . . because she loved her son, she would try her best to fulfill his wish.

Before the time came for him to leave this world, Prasad looked forward to meeting Ragini just once to thank her for what she did for him. She failed in fulfilling that wish. Even before they had reached her place, Ragini left this world in a hurry.

Now Prasad is yearning for mercy killing. She should at least fulfill that one wish of his.

Saroja resolved her mind.

The next day, Saroja met lawyer Ramanadham who she knew.

Saroja filed a petition in court seeking mercy killing for her son, Prasad.

*   *   *

The verdict was out in Dr. Siddhartha's case. The court finding him guilty sentenced him to ten years rigorous imprisonment.

'Here is another feather in your cap! You are sure to be promoted very soon as High Court judge,' Kiran said treating Akshara to a piece of sweet.

'What else do I need except fulfilling my wish of giving historical verdict at least in some cases? I am happy I fulfilled *Amma*'s dreams . . . enough, I consider my life as blessed!'

'Tomorrow Prasad's case for mercy killing is coming for hearing. Since the case bears much resemblance to Siddhartha's case, success is going to be yours in this case too!'

'How can we declare it before hand? The lawyer from their side, Ramanadham is a very senior lawyer. We cannot compare Dr. Siddhartha's case with this. In that case, the doctor resorted to killing of an innocent life and so committed a criminal act. Here, in this case, Prasad is seeking permission to kill himself.'

'There are very few cases which sought permission for mercy killing, is it not so especially in our country?' Kiran asked.

'It is because many are unaware, that we need to take permission from the court even to take our own life. People instead resort to suicide if life seemed miserable. That is all. Even so, in recent times, cases seeking mercy killing are on the rise. A girl by name Seema Sood from Himachal Pradesh who studied engineering course up to postgraduation and over that won a gold medal wrote a letter to the President seeking mercy killing. The couple from Mirzapur, Jeet Narayen and Prabhavathi, applied for permission from the President to kill their four children. They claimed all their four children were suffering from Muscular Dystrophy,' Akshara remarked.

'It is unfortunate there are no recognized institutions in our country to care for patients suffering from incurable diseases. The affluent can go to corporate hospitals. Who will bother about the poor? I think since government does not come forward to take care of patients suffering from long term diseases such as Muscular Dystrophy, there are more people seeking mercy killing.'

'Whatever the reasons, either physical or financial, it is not proper to ask for mercy killing. I am a staunch opponent of mercy killing. There is an institution in America called 'Too Young to Die'. It is fighting against mercy killing. I too plan to start an institution on similar lines in our country. Send for our auditor, let him draft the trust deed,' Akshara said.

Next day, the arguments in Prasad's case commenced.

'Your Honour! The term mercy killing is an oxymoron. Where is room for mercy when killing is in itself cruel? Under IPC 306, even if a person is killed with his approval, it is a criminal offence,' Akshara began her argument.

Lawyer Ramanatham rose on his feet to interrupt Akshara's argument. 'Your Honour! The Public Prosecutor is repeatedly stating that the term mercy killing is meaningless. I have a request. Instead of terming it as mercy killing, treat it as merciful death. If mercy killing is legally untenable, then countries such as Netherlands, Albania, Germany and Switzerland would not have made laws upholding it. With changing times, there is need for laws to change, Your Honour. There has been already an inordinate delay in our country in bringing about a law permitting mercy killing. There can be no worse miserable condition than of Prasad's as sufficient reason for promulgating the new law to uphold mercy killing. In Prasad's case, living itself is the worst possible punishment. Even an accused charged with multiple murders, does not receive such a ruthless punishment under our legal system. If that is so, is it just to subject a person to such miserable suffering who is not guilty of any crime? Considering the just aspects of Prasad's plea, I request the court to take a humanitarian view and grant him mercy killing.'

'The respectable lawyer, mentioned about countries permitting mercy killing, but forgot to mention the countries where it is opposed. In recent times, in countries such as Western Australia, Hawaii, Israel and France the bill introducing mercy killing has been defeated.

'In a poor country such as India, if laws are promulgated for mercy killing, there are chances of misuse. All those who cannot afford treatment for patients with incurable diseases may, to escape duty and responsibility, resort to mercy killing. The lives of those born with physical deformities and old and infirm may also come under threat of mercy killing. In addition, people may abet patients to accept mercy killing, for property or for financial gain.

'Why go that far? Lawyer Ramanadham mentioned a while ago, of the law in Netherlands. That government was stunned coming to know what atrocities had been committed in the name of mercy killing in the country. In spite of having stringent laws in place to see that mercy killing could take place with only the patient's permission, more than thousand patients were killed without their approval in 1990. Through stopping medical treatment another 14,175 died. Yet another 1,701 patients died due to disconnection of life support systems without their knowledge. Then in a poor country like India where there is a large illiterate population, if law for mercy killing is upheld, there is ample scope for killing people systematically and escaping in the guise of mercy killing,' argued Akshara.

Lawyer Ramanadham put forward his argument. 'None of the arguments that the Public Prosecutor put forward will stand to reason with regard to Prasad's case. It is a fact he is suffering from Muscular Dystrophy. The medical world says there is no medicine for the disease and that the disease only grows worse as days pass by. Prasad now is close to death. He is on ventilator for artificial breathing, unable to swallow food he is supplied food through a tube. He is leading a miserable life with each organ failing one at a time. The court in certain cases grants death sentence as punishment, but in this case living itself is a merciless punishment, Your Honour! Death too is a gift, and I request the court to grant him that wish and release him from physical pain. If both his mother Saroja and his grandmother Jayamma are also seeking mercy killing for him, then you can realize the unbearable condition of his health, and what distress and mental trauma his close relatives are facing.'

The judge adjourned the case for the next day.

The court heard to arguments on that day also.

The day when the case came for final hearing, the judge asked Akshara to put forth her final argument.

'In the context of Prasad's petition for mercy killing, Your Honour, I find it necessary to quote the case of Karri Basamma from Karnataka High Court. She is aged seventy . . . for the past twelve years she has been fighting for her right to a respectable death. She is suffering from slip disc and excruciating pain in her legs. She argues Section 306 and 309 are unconstitutional and that Article 14 and 21 are a mockery of one's right to a life of dignity.

'But Your Honour . . . if mercy killing is granted because of slip disc or arthritic problems ten per cent of world's population has to die. What we need are not laws that permit mercy killing . . . but decisions that allow governments to give care to the old and patients suffering from chronic diseases . . . bring better medical facilities within the reach of people for pain relief . . . Prasad's case too is similar. Is it not the doctors who have to decide that his pain is unbearable and that medicines meant to control his pain are unavailable . . . a medical knowledge that the patient lacks, doctors possess.'

At this point, lawyer Ramanatham came in with an observation interrupting Akshara's argument.

'If it is so, I request the court to constitute a committee having a team of doctors on it to go into Prasad's case and as per its advice permit mercy killing.'

'Unfortunately, Your Honour, we cannot consider the opinion of the team of doctors as impartial! They are not above various types of temptations. We have no mechanism in our country for strict implementation of necessary laws and rules to precision. When poverty and corruption are reigning supreme in our country, it is too early to permit mercy killing. We have not reached a mature stage Your Honour, to handle mercy killing.

'Mercy killing is not just an issue related to justice. According to the prevailing philosophical and ethical norms in our country, mercy killing is an issue the court has to decide subject to norms of the society.

'It is not proper for a patient to seek mercy killing, on the pretext that a particular disease has no medicine or that the medical world has no required knowledge to reduce his pain . . . Some day, the medical world is sure to come up with a cure or ways to controlling the disease.'

At this stage, lawyer Ramanadham intervened.

'There is no cure for Muscular Dystrophy. Prasad is close to dying . . . a few days or at best one or two months . . . before that there is no hope that the medical world will discover a medicine, Your Honour. If there are records of the medical research's attempts to find a cure or proof of its anticipated success, I request the Public Prosecutor to bring it to the court's notice.'

'What lawyer Ramanadham said is true. There is no medicine today for Muscular Dystrophy. Yet I cannot wish every sufferer of Muscular Dystrophy to die, Your Honour. There are many in the society who are fighting the disease bravely and are leading purposeful lives. I have ample proof of it to offer.

'A person by name, P. Sudhakar Reddy is living with Muscular Dystrophy. He is running an organization called 'Society for Equal Opportunities for Persons with Physical Disabilities'. Way back in 1980 itself, he took his postgraduate degree in engineering from Jawaharlal Technological University, and selected for a post on merit in Bharath Heavy Electricals. I will tell you what he said of himself:

'When compared with many others, I don't appear different from them. I work twelve hours a day in my office. The only difference is I use a wheelchair instead of two legs.'

'He says that by leading a constructive and socially productive life, he is trying not to succumb to Muscular Dystrophy.

'Another living proof is standing before you Your Honour . . . it is I!

'Even before I reached the age of sixteen, the doctors had declared three times that the time had come for me to die. I defied death three times. Now I am forty years old . . . and I am still going strong. Had I believed the opinion of doctors and succumbed to despair, attempted suicide or sought mercy killing inviting death, there would not have been a Public Prosecutor by name Akshara. That is all, Your Honour.'

The court adjourned the case to the next day.

*   *   *

Prasad's health further declined that morning. Saroja called Dr. Murthy for his opinion. As Dr. Murthy arrived, he understood Prasad's condition. 'At best a few hours, that is it . . . there is not much we can do,' he remarked.

Saroja was not saddened hearing those words. She knew that such a day would come and so she had been bracing herself for that eventuality. To tell the truth, she had been looking forward to that day. She wished for the day to arrive sooner than expected, but it did not. Death was coming to Prasad only after ensuring that he suffered physical pain enough for ten lives.

Saroja waged some sort of a war itself with law courts for the grant of mercy killing for her son, but in the end, she lost the battle. It had been close to a month since the verdict went against them. . . . Saroja tried not to tell Prasad of the verdict.

However, Prasad was not dull to fail in guessing the outcome of the case. Since the laptop was within his reach, long before his mother told him of what transpired he browsed the Internet for the news.Seeing his mother get back from the court wearing a long face and weary, Prasad did not exchange a word.

Saroja waited long for Prasad to make a mention of what went through his mind. Prasad instead, withdrew further into his shell as a snail. From then on, Prasad's health went downhill rapidly.

Saroja could not stomach the fact even now that she lost the case. She did not want to give up on it so easily. She waited patiently for this day to come her way.

She took a determined forward step.

'*Amma* . . . I have some small work to attend. I will be back in a while. Look after Prasad with care until I get back,' she asked her mother.

Jayamma who sat with a distraught face, felt alarmed.

'What is that . . . didn't the doctor say that his end is approaching in a few hours? Why are you going out at this hour . . . shouldn't you be there when his end comes?'

'I will not take long *Amma*. He is my son . . . he knows how determined I am. Until I achieve what I intended he will not allow the end to come anywhere near him.'

'I don't get what you are driving at,' Jayamma expressed her doubt in surprise.

Before stepping out, Saroja looked into Prasad's room. He was struggling for breath. He was a poignant picture framed, an illustration before one's eyes of how torturous death could be.

Unable to withstand the sight, Saroja turned away her eyes. Looking into some corner of the room, she addressed Prasad. 'We have lost the court case Prasad, but I decided not to give up. I have been looking forward to just this day. Don't be in a hurry to leave until I achieve what I intended. I will be back soon.'

Saroja did not pause to think if her words reached Prasad's ears. Even though she knew that Prasad was in no condition to hear her, she still articulated her mind since she wanted to. She did not know what her words could gain . . . just a crazy belief . . . that her son would stay alive until she got back.

The time was six-thirty in the evening when Saroja stepped out of the house. She went straight to Akshara's house . . . a half-hour drive. . . . When Saroja reached, she found Akshara and Kiran discussing a case between them.

Akshara recognized Saroja instantly. She remembered Saroja well as it was only a month since the verdict came in her case and that too it was a rare case.

When the verdict came, seeing Saroja's sorrow erupting like volcano's lava, Akshara got scared . . . she feared Saroja would corner her in the court to take her to task then and there . . . such instances were not uncommon in court halls.

Akshara expressed her fear in a whisper to Kiran. 'Don't worry . . . I am there,' he signaled her through a look.

However, nothing of the sort happened, yet the glance Saroja threw at her while leaving the court hall, hit her as a burning shaft . . . that anger in her eyes . . . and that glance so piercing seemed afresh now when she saw Saroja standing at her doorstep.

Akshara did not get why Saroja came looking for her office so long after the case had closed. Thoughts flashed across her mind in quick succession.

Perhaps Prasad expired. She might have come in that anger. She was sure to scream and abuse her now . . . would she . . . not stopping with that would she even hit her in fury.

Akshara threw a look at Kiran as if to ask what was coming on.

He exchanged a similar gesture, 'You wait . . . I will find out!'

Saroja until then remained standing. 'Don't you observe common etiquette of offering a seat to those who visit your office?' she said continuing, 'Oh, is that because I belong to the opponent party that you don't care to welcome me with a smile?'

Akshara looked into Saroja's face curiously. There were no traces of any anger in her. She only projected a picture of sorrow. In her eyes could be seen hardened grief.

'Please take your seat. Aren't you Prasad's mother, whose case Akshara had argued on mercy killing . . . if I am not mistaken?' Kiran said.

'Yes. You have recognized me rightly. I am Saroja,' she said taking a chair.

'Tell us, what brought you here?' Kiran said again.

Even so, various doubts had been hissing in Akshara's mind as hooded snakes.

'I have come to you for some help,' Saroja said looking at Akshara.

'Oh, so you have come now as our client. We feared you came to lodge a complaint,' Kiran said smiling.

'Justice has not been done to me in the court. You too know that,' Saroja began.

Akshara responded quickly. 'I did my duty as a Public Prosecutor. Lawyer from your end too argued to the best of his ability. That is all. However, the responsibility of giving a verdict rested on the judge alone. We don't have any hand in it. If you felt you did not get justice, you could have appealed to the higher court. I am afraid we cannot be of help to you in that regard now.'

'The reason I came here now is not for a court's verdict. That is a verdict according to law . . . what I came to seek now is a verdict based on the *dharma,* of humanitarian concern.'

'Let us know more clearly what you want. If it is something we can do, we will certainly,' Akshara said.

'It is a help I am sure you can render . . . very small help . . . my son is dying. The doctor said he is not going to survive more than a few hours. I have come to request you to fulfill his last wish.'

'What is that last wish?' Kiran queried.

'I have come to request both of you to come to my house. His wish is that you two should be next to him in his last moments. That is all.'

That last wish of Prasad intrigued Akshara. What do they stand to gain from that visit? What did Saroja expect asking such a wish? Akshara looked at Kiran as if to ask what was on hand and what they were to do.

'Please allow us to think awhile. Leave behind your address and your phone number. We will get back to you soon.'

'Where is so much time on hand? In truth, he may breathe his last by the time I get back. You don't have to stay for long; there is no need for it. Even if he lives, he may last at best for another two hours. Please don't refuse. You simply have to just sit by his bedside . . . that is all.'

Kiran was lost for words.

As for Akshara, the request seemed absurd. She wondered if there was any hidden plan behind the request.

'Okay. Can you wait outside for some time? We will soon inform you of our decision,' Kiran said.

'Thanks . . . I will wait. I expect you will not disappoint me in this regard. I don't have to tell you how important it is to fulfill the last wish of a dying person.' Saroja walked out and waited sitting in one of the chairs placed there.

Following Saroja out, Kiran came back closing the door behind him. 'What shall we do?' he asked Akshara.

'I have a suspicion. What she is asking for may not be her son's final wish. That must be her own,' Akshara observed.

'It is irrelevant now to debate as to whose wish it is, think of what we should do.'

'Could there be any conspiracy behind this, Kiran?'

Kiran smiled looking at Akshara. 'Your suspicions such as these are on the increase as your success rate is increasing.'

'Is it not an occupational hazard, Kiran? As successes go up in numbers, proportionately our enemies too grow in numbers. Don't we have to be on our guard?'

'There is no such fear in this instance, Akshara. I see sincerity in what she is asking. I don't think there is scope for any danger or loss of any kind by our going there,' Kiran said in an assuring tone.

'Why should we go there at all? What relationship do we have with her family? I took up many cases as a Public Prosecutor. We do not evince any personal interest in any of them. Then, why should we treat this case as special? I have no need to oblige her request, Kiran,' Akshara reasoned.

'There is. What she asked is a very small request . . . just sit in the presence of a person dying in the next hour or two . . . that is all she is asking. It is our minimum duty to fulfill the last wish of a dying person. Let us go.'

'Okay, Kiran. I am agreeing to come since you are suggesting. It is not possible to stay until his moment of death. I will not stay a minute beyond an hour. Is that okay . . . it is now half past seven. Even if it takes half an hour for travel, we will return by nine.'

'Okay . . . shall I call Saroja in?'

'Call her . . . tell *Amma* that we are going to be late for dinner.'

Kiran opened the door and asked Saroja in. He then went in to inform his mother-in-law that they were going out and would be back by nine for dinner.

By the time Kiran returned, 'thanks a lot for agreeing to come to our house as per my request,' he heard Saroja saying to Akshara.

'I am telling in advance . . . there should not be any discussion or criticism of my arguments regarding your son's case.'

Saroja assured, 'There is going to be no reference whatsoever to those things.'

'I strongly oppose mercy killing. Once I come to your place, you should not pressurize me to change my opinion regarding mercy killing.'

'I am promising you that no one will talk about mercy killing. No one will speak to you regarding any subject. You don't have to speak at all. It is enough if you spend a few hours in his room.'

'Okay, let us leave. Shall we go Kiran?'

As they reached, Jayamma was anxiously looking forward to her return.

'Thank God! You have come . . . I was scared stiff if anything would happen to him before you returned. Is it for these people you ran in a hurry? Even so, who are they? Are they doctors?' Jayamma asked.

Akshara thought Saroja would introduce them as lawyers who argued in Prasad's case.

'This couple is quite close to Prasad, *Amma*. It is Prasad's final wish that they be there next to him at the time of his death. That is why I went to fetch them.'

'Oh is that so . . . then take them in fast. It looks the end would come anytime now,' Jayamma said controlling her tears.

Saroja placed a chair beside Prasad's bed for Kiran to sit. 'You also sit down,' Akshara said as Saroja was about to leave the room.

Akshara noticed sorrow rise as tidal wave in Saroja, 'No mother in this world has the courage to watch her son struggling to reach his end while suffering torturously. No woman would be so stone hearted to remain unruffled when her son was dying,' saying so, Saroja left the room.

Saroja burst into sobs placing her head in Jayamma's lap who was sitting outside the room with tears in her eyes.

Inside the room . . . sound of oxygen gushing from the ventilator . . . sound of the fan whirring above . . . various strange sounds escaping from Prasad's throat in his deathly struggle . . . evoking a dread. Tinkling sound of death as of ankle bells heard wherever one looked in that room. . . . Death's last monstrous dance . . . odour of death . . . spread of burning fetid smell of death . . . Akshara sat watching Prasad.

Akshara had not a chance to see until then death from such close quarters. To sit in that room watching a dying man was an entirely new experience for her . . . a little scary too.

There was an endless struggle in Prasad's face. His chest expanded and contracted from time to time in a struggle for breath. Did death face so much pain and resistance? Should life struggle so much while leaving this body . . . should body put up with so much torment?

Time seemed to move very slow . . . as though involved in a struggle of death for moments to turn to hours . . . and for seconds hand to change from one number to another . . . as if it had its legs broken, it is crawling to reach its next moment . . .

A snore-like sound was struggling to escape Prasad's throat. The sound was frightful . . . as a shudder passing down the spine as one watched a terrifying horror film sitting inside a dark room . . .

Ten minutes passed . . . heavily . . .

Akshara fidgeted uneasily in her wheelchair.

She looked at Kiran. His condition seemed none too different.

'Kiran, I cannot take this anymore. Let us go,' Akshara murmured.

Kiran looked at his watch. 'It is not even ten minutes since we came here. Didn't you say we will be staying for an hour . . . there is lot of time left for one hour to pass.'

'Is it only ten minutes . . . do we have to sit through this for another fifty minutes . . . I can't bear this sight.'

'Can't help it, Akshara . . . we gave our word to her.'

Akshara stopped looking at Prasad and began to stare at the ceiling fan above and the corners of the room.

Yet those sounds . . . the sound of the footsteps of death . . . as drum-beat of death . . . the more torturous gloom of death . . . those sounds seemed frightful . . . the pain of death as each organ in the body died . . . the moments when life resisted leaving the body . . . an intense struggle when the body fought against forcing life out . . . an unending torment. Prasad's harrowing struggle was clearly visible even to closed eyes . . .

Unwillingly, Akshara's glances turned to Kiran . . . each time Prasad's body shook as coming under the effect of an earthquake she too shuddered.

'Kiran . . . can death be so frightful?' Akshara asked. She said that as if she was asking herself a question without expecting an answer.

'Even I am watching it for the first time, Akshara . . . with the death of my father, I experienced directly what sorrow my family suffered when an earning member died all of a sudden, but watching death from so close is a new experience even to me.'

'Kiran, I cannot remain here any longer. I am not able to see his pain. Let us leave this place, please.'

Kiran looked at his watch one more time.

'Six more minutes have passed. That means we have spent here a total of sixteen minutes, but we are not done yet.'

'Oh is that all! I wish his end would come soon . . . poor man, see how much he is suffering?'

'Even I am unable to watch this, Akshara . . . it appears Saroja has given us this punishment by way of vengeance since the verdict went against them. Now I understand what a grievous mistake we committed by accepting to come.'

'Let anyone say anything . . . let us leave this place, please!' Akshara begged him.

'Going by his condition, it appears his end would come any time now. Let us bear this at least to fulfill his last wish,' Kiran said.

Restlessly, Akshara looked at the bed. Was he dying . . . in a few minutes . . . yes . . . his heart did not seem to be beating. The body was not shaking violently as before except intermittently. Perhaps that way those shudders would stop altogether . . .

He began frothing at the mouth . . . froth, not white in colour, but red . . . the air escaping in bubbles . . . the bubbles initially small, and then growing in size bursting . . . does life bubble away in the end . . . .

'Kiran, it is impossible for me to stay. Please let us go. Get up!' Akshara said with her eyes wide with fear, as she concentrated her looks on Kiran.

'It is now twenty-six minutes . . . a little longer . . .'

'No' Akshara yelled out aloud. 'If I stay here longer, I am sure this experience would haunt me through out my life as a nightmare. Not even our enemies should have such painful death, Kiran. That is why I said many times, there is no one by name god. If one were there, he would not take away life of people so cruelly, frighteningly and mercilessly. Even if he is there, there can be no worse sadist than him.'

'Now I come to understand why they say easy death is a blessing,' Kiran commented pensively.

'Let us first leave this place. I am sure to go insane if I tarry here longer.'

'Okay, let us go!' Kiran came out pushing Akshara's wheelchair.

Saroja, who till then was weeping with her head in her mother's lap, seeing them, sat up. She appeared a goddess of sorrow. Weeping incessantly, she appeared to drop off as a tear drop. 'Is everything over?' she asked Kiran.

Kiran was very embarrassed to give any reply. Gathering words he said, 'No . . . it is we . . . unable to stay are leaving. Sorry, we are unable to keep up our word,' saying so he folded his hands in a *namaste*.

Saroja stood in silence for some time. Fighting back her tears, she said, 'I wonder how long that body is fated to suffer . . . what can I do except pray god that he grant him a quick death?'

She accompanied them till the gate. As they took leave of her, she said, 'I thank you for keeping your promise and coming to spend at least this half hour with him. Finally, I would like to say only one thing, especially to Akshara. . . . You do not have any relationship or attachment whatsoever with Prasad. Even then you could not bear to see him suffer for more than a half hour, then how did you expect me as a mother, to keep watching him writhing in pain and losing a bit of life every minute? How heart-breaking . . . as if shredding my womb into pieces . . . if you can understand how punishing it is, that is enough!' saying *namaste*, bringing together her hands, Saroja saw them off.

Akkshra came back home, but felt sick at heart. She never before saw so much agitation raging within her.

Akshara could not taste her food. In spite of her mother pleading and Kiran consoling, she could not take even a morsel.

That night she could hardly snatch a wink. Thoughts . . . chased her as hunting dogs . . . nightmarish thoughts.

She lost her peace . . . not just that day . . . for many days that followed . . . .

*   *   *

Two hours after Akshara had left, Prasad passed away . . .

Prasad's agonizing death . . . Saroja's fight for justice, plea for grant of mercy killing to her son, did not quite go waste. A few years after Prasad's death, in Aruna Shanbagh's case, the Supreme Court gave a historic ruling in favour of passive euthanasia.

*   *   *

The End